THE SUM OF ALL MAGIC

THE SUM OF ALL MAGIC

DRAGON'S DAUGHTER™ BOOK 6

KEVIN MCLAUGHLIN
MICHAEL ANDERLE

DISRUPTIVE IMAGINATION

Copyright © 2021 LMBPN Publishing
Cover Art by Jake @ J Caleb Design
http://jcalebdesign.com / jcalebdesign@gmail.com
Cover copyright © LMBPN Publishing
A Michael Anderle Production

LMBPN Publishing
PMB 196, 2540 South Maryland Pkwy
Las Vegas, NV 89109

Version 1.00 April 2021
eBook ISBN: 978-1-64971-710-8
Print ISBN: 978-1-64971-711-5

THE SUM OF ALL MAGIC TEAM

Thanks to the JIT Readers

Dave Hicks
Veronica Stephan-Miller
Deb Mader
Diane L. Smith
Daryl McDaniel
Dorothy Lloyd
Wendy L. Bonell
Paul Westman

If we've missed anyone, please let us know!

Editor
The Skyhunter Editing Team

CHAPTER ONE

Kristen Hall was ostensibly the most powerful being on the entire planet. It therefore wasn't unreasonable to expect that her position meant she could take her cellphone out in the middle of a meeting of the Dragon Council if she wanted to. Despite the power she supposedly wielded and the fact that the current topic of discussion had dragged on far longer than she had hoped it would, she did not dare to touch her phone.

The members all sat in the Council's chamber, a massive, ornate room that occupied the main floor of the Chrome Castle she had ordered constructed at the top of the skyscraper she paid to be built in the middle of Detroit. That she had done either of these things still felt bizarre to her.

She had grown up in a tiny, three-bedroom house in a suburb of Detroit and had never fantasized about homeownership. The idea of owning a chromed castle at the top of the tallest building in the city was so far beyond her that she might as well have dreamed it. Unfortunately, dragons valued appearances, which meant she had to as well.

When dragons came to visit, they landed on a drawbridge that was higher than the tops of any of the other nearby buildings.

They walked down a hallway that was inlaid with carved stonework to reach the massive doors at the entrance to the chamber. The stonework hadn't been commissioned because she particularly liked it but because having carved stone in pristine condition in a castle that was often higher than the clouds was somehow impressive.

Exactly like having a chair carved of a single piece of wood was impressive. Despite her preference for a normal one that didn't involve a centuries-old tree being felled, she had to have the fancy one because appearances were everything.

This was also one of the reasons why she couldn't check her stupid phone,

The problem was the issue of precedents. She had discovered it on the first day of the job. If she took her cellphone out, the other dragons would think they could also receive communications during a meeting, which would only slow the already glacially paced meetings.

So, while she was very anxious to see if Lady Amythist had any more news about the return of an evil dragon goddess, she forced herself to pay attention to the particulars of the current debate.

"The precedent was set in Antarctica," Lord Orenclaw stated through his mustaches, his tone slightly offended. "Dragons cannot destroy habitats that are governed by human law, even if there are no humans currently there." He had made a massive fortune on factories and refineries. As a result, he understood that his fortune was entwined with humans so he often argued on their behalf, albeit for selfish reasons.

"Humans have made rules about every inch of the planet," Lady Jade protested. "We cannot expect to respect their rules in every single happenstance." She turned to Kristen for confirmation or refutation but before she could answer, another spoke.

The interruption suited the Steel Dragon, honestly. She knew these issues were important but she could not stop thinking about Amythist's message. The headmaster of the Lumos School had said she was unhurt—although she had been turned briefly to stone—and that the students were all right. But honestly, how could someone be expected to absorb that kind of information and still pay attention to territory disputes?

At the crux of the whole matter was the idea that Tiamat had somehow returned to life. Kristen had familiarized herself with dragon mythology, such as it was, and never came away with a strong sense that any of it was real.

Now, however, Amythist claimed exactly that—the dragon who had been killed millennia before and whose blood had given magic to this world had returned and had chosen one of their interns as a target. The headmaster had said she was not sure how much of it could be believed as it came from students, which was frustrating. Kristen felt like she could neither act on it nor ignore the information. She had sent Amy Williams—her most powerful mage and most trusted advisor—to investigate. It was her call she now hoped to receive.

Finally, Lady Jade and Lord Orenclaw stopped their bickering and agreed to move on to the next item.

The Steel Dragon perked up immediately. The next topic was the Followers of Tiamat. "Lords and Ladies of the Council, I would like to address the current rise in activity by the Followers of Tiamat. As you all know, they have previously attacked students from the Lumos School."

"And been dealt with," Orenclaw retorted sharply.

She glared at him and the old fop withered under her steely gaze. "I have received another report from Amythist. There has been an attack on the Lumos School."

Mutters and discontent followed this but no true outrage. None of the councilors had students enrolled at the school. In that way, dragons could be as narrow-sighted as humans. She was certain that if a deranged cult had attacked the school one of their children had been attending, they would have done far more than mutter.

"How did this…attack play out?" Lady Jade asked.

"Amythist says a group of students were able to drive the Followers back."

"Well, then, if the issue is settled, perhaps we could move on to more pressing matters," Lord Gilt said. He had a tax proposal he wished to get to.

"I don't think it's prudent to dismiss attacks on the school by the Followers," Kristen pointed out.

"Call them what they are, Lady Steel—cultists." Orenclaw snorted.

"On this, the lord and I agree," Lady Jade added. "The cultists of Tiamat are dragons who never found a way to put their bizarre powers to constructive use. Rather than interact with the real world, they would prefer to pretend they are pieces of a dead dragon's blood. Honestly, the mythology is exhausting."

Kristen was undeterred. "The headmaster said they brought a formidable force to the school. She said they were led by a powerful dragon who called herself Kishar. They were trying to bring Tiamat back, according to Lady Amythist."

A moment of dead silence followed before, for the first time since she had been a part of Council, the entire group of dragons burst into laughter.

"You can't truly believe this nonsense, can you?" Lord Gilt seemed to forget that he would need her help as the head of the Council to raise his tax proposal. "Tiamat is a child's fancy. A way to make the unusually gifted feel valuable."

"Lady Amythist said she was quite powerful."

"This has happened before, you see," Orenclaw said. "These cultists get a little wild every few centuries and claim they've uncovered the Sum of All Dragons or some such nonsense. They no doubt choose a strong dragon as any other would not stand up to any scrutiny. I promise you this will blow over as it has before. I'm sure you don't seriously believe that this is the real Tiamat." He chuckled dismissively.

His humor was short-lived, however, as the doors to the massive wooden doors of the Council chamber were flung open.

"Excuse me, but are my ears burning?" A beautiful woman strode in, with dark, full hair, copper skin, and a golden nose ring. She wore a black gown that sparkled in the light and revealed a myriad of colors.

"You have no business here!" Orenclaw protested.

"But you were discussing me."

"We were discussing no such thing," Lady Jade retorted acidly.

"But you asked if Tiamat was real and I can assure you I most certainly am."

CHAPTER TWO

Kristen rose from her place at the head of the table and turned her skin to steel. "I don't know who the hell you think you are, but you can't simply barge in here. Leave willingly or I'll make you."

"Oh, I forgot myself," the woman said and placed a hand upon her perfect chest in mock consternation. "But it's so exciting to be back in the thick of it all. I never imagined buildings would ever get to be this tall, and you've put a shiny silver castle at the top of this one. Truly, it is too much."

"Leave. Now," she ordered.

"Right. There are procedures to be followed. If one of your most trusted guards were to announce me, I might have a place here but otherwise, I'm merely barging in." The way the woman said the last two words made her think she was trying to make her regret using them.

She was about to rush the woman and inflict her version of discipline—dragons recognized strength even more than humans did—when Heartsbane entered.

The dragon in human form bowed stiffly and cleared her

throat. "I hereby announce Lady Tiamat and ask the Council to hear her humble request."

Kristen studied Heartsbane warily. The woman seemed like herself. She wore her typical scowl and her fists were clenched at her sides as they often were, but something was off about her. After a moment, she realized it was her aura. It always poked and prodded at everyone to sense their emotional states and tweak them as she saw fit. If she barged into a Council meeting—and she had before—she did so while using an aura that was stronger than any other dragon's.

For some inexplicable reason, she made no effort to do so now. The leader of the Dragon Council didn't know what that meant, exactly, but she didn't like it. Still, she leaned back in her throne and decided to deescalate the situation if possible.

"Your request is denied. Leave now. Guards!" She looked at the door. Two guards were always posted outside, a human armed with dragon-slaying bullets and a mage. She could barely see them on either side of the open door but neither of them moved at all. Something was very wrong. She could feel it.

"Now, now. This young woman comes here without a force or any cultists. It is the right of the Council, not the head, to decide if we shall hear her request," Orenclaw smiled through his mustaches. He had always been a sucker for a pretty face.

"I agree," Lady Jade all but purred. "Let her speak. I have heard of you, Lady Kishar, although the last my sources told me you were known as the First Walker of your religion, not Tiamat."

"Fine," Kristen grumbled before the intruder could speak. "A vote. Shall we hear this intruder's request?"

"I don't see why not. If she had Heartsbane's trust, the least we can do is hear her out," Lord Gilt said.

She was the only one who voted against hearing the woman. It seemed reasonable that if Heartsbane trusted her, it should have been enough, but something still unsettled her. Why hadn't the guards moved? They were well trained, yes, but the door was wide open and neither one of them had so much as twitched, even to acknowledge her call. Reluctantly, she resumed her seat.

"Lords and Ladies of the Council," the woman began, her tone soothing, placating, and oh so very polite. "I am Tiamat. Yes, the Tiamat of legend. It is I who was killed by the hand of a human and it was my blood that gave rise to all of you. I was freed from my prison and given this body by one of my most loyal Followers."

"Why did you attack the Lumos School?" Kristen demanded.

"That was an unfortunate misunderstanding perpetrated by Lady Kishar before my return," Tiamat said smoothly. "I assure you, no one will witness such a thing take place again."

"But why?"

"She thought a girl there was the Sum of All Dragons. She was right in a way, but I have since reclaimed the powers that were denied to me for so long. All of them. Every. Last. One." Tiamat extended her fingers and lightning danced from their tips, then fire, then pieces of metal, frost, light, shadow, and a dozen other types of magic. "Now that my power is returned, I intend to wield it as is my right as the mother of you all."

"You are not my mom," Kristen snapped.

"Yes, I've heard you were raised by a human. How wonderfully quaint. I don't demand you call me Mother, though. Even though I did grant you the life that you have, I can see how that might be awkward for you. I would settle for you calling me your queen and swearing your allegiance. Now. In blood. Exactly as I have done for all of you."

At least everything made sense now. "Lady Kishar," she began. "I don't know what kind of brain damage you suffered when battling a group of kids or what you did to Heartsbane to convince her to allow you here—I assume chocolate was involved —but I can assure you that my best medics will help you get well again so you can get back to your little cult. Sorry—club? Whatever you dragons call yourselves."

"Excuse...me?" Tiamat growled with displeasure.

"See, that's better," she said. "If you had started your little presentation with more respect, we might have listened for longer. But given that it was rather unimpressive, I would say it's too little too late."

"We don't have a queen, madam," Orenclaw added.

"And we don't wish to," Lady Jade did not look amused.

"Now, if you'd please see our guest out before the guards get here, that would be great," Kristen said to Heartsbane, who didn't budge.

Instead, she looked at her in the same way she looked at almost anyone else. It was not a kind expression.

Tiamat laughed. It was a high, tinkly sound that matched the beautiful woman perfectly. Instead of leaving as she had been ordered to do, she approached Lord Orenclaw, who was seated on one side of the table and closest to her.

"How does one go about getting a seat on the Council these days? I've been gone a long time, you understand. I believe I might need a refresher," Tiamat said with saccharine sweetness.

Kristen fought the odd compulsion—one that was surprisingly hard to resist—to think of her as Tiamat despite the fact that she wanted to think of her as Kishar.

Lord Orenclaw chewed thoughtfully on his mustaches. "We have implemented a democratic system. You may rise to represent a group of dragons if you can get at least a hundred supporters. I would be happy to—"

"And is that how the Steel Dragon ascended to power?" the interloper asked and sauntered past him. His gaze followed the sway of her hips and the way they made her black dress flow through a thousand colors. "I can't imagine such a young hatchling convincing esteemed dragons such as yourselves to submit to her power."

"I did it the old-fashioned way," Kristen said coldly. "I killed the asshole who tried to rule all on his lonesome."

"Ah...the old way," Tiamat said appreciatively. "Rulership from combat. Now that is an idea I understand—and approve of, in fact. After all, power is power. If one cannot enforce their will upon one of their subjects, why should they rule them? It's a philosophy I can live by."

"If you're trying to challenge me to a duel, this is a round-about way of doing it," she said, her voice as hard as her steel skin.

The interloper approached until she was only a few feet away and stared at her while she stared into her eyes from her throne. Her eyes were dark-brown, almost black, but they sparkled with the same iridescence as her dress. They were full of confidence. Normally, when Kristen was seated and others stood, they were uncomfortable as if her state of relative relaxation gave her more authority, but this dragon's aura made it feel the opposite. She could not help but think of her mother standing over her as if she had raided the cookie jar.

"I don't wish to fight you, little hatchling," Tiamat responded. "I wish you to submit." Her aura surged into a tsunami and swamped the Steel Dragon. Immediately, she understood what had happened to Heartsbane—despite her being more skilled with aura magic than possibly any dragon alive, this dragon was even stronger. Much stronger, in fact, and her will was unlike anything she had ever experienced.

It made no sense to resist it. What made sense—for Kristen, for the Council, and for all the people she represented and protected—was to slide out of her throne and drop to her knees before this godly power. Her divinity now seemed plain. How else could an individual be so strong? This must be the real Tiamat or something equivalent—a progenitor dragon whose power was greater than any that had come after her.

But—a tiny part of her mind thought with fierce independence—none of this was right. This was how people felt when Heartsbane overpowered them. Tiamat—no! this woman's—aura was strong but that didn't mean she was a god any more than her steel skin meant she was one. If she could not resist, then perhaps Tiamat—Kishar, her rebellion asserted—would take her place. But if she could resist, the dragon was nothing but another self-important usurper.

Kristen leaned forward, grasped the arms of her throne, clenched her teeth, and met Kishar's gaze. Oh, how she wanted to please those beautiful brown eyes. There was nothing she wanted more—but that was a lie. It was Tiamat's—no, Kishar's—lie.

"We will...not...give in to your demands," she said through gritted teeth. It was a struggle to even say that much. Every fiber of her being wanted to please this woman, to kiss the ground she walked on and thank her for it, but she knew that for the lie that it was.

"You cannot even beat...a hatchling...like me," she stated grimly, every word an effort.

As suddenly as it had been invoked, the aura was gone and the intruder bowed in respect. "You are more powerful than I thought," she said. "I had hoped you would join me, but I can see now that it was never to be."

Kishar sighed, a sad sigh of defeat that seemed to deflate what strength she had possessed. Kristen smiled, confident that she had defeated yet another challenge to her title. It had not been easy as aura battles were not her forte, but she had weathered it well enough.

She only realized belatedly that her sense of victory also came from Tiamat. It was vivid enough to give her the confidence to look at the Dragon Council and assure herself that she was still their leader. Unfortunately, that sense of triumph stole her attention away from the black smoke that poured from Tiamat's nostrils when she sighed.

By the time she realized the interloper was doing something to her, it was too late. Her entire body was wrapped in the black mist. Every part of her that touched it was frozen solid. Not frozen—petrified. Tiamat had turned her body to stone. Only her head was still under her command and she could feel that turning to stone as well.

"Council, we are under attack!" she roared and—despite being in her human form like the rest of the Council—exhaled fire into Tiamat's face.

The woman held a hand up and a pane of ice appeared to block the fire as if it were a gentle breeze blowing against a well-made windowpane.

"This won't stand!" Lady Jade said and took her dragon form. She attacked with claws of stone, a whirlwind of death that Kristen knew from experience was quite formidable in combat.

Tiamat breathed her mist at the dragon and petrified her before she was even able to get off the ground.

"This is not how it's done!" Lord Orenclaw protested and also took his dragon form. He accomplished even less before the mist turned him into the statue of a dragon, complete with long dropping mustaches rendered in perfect detail in black obsidian.

Lord Gilt made no such attempt. He simply ran to the door. The light reflecting off his scales revealed to Kristen what had happened to the two guards—the same thing that had happened to the Dragon Council and was happening to her. Tiamat froze him in his human form in midstride, a look of panic on his face. It was a small miracle that he did not pitch forward and shatter into a thousand pieces.

The other members of the Council seemed to think their odds were better in combat than in retreat. They took their dragon forms and blasted their adversary with fire, but their flames did nothing to the insidious black mist. It enshrouded them all and soon, every Council member was petrified in black stone. At least their poses were ones of courage. Kristen could make no such claim about her reclining posture and Lord Gilt was even worse.

"My guards will put an end to this," she said.

Tiamat only laughed. "Why do you think you are not yet completely frozen?"

A dozen guards—comprised of Kristen's most powerful mages and dragons—raced down the hall toward the open door of the council chamber and past the obsidian statue of Lord Gilt. If the look of terror on his face frightened any of them at all, they did not let it show.

They entered the chamber and surrounded Tiamat. The dragons took their dragon form and the mages wrapped their hands in shields of telekinesis, a power that no dragon but Amythist had ever had and was thus useful against them all.

"Bow to me," Tiamat ordered the guards imperiously.

Struck by her aura, every single one of them knelt and rested their foreheads on the floor.

"No!" Kristen shouted. Her nemesis only laughed as the black mist rose to touch her cheeks. "No!" Her face was petrified in a rictus of rage. The last thing she heard was the ancient dragon's twisted laughter before blackness swallowed her.

CHAPTER THREE

Despite being surrounded by her best friends, powerful mages skilled in the arts of healing and defense, and dragons who excelled in combat, a chill rippled down Kylara's spine. She didn't know why or where it had come from, but after everything that had happened recently, she was willing to bet Tiamat had a part to play in it.

"Is everything all right, Ky? You seem...colder." Sam smiled and the feeling of dread faded as quickly as it came. He hadn't released her hand since they'd reappeared at school and even went so far as to stand up to the head nurse, a fearsome woman if ever there was one.

She noticed that she had changed the temperature of her skin and had made herself so cold there was frost on top of the sheets in the infirmary bed where she lay. The air in the small room had become colder too.

"Sorry, I don't know what came over me," she said.

"Did you notice anything?" the headmaster asked the head nurse. Quite a few people were crowded into the tiny room. The young dragon mage didn't understand why the space was so small, to be honest. Many of the classrooms at the Lumos School were enchanted to be larger on the inside than the outside. This one seemed to have been crafted with the opposite effect. If the purpose of the tight confines and windowless brick walls was to stop crowds from gathering, it wasn't working.

"No, Lady Amythist," the woman replied to the headmaster. "Nothing other than Miss Diamantine activating a power, although—"

"Although what?" the old dragon snapped. She was a tiny woman, smaller than the head nurse although in her dragon form, she was a truly fearsome being. It was hard to imagine that this wrinkled woman who normally had flowers poking from one pocket and seeds falling out another was a deadly combatant when she had to be. Kylara had seen her fight at her full potential for the first time only a few hours earlier.

With that said, it was mind-boggling to realize that she now had far more powers than even the headmaster had at her disposal.

"Although Miss Diamantine was possessed by a goddess," the nurse snapped in response.

"Whatever that being we fought was, it was no goddess," Sam protested.

The nurse brushed his comment off as if it were nothing more than a speck of dust. "I'm here to assess the health of Miss Diamantine and yourself, headmaster, not quibble about semantics. I have never seen a dragon take a spirit form and possess the body of another, but if you wish to call her something other than what Kylara said she called herself, who am I to argue?"

"Your point is well made," Amythist replied begrudgingly. "You were saying—before you were interrupted?" She looked at Sam as if he had been the one to interrupt the woman, not her.

"My point was that I have no experience with any of what she claims happened," the nurse said, speaking over Kylara's head.

KEVIN MCLAUGHLIN & MICHAEL ANDERLE

"Every word of it was true. I saw it myself," Sam said. "Professor Sharra and Kor were there, they can corroborate—"

"I'm not interested in corroboration," the woman said. "Keep an eye on your friend, all right? She seems healthy to me, although in need of food and rest—as are you, headmaster. How that can be after being turned into stone is again something I have no experience with. Please, if either of you notice anything unusual, let me know." With that, she spun on her heel and marched out of the tiny infirmary.

"Well then, Miss Diamantine, I suppose you're free to return to your dorm," Lady Amythist said. "You will tell me if anything is amiss?"

Kylara felt the headmaster's aura prod her, willing her to want to do exactly that. She might have minded it once but after battling with Tiamat, the headmaster's aura did not seem nearly as formidable.

"I will, headmaster." She climbed out of the bed and bowed politely. It was tempting to add, "and if you get frozen in stone again, you know how to call for me to get you out," but instead, she merely said, "Perhaps I can come for tea sometime?"

"That would be lovely, dear, yes," Amythist bowed so slightly it was almost imperceptible. Still, it was a sign of respect that the headmaster had not previously shown to her. Even if she had not been a part of the jungle battle where she freed herself from Tiamat's clutches, the ancient dragon understood that it was Kylara and her unusual powers that had freed her.

"Come on, Ky. Tanya's probably dying to know if you're all right." Sam took her by the hand and pulled her out of the infirmary and into the U, a large lawn in the center of the three main buildings that made up the Lumos School.

"Oh. My. God! Kylara!" Tanya screamed the moment they stepped outside, ran to her roommate, and wrapped her up in a hug. The embrace was augmented with so much dragon strength that for a moment, the dragon mage was worried she might need

16

to be checked into the infirmary again, this time for a cracked rib. She had no idea how long she had been there although it could not have been more than a half-hour. In that time Tanya had showered, put on a new dress, and redone her makeup. She looked amazingly overdressed, as usual.

"We thought we might have lost you," Karl Midnight said. He had an arm draped over Jasmine Patel's shoulder, which was a new development.

Tanya did not fail to see Kylara noticing this.

"Oh yeah, they're a thing now. Like officially." Her roommate winked.

"Is that right?" Sam asked and grinned at Karl. The two boys —despite both being Kylara's closest friends—could not have looked more different. Sam was broad-shouldered, blond and tanned, with a smile that could have made most normal humans aspire to a modeling career. Karl was skinny, pale, and had long black hair that was perpetually greasy. He might have had a nice smile but she wouldn't know as he perpetually wore a frown.

"Jasmine kicks ass. I like people who kick ass. I don't see a problem." Midnight shrugged and neatly bypassed the whole mage and dragon relationship subject.

"You don't think your dad will be mad that I kind of—"

"Kicked his ass?" Karl snorted in amusement. "Nah. My old man may be a Follower of Tiamat but he knows what power means. My guess is that you'll be in his good graces as soon as he doesn't have to keep pretending to care about her."

That soured the conversation like lemon juice. Kylara had thrown Tiamat's spirit out of her mind but that had not stopped the dragon. Instead, she had taken the body of one of her Followers and fled. Not that she counted that as a victory. Her only question about the self-proclaimed goddess's intentions was if she planned to steal her body again or simply kill her.

"So, who's hungry?" Tanya clapped her hands and smiled. She

was the best at moving conversations along. "Or did the four of you think more of a double date situation?"

The young dragon mage was still not accustomed to always being able to feel dragon auras, although in this case, she liked it. She could feel that Tanya felt a little left out and much like a fifth wheel, but she could also feel her genuine joy over the fact that her four best friends were finally being honest about their feelings.

Karl and Sam must have felt her aura too as they both reacted quickly and spoke over each other to invite her with them. Kylara felt their misgivings at this too. Both the boys wanted to be alone with the girls to flirt, but they also valued their relationships with Tanya and the group as a whole.

"Kylara, are you all right?" Tanya asked. "You're feeling a little…"

"Overwhelmed," Sam finished.

Jasmine sighed in annoyance. "This is a dragon aura moment, isn't it? I think I liked it more when Ky still had that amulet so two of us non-dragons could communicate normally."

Kylara laughed. "Me too! Maybe we should get some food. I can tell that the dragons at least—"

"I'm hungry too," the mage interjected.

The five friends set off across the U and hurried to the dining hall. Truly, it was so much more than that. With carved pillars, a ceiling of historical frescoes, and a mosaic floor that showed two dragons locked in eternal battle, the room where the student body of the Lumos School ate would have worked as a museum hall equally as well as a place for kids to eat.

It wasn't only the look of it that Kylara loved but also the smells. As soon as they opened the grand, oversized doors, her nostrils were assaulted with the aromas of beef and barley stew seasoned with herbs from the headmaster's garden and freshly baked bread.

The five of them hurried across the room. They were barely

halfway across before some of the lower classmen noticed who had entered.

The dragon mage added the sounds of the room to the reasons she loved it as the students cheered and clapped for the triumphant return of the victorious students. She knew the victory was temporary at best—Tiamat was still out there—but it was hard to feel that as a pressing concern when over a hundred dragon auras rallied her with their excitement. This was a huge advantage of being able to sense auras, she decided with a grin.

With smiles plastered on their faces—even Karl, who had always been a sucker for fame—she and her friends stacked their trays with herbed rolls and filled bowls of soup.

By the time they found a table and sat, the applause had died down although the emotion in the room was still one of triumph. Despite all the stress they had been through, the sensation of everyone's aura was enough to almost make her want to relive everything they had been through.

"I still don't know how you all managed to send me energy inside Tiamat. That was a huge risk." Kylara ripped a piece of roll off and dunked it in her soup.

"That was all Sam," Karl said. "My vote was to let you stay a goddess."

They all laughed at that except Tanya, who stared at her phone.

"Tanya, your power was there too," she said warmly. "It was your leaves and vine which gave structure to the beam of energy that saved me. I don't think the light and dark powers would have worked together as well without you in the middle."

"Huh?" her friend said and looked up from her phone.

"Kylara was laying it on thick, is all," Jasmine said.

"Oh, sure, yeah." The girl returned her attention to her phone.

"Is something going on?" Sam asked her.

Tanya looked up again, took a deep breath, and turned her

phone to face her friends. "I got a text from a number I don't have saved."

"Well, what does it say?" Karl demanded.

Jasmine—seated next to Tanya—leaned closer and read aloud. "I need your help. Can you meet me outside campus near the dueling ground? Galen."

CHAPTER FOUR

Karl was the first to break the moment of silence. He chose to sum up how he felt about the text with a derisive snort. "That's what has you all freaked? So what? Some dude got your number and is pranking you. They're probably at another table laughing their heads off about that stupid look on your face right now."

His words shifted Tanya's aura to frustration but also made her doubtful about the authenticity of the text. "I don't know. Why would anyone try to trick me like that?"

Sam shrugged. "Okay, well...it is common knowledge that you and Galen got your powers in the same place. Both of you snuck off and came back with new abilities. Maybe someone is jealous?"

"I wouldn't put it past some of the mages," Karl said out of the corner of his mouth while he chewed a roll. "It's getting better between dragons and mages, but some of them think it means mages should be able to mess with dragons the same way dragons have messed with them."

"Sending someone a text as a joke is hardly the same as enslaving people for millennia," Jasmine said to him and pulled away so they no longer sat as close.

"I know that. I'm only saying it makes sense. Come on. Galen's dead. Who else could it be but someone messing around? It could be a dragon for that matter."

Tanya felt a pulse of guilt from Kylara. She looked up and saw her friend biting her lip. It was insane to be able to feel her aura after it had been faked for so long. She had grown accustomed to not being able to read her roommate. The pendant she had always worn did little more besides reflect the aura of the dragons around her. Although she had made some progress in being able to read her friend's facial expressions, biting her lip had always been inscrutable. She thought she did it to hide her expressions but now, with her aura, it was obvious that she was trying to hide more than her feelings.

"Kylara?" she asked and drew her friend's name out into a question by augmenting it with curiosity from her aura.

"Galen…might not be dead," the dragon mage said after a long moment of hesitation.

"Wait—what do you mean might not be dead? He died fighting Boneclaw," Sam protested, his aura heavy with concern and directed at Kylara. Tanya couldn't help but think of the summer when she and Sam had tried to date. Looking back, it had been ridiculous. Now that she could see Kylara's and his auras, it was obvious that the two cared about each other. Even with the prospect of someone coming back from the dead, he was squarely focused on her. She wondered if the girl knew how much he cared about her.

Kylara shrugged. "He didn't, though."

Everyone stared at her and she swallowed hard.

"You need to keep talking," Tanya implored.

"When I fought Boneclaw on the mountain top, Galen arrived to help. I wouldn't have been able to gain the victory without his help, honestly," she said.

"I thought you defeated Boneclaw in the void?" Karl asked.

"I did." Her aura made it clear she was telling the truth. "But I could never have been able to get him through the portal without Galen's help."

"Why didn't you tell us?" Sam asked. "His family...they don't know either?"

She shook her head. "He asked me not to tell them. He's...not the same." Kylara sighed and her aura made it clear that she struggled with what to say. She had very little control over it. It was cute but Tanya knew she wouldn't see it that way.

"What, he's no longer a jerk?" Karl asked.

"Like you're one to talk," Sam retorted.

"I'm not." Karl grinned wolfishly as Jasmine slapped him on the arm.

"Honestly, he's...uh, not human anymore. Or dragon," Kylara said. "Boneclaw did something to him. When I last saw him, he was...I don't know—trapped between the two forms, I guess. It wasn't pretty. He said he knew his family wouldn't want him if they saw him like that."

"I don't think the Stormwings would care what he looked like if he could control the skeletons of the dead," Karl pointed out.

Kylara shook her head. "He can't. Not when I last saw him, anyway."

"Do you think this is him?" Tanya asked.

She shrugged, doubt and certainty at war in her aura. "I don't know. I think it could be. The last time I saw him was near here. Plus, I don't see why anyone would use him to mess with Tanya."

"Who cares if it is Galen?" Karl asked. "The dude was a jerk when he was still a vanilla dragon. He became an even bigger jerk when he got weird powers. He's probably still one now."

"He fought with Kylara against Boneclaw, though," Tanya said and her gaze wandered to the text message still open on the screen of her phone.

"He realized that she was more powerful than Boneclaw and took a gamble. There's nothing noble in that," Karl said.

"Oh yeah. Are you speaking from experience?" Sam taunted.

"I hope all of you know that I wouldn't be friends with you if you were half as powerful as you are now. I'm here because you're the only people I know—dragons or mages—who can keep up with me." Midnight grinned until everyone pelted him with rolls.

"I think I'll go check it out," Tanya said and pushed her chair out so she could stand.

A tendril of shadow caught the chair and blocked her before she could step away. Tanya glared at Karl before she realized that Kylara had stopped her.

"If you're going, I'm going with you," the dragon mage said.

Tanya smiled at her. "I won't argue with the Sum of All Dragons."

She smiled. "If you want to use one of the weird titles people have given me, the Big Pixie is my preferred moniker."

"I'm coming too," Sam said. "If Galen is alive, it makes sense that he'd reach out to us and Tanya specifically. You two did get your powers in the same place. But we can't be sure it's him. The Followers of Tiamat are still out there. If one of them discovered that Galen was still alive—hell, if one of them guessed that Galen was still alive—this could be them."

"How could they possibly know about him?" Tanya asked. "We didn't even know about him and we're Ky's best friends."

"I'm not the only kid whose parents belong to that cult," Karl said. "The Lumos School has historically been a school for dragons with unusual powers. If someone—anyone—saw him wander off, they might have told the wrong person. I'll come too."

"I agree that we can't face problems by running away from them," Jasmine added. "Count me in."

Tanya smiled at everyone at the table. "I guess I shouldn't be surprised that the four of you are willing to leave campus based on a text."

Kylara smiled. "It's good to know I've been a bad influence on all of you."

"Says the girl who never left the piece of land she grew up on for sixteen years," her roommate teased.

They left the dining hall and hurried across the grounds toward the dueling fields. Despite it being fairly late in the day, the lengthening daylight of late spring set the sky afire with red light. Tanya found it so beautiful and tranquil that it was almost possible to forget that only hours earlier, they had fought for their lives and Kylara's soul.

They reached the dueling grounds to find them unsurprisingly empty. It was late, after all, and the events of the morning had been a little much, even for a school tasked with training dragons and mages in the particulars of combat.

"I don't see him," Karl said. "If the sprinklers turn on, I swear I will use my shadow powers to keep me and Jasmine dry and let the rest of you get soaked."

"Tanya has plant powers, dork," Sam reminded Karl. "If anyone planned a prank, they wouldn't use water."

"So what, then? Is someone simply wasting our time?" the shadow dragon asked and looked around the empty field.

"I don't think so..." Tanya said warily. She peered into the woods on one side of the large area. "Do you all feel that?"

Sam nodded after a moment. "Yeah...it feels like an aura but I don't know...muffled somehow?"

"It could be a bear or an elk or whatever," Karl said unhelpfully.

Kylara only shook her head. "Honestly, between Karl not wanting to be here, Tanya's curiosity, and Sam's...feelings for me, I can't feel much else."

Tanya smiled. Her friend was a beast in battle but her aura was so weak. Still, it was stronger than whatever emanated from the woods.

"Come on," the plant dragon said and took the lead. "Let's investigate."

They entered the woods and the warm light of late afternoon became the darkness of early evening. It was quiet in there, save for the chirp of desert creatures and the occasional bird thankful to call this forest in a canyon their home.

"I don't see anything," Karl said.

"Honestly, I'm with Karl. Unless you want me to light it up?" Sam asked and his eyes started to glow with his light powers.

"No, no. Give Tanya a minute," Kylara said. "Do you think you can use the roots to sense for someone?"

The girl closed her eyes and tried to do exactly that. It had taken a ton of practice but given that she was the first dragon to ever be able to communicate with plants, she did not mind exploring and perfecting her ability. She reached out to the trees now, especially the larger ones whose roots extended a long way just under the surface of the soil. She asked them if anything felt unusual.

As always, it took a while for them to answer. Trees—despite being shorter-lived than dragons—were masters of patience. Something stepping on their roots didn't register immediately, which made sense. Even if an elk slept on them all night, it wouldn't count for much of anything in their lifetime. Tanya had even met some who had yet to notice a new pile of rocks that had been dropped onto their roots.

But now that she had asked, the trees responded. They always did. That was part of her power. While she could tell plants what to do, it was more of a collaborative effort than a command. She thought it was because she had learned the power in the pixie realm. Most dragon powers were overwhelming, fearsome things. Hers was more about asking if plants wanted magic to grow in certain ways and waiting for them to say yes so she could then help them do what she wanted.

So, while Karl fidgeted and Sam stopped himself from shining a spotlight into the woods, she felt to determine if any of the trees needed something removed from their roots. After a moment, she had a reply from a small cluster of junipers deeper into the small forest. It seemed they were unhappy about something heavy with pointy parts. That was good enough for Tanya.

"This way," she said and led the group deeper between the trees.

She saw it through the gloom and realized how wrong she had been. It was one of the guardian statues that had been erected around the perimeter of the campus. In the shape of a griffin, it appeared to be solid stone but Kylara had told them the statues sprang to life if someone tried to cross the perimeter.

"Sorry, y'all. False alarm," she said.

Tanya was about to reach out to the trees again when something else stepped from the gloom.

Her first thought was that it was another of the statues—one of the hideous gargoyles like those atop the main gate of the Lumos School. But as it came closer, she saw that it wasn't made of stone but flesh.

Karl managed to speak first. "Holy crap, Galen? Is that you? Dude...you look like hell."

"It's good to know my brother's buddy is still a jerk," the figure who could only be Galen replied.

"Oh, sorry, man," Midnight said and his aura surged with genuine remorse. "I stopped hanging out with your brother a while back. He was a real jerk."

"We can agree on that, anyway," Galen took another step closer. "Hi, Tanya. Thanks for coming. Kylara...good to see you too. And thanks for keeping this a secret." He gestured to his body with fingers that ended with claws that were much too long for his mostly human form. "Lumos, you might as well give everyone some light so we can get the whole 'take a look at this disfigured freak' part over with."

Sam nodded and his skin glowed with golden light to illuminate the small area in which they stood.

"Oh, Galen, I'm so sorry." Tears trickled from Tanya's eyes. She couldn't help it. Galen had never been the jaw-droppingly handsome young man Sam was, but she had always found him attractive. Now, the parts she recognized only served to remind her of how different he was.

The boy's body took the general shape of a human, except he had dragon claws and dragon wings, which both looked uncomfortably large. His skin was a mottled mix of scales and skin, with scabs where the two met. But his face—oh, God, his face.

His mouth extended like a dragon's snout but the teeth inside didn't quite fit—as if all his dragon teeth had been crammed into this foreshortened version. Rather than having a snout with two holes like most dragons, he had a human nose crammed on top of his face. Unlike his snout, which was scaled, his nose was incongruously fleshy and skin toned, which honestly wasn't appealing. It was also covered in scratches as if he had tried to remove it with his claws.

He had no ears which, given everything else, should not have even been a footnote, yet Tanya couldn't help but feel like his head was missing something. Ragged patches of hair looked like he might have tried to shear off as much of it as he could.

Worst of all were his eyes. They had changed considerably. Although they were the pale gray of a winter sky, they were human eyes without a doubt. Like a human, they expressed pain in a way dragon eyes simply could not. She honestly didn't remember what color they had been when he had still been fully human, but she recognized these as his.

"I know I have no right to be here," Galen began and hung his head in shame. "I don't deserve any of your help. Kylara, it was charity for you to let me live."

"I wasn't about to kill you after you helped me with Boneclaw. We'd all be living under his rule if not for you," the dragon mage said. "I said I would help you and I meant it."

He nodded, straightened his spine, and tried to look her in the face but could not manage it. Instead, his gaze found Tanya's and she could not look away.

"I don't know who else to go to. I tried to go to my family but the defenses they have in place..." Galen shook his head. "I couldn't even make it past the wind."

"How did you get in here?" Sam asked, ever the pragmatist.

"Honestly, I didn't know if it would work at first. These guard statues are fearsome. I've seen them foil a few dragons who tried to sneak in."

"You've been in the area then?" Karl asked.

The boy nodded. "I can't let people see me like this. I can't let anyone see me like this. The desert has been tough, but at least... at least there's no water so I don't have to see my...my reflection." He began to weep and before she realized what she was doing, Tanya embraced him.

"It's all right, Galen. We're glad you came."

He cried harder. "You're the first person to even touch me since...since I became this...monster!"

She hugged him tighter and let him cry.

After a moment, he pulled himself together. "Sorry. It has been so long since I've talked to anyone." He went to wipe his eyes but Tanya stopped him. She assumed that was how he had gotten those scratches. She took a handkerchief out and dabbed them for him instead.

"You were saying?" she asked gently.

"Well, eventually, I got so desperate that I decided I might as well try to break into campus and let the statues finish me off, only they didn't. They didn't even budge."

"They must recognize you as a student," Jasmine said.

"How is that possible?" Karl asked, which was a little rude for Tanya's taste but she knew better than to point it out.

"Mage magic is weird. These defenses are wrapped in identity.

Honestly, you getting past them proves that you're Galen better than any test I can think of," Jasmine explained.

Galen nodded. "When I found out they wouldn't simply kill me, it changed everything. I couldn't stop thinking about you." He looked into Tanya's eyes. "All of you," he added belatedly. "I think you're the only people who can help me."

"Help you with what?" Tanya asked.

"Boneclaw did this to me in the pixie realm," he said, his eyes pleading as he stared at her. "Maybe if I can go back there, I can undo this somehow."

"Are you sure this isn't about becoming a bone lord again?" Karl asked.

"It's not. I swear it's not," Galen said, his voice firm for the first time since they'd been talking. "Boneclaw took those powers from me and I'm glad he did. They weren't right. Nothing about them was right and I'm glad they're gone."

"You only want to be normal again," Tanya said softly.

"More than anything." He choked on a sob before he began to weep again.

Tanya went to embrace him but before she could, a dark tendril on her shoulder pulled her away. She looked at Kylara but this time, it was Karl who had done it.

"Galen, you understand that we'll have to talk about this amongst ourselves—right, buddy?" Karl said.

The boy nodded. "I've been alone for so long that a few more minutes is fine. If you can't, I understand. I truly do. I only...I didn't know where else to go."

Midnight beckoned for Tanya to come closer to the others and created a sphere of shadow all around them. The sounds of insects vanished, muffled by the web of shadow.

"Golden boy, do you mind?" he asked.

A ball of light appeared in the darkness and levitated above Sam's palm. The light was dim but still bright enough to make the interior surface of the shadow web crawl in the glow. It said much about how far the two had come that Karl could regrow a shadow web at the right rate to compensate for Sam's power. It seemed their powers weren't the only two things in sync.

"This has to be a scam, right?" Karl asked. "Seriously, he wants us to go to the pixie realm? I'm willing to bet there is a certain pond he thinks will be a good place to try to 'heal' him, too."

"I agree with the ink stain," Sam added. "It seems like a good ploy to get us off campus."

"But Boneclaw is gone," Kylara said. "I finished him myself."

"It could be the Followers of Tiamat," Sam pointed out, which earned him a smidge of annoyance from Kylara's aura.

"Well...I don't think so," Karl said. His aura made it known that he didn't want to say this but thought it to be true. "Galen was always a vanilla. Followers of Tiamat don't have time for them. Plus, in his current condition, they'd like him even less. They're horrible about stuff like that."

"Then do you think we can trust him?" Jasmine asked him.

The shadow dragon curled his lip. "Just because he's not with the cult doesn't mean we should trust him."

"I trust him," Kylara said. "He can be a pain but he came through for us—for the whole world when you think about it—when it mattered most."

"Plus, maybe we can help him," Tanya said. To her, this was the part of the entire equation that made the most sense. If Tiamat wanted to send an agent of some kind, there was no reason to think she would have chosen a disgraced dragon in hiding. Galen coming to them made sense precisely because Kylara was the only dragon on the planet who could take him to the pixie realm. For that matter, Tanya was the only dragon who had obtained her powers in the same way he had.

"I agree with Kylara and Tanya," Jasmine interjected. "I don't think this is a trap. Why would Tiamat try something on the same day we defeated her? How could she even have the energy?"

Everyone smirked at that. Tiamat may have styled herself a

goddess but they had beaten her. What did that make them?

"Then we help," Kylara said. "Three to two. Majority rules."

"Fine," Karl said and began to unravel the web of shadow around them.

"Now wait a minute," Sam protested and the other boy stopped. "If you all want to help him, that's fine, but it doesn't mean it's a great idea for Kylara to leave campus and go to the pixie realm right now. The nurse said you needed food and rest."

"Yeah, and I ate," Kylara said although her aura betrayed her weariness.

"Ky, you're tired," Sam said. "We can all feel it on you."

She looked like she wanted to protest but Jasmine spoke first. "Even I can tell you're exhausted, Kylara."

The dragon mage nodded and let her shoulders sag. "I want to help Galen, I truly do. I think it's the right thing to do…"

"But?" Tanya could hear it coming.

"Well, frankly, the idea of going back to the pixie realm right now sounds exhausting. And if Karl's right and we have to return to that pond…" She shook her head. "I faced Boneclaw there and the Cult of Tiamat." She bit her lip and Tanya felt fear creep into her aura.

Sam nodded. "Plus, Tiamat is still a threat in this world. We may need you here."

"Now there's a depressing thought," Kylara joked cheerfully but they could all tell that the idea had already occurred to her and she did not find it pleasant.

"Why does Kylara have to go?" Tanya asked.

"She's the only one who can open portals." Karl snorted.

"So open one for us."

"That…that could work." The dragon mage nodded.

"So, we're agreed, then?" Tanya asked. "We're helping Galen."

Everyone looked at each other but eventually, they all nodded.

Karl lowered his shadow shield. "It's your lucky day, Galen. It turns out my new friends are far nicer than my old ones."

CHAPTER FIVE

With her aura no longer shielded, Kylara could feel Galen's relief at being told they would help him. It was like an enormous weight lifted from him. He didn't change physically yet somehow, he seemed less monstrous as if whatever had haunted him had been pushed back, at least for the time being. His eyes didn't look as pained and his back didn't look as twisted.

"Thank you. Thank you all so much," he said haltingly. "Kylara, when do we leave? I would like to go as soon as we can but have waited a long time. I can make it another few days."

"Now hold up," Sam said. "We agreed to help but that doesn't mean Kylara will go with you."

The boy looked confused. That put to rest any doubts that Kylara still had about him working with Tiamat. He did not seem to be aware of everything that had happened to her at that pyramid in the jungle.

"Kylara has had quite the day," Tanya said. "She'll open a gate for you and me so we can try to solve your ailment, then open another one to bring us back when we're done."

"And how exactly is that supposed to work?" Karl asked.

"We'll have to time it," Sam said.

"That will be tricky with the time distortion," Kylara said. "Time passes faster over here than over there."

"But that's a good thing," Tanya pointed out. "If you give us an hour here, that should be way more time over there. We should be able to accomplish whatever we need to and come back before your bedtime."

If I'm still awake, she wanted to say as she began to feel the fatigue weighing her eyelids down, but she remained silent. Opening portals was easy. She could do that and if she fell asleep, Sam or Jasmine could wake her.

"There's also the issue of Tiamat," Sam said.

"Galen's not with her, I'm telling you," Karl said.

"Tiamat?" Galen asked. "You mean like the fairytale?"

"It's a long story," Tanya said. "I can tell you in the pixie realm."

Sam shook his head. "What I mean is we can't pretend like we're completely safe over here. Tiamat could attack and delay us, or worse. If that happens, you two would be stuck there."

"Don't talk like that!" Tanya snapped, which Kylara loved even though it was profoundly naïve.

"Sam's right," Jasmine said. "Ky is the only dragon who can open a gate."

"But not the only pixie," the dragon mage added. "If the worst happens and I can't open a gate, you'll have to find a pixie. They can all open gates. It's their magic that lets me do it."

"I don't know. I tried that," Galen said. "They don't want anything to do with me."

"Yeah, the whole resurrecting the dead to make an army can have that effect on people," Karl quipped.

The other boy didn't try to defend himself and simply nodded.

"I have plant powers, which the pixies seem to appreciate," Tanya said thoughtfully. "I hope you don't leave us stranded but if something happens, I'll have to make it work."

"Maybe this is all too much." Galen looked worried. Kylara could sense his aura but compared to everyone else's, it seemed muddied.

"It's too late now." She grinned and tried to not let her fatigue show before she realized yet again that her aura made it painfully clear. "None of us could live with ourselves knowing you're out there barely managing to survive."

"So, we meet at this same place tomorrow at dawn. It's a Saturday, so we should be able to all hang here for the hour while you two are gone," Sam said.

"Sam, I can do it now," Kylara protested.

He shook his head. "No way. You need rest. Galen, you can wait another twelve hours, I trust? I'll bring you soup and bread."

"I could wait three days for soup and bread," Galen stammered.

"Great. We'll see you then. Now come on, Kylara, it's bedtime."

Kylara had not liked being whisked off to bed like a little kid—not until her head touched her pillow. Ten hours later, with a full night of wondrous, dreamless, and nightmare-free sleep behind her, she felt much better.

Her eyes fluttered open and she paused, surprised that Tanya was already awake. "Good. You're up. Oh, my God, Ky—how do you wear these? Everyone can see my legs."

"They're jeans, Tanya. It's not like they're transparent."

The girl snorted. "I thought this was the smarter choice if we have to go into the swamp at all, but I don't know... I look ridiculous."

"Normally, you look ridiculous. Right now, you look normal. There's no reason to wear a ballgown on a mission like this."

"Oh, honestly, Ky! I only own three ballgowns and I wouldn't

35

wear any of them for something like this...although the green one might do the trick—"

"Tanya, no." Kylara pushed out of bed. "Can you get me breakfast and meet me where we saw Galen yesterday?"

"You're sending me on an errand so I don't change," Tanya accused her.

She grinned. "Guilty. You wouldn't want the Big Pixie to go hungry before she opens a portal for you, right?"

Her roommate rolled her eyes. "Great, now my best friend is referring to herself in the third person." But she responded well enough to the request. She changed her top a final time and hurried to the dining hall.

Kylara dressed and proceeded to walk across campus. She loved how quiet the school was early in the morning. The birds hadn't even woken up yet.

She found Sam waiting for her at the edge of the woods with a thermos of coffee. "Hey," he said warmly.

"Hey yourself. I'm cold," she replied. Despite it being late spring, nights were almost always cold in the desert.

He didn't miss a beat and slid an arm around her shoulder. "I'm cold too."

In response, she heated her skin and he seemed to melt against her.

"Ew, gross—you're both glowing," Karl said but even his sneer couldn't ruin her good mood. There was something wonderful about a night of sleep without nightmares.

He and Jasmine came across the field, each holding coffee. Tanya was on the far side of and carried a bag that already had dark spots from where either butter or bacon grease had touched the brown paper. Kylara's stomach grumbled at the prospect.

United once more, the five set off through the woods. She wondered if seeing Galen had all been a dream, but when they reached the statues at the perimeter of the school and one of them unfurled the wings around it to reveal their magically deformed former classmate, she accepted that her reality would forever be as strange as any dream.

Tanya passed food out to everyone—including Galen, who thanked her profusely before he all but inhaled the biscuits and sausage—and they discussed the final details of how to help the boy.

"We can't open a portal on campus too easily," Tanya pointed out. "And I hadn't planned to dig."

Karl pulled some shadow tendrils up, but Kylara could see that he was doubtful about how much work it might be.

"I can handle that," she said and called on one of her many newfound powers. The ability to move earth was something Tiamat had used with great success. She discovered that after spending so much time sculpting and shaping things with the shadow powers she learned from Karl, creating a tunnel under the perimeter of the school wasn't all that difficult. It was a relatively simple matter to force the dirt to pull itself out the far end of the tunnel. The great snake of earth mounded itself into a pile behind a cluster of boulders. She made sure to not scatter it. If all went well, she would replace it in sixty-one minutes.

The five friends plus Galen walked through the tunnel and emerged outside the protective shield and ring of guardian statues around the Lumos School.

"All right. Is everyone ready?" she asked.

"Are we sure the time distortion will work?" Sam asked.

"Kristen Hall's reports of the pixie realm made it sound like days or even weeks had passed when she tried to get a new power," Kylara pointed out. "If anything, we'll give them too much time."

"An hour is fine," Tanya said. "Intention is everything, right? We can do this in an hour."

Galen nodded. "If we can't, then it's okay. You all helping me —well, it means a lot."

"Can you open the portal before we all start singing 'kumbaya?'" Karl groaned.

"Let's do it," Kylara said and a portal into the pixie realm blazed into existence.

Tanya looked at her, nodded once, and took Galen's claw to lead him through.

The dragon mage waved farewell and was about to close the gate when Jasmine pulled free from Karl and followed them.

"Jasmine! What are you doing?" Midnight demanded.

"Helping someone who needs it!" the mage responded. Her voice sounded strange echoing out of a world with different rules than the one the others stood in.

Karl cursed under his breath and hurried toward the portal.

"Midnight?" Sam asked, flabbergasted.

"Well, someone has to keep them all in one piece. Don't forget about us, okay?" the other boy said through clenched teeth and followed Jasmine into the clearing on the other side of the gateway.

"I won't," Kylara said. "You have fifty-nine minutes and fifteen seconds. It will feel way longer for all of you but that's all you're getting before you come back."

"Not a second longer," Karl said with no humor in his voice and his eyes serious. "If you're late because you start making out, I'll tell Hester Diamantine."

She smiled, nodded, and closed the gate behind her friends.

CHAPTER SIX

Kylara had enough time to sip her coffee and smile somewhat awkwardly at the fact that she and Sam were now alone in the woods. Before either of them could speak, the magical shield around the Lumos School failed and the statues on the perimeter of the grounds came to life.

Seeing statues of mythological beasts staring sightlessly out into the desert was disconcerting, but it was nothing compared to seeing them come to life and prepare for battle. They couldn't detect any signs of immediate attack but the statues wouldn't animate without a threat.

"Crud," Sam said and glanced at the gold watch on his wrist.

"At least I had a good night's sleep." She smiled weakly as she prepared herself mentally to fight and defeat a goddess who had stolen her body and ransacked her mind. As things stood, she only had fifty-eight minutes and forty seconds to spare.

"Come on. We need to get back with everyone else," Sam said.

She nodded. They would have to return in an hour but that would be meaningless if there was nowhere to come back to.

They hurried out of the woods, across the dueling grounds,

and to the U. She was prepared for a fight but what she saw in the U didn't put fear on her face. Instead, she smiled.

"Amy Williams?" The question was more about what the woman was doing there.

"Kylara!" The world's most powerful mage hopped off her skateboard and wrapped her in a hug.

At the behest of Professor Sharra, the team of security mages recast the security spell that protected the Lumos School from the air. In an instant, Kylara was able to breathe again, her fears about an attack laid to rest.

"What are you doing here?" she asked Amy.

"Kristen sent me to check on you. There was an attack on the Lumos School and you were a part of it?"

"Yes, ma'am. I'm sorry about that," she said.

"It's fine—well, as long you never call me 'ma'am' again." Amy grinned. "I've been in touch with your headmaster and she said that the campus has been secured. I went to Mexico to see the battlefield. I have to say, Kylara, I've never seen anything like the aftermath of what happened down there. Are you all right?"

She nodded. "I am, thanks to my friends."

"Where are the rest of them?" Amy asked.

Kylara and Sam shared a look before he glanced at his watch. "They wanted to sleep in," Sam mumbled. "No light powers, you know?"

It was appealing how obvious it was that Sam was lying. His aura made it as plain as day yet to Amy—despite being able to best almost any dragon in single combat—his deception was invisible and hidden behind his perfect smile.

"Well, you snooze you lose, I guess," the woman muttered. "I thought with everything going on, it might be best if you come with me to Detroit, at least until this cult nonsense is settled. We can keep you safe there. I planned to invite your little cadre too, but I guess only young Mr. Lumos will join us."

Sam and Kylara shared a look and an exchange of auras. He

was conflicted. While he thought going with Amy would be the safest thing for her, he didn't want to abandon his friends.

"I can use my powers anywhere," she said. "And if Tiamat decides to attack Kristen, I would like to be there to help."

"Of course, you would," Sam said, his aura both proud of her and letting her know he felt she was ridiculous.

"I don't think she would dare," Amy said with a shrug. "But honestly, I'm in rather a hurry. I haven't been able to make contact with anyone in Detroit—not even Brian, and he practically lives on the Internet. I guess it's my phone but there's a landline in the headmaster's office."

"That's odd, isn't it?" Sam asked and furrowed his perfect brow.

The mage both shrugged and nodded. "Kristen's not above doing blackout drills. She came to power against a force that was better at tech than her team was and isn't one to trust it implicitly. Still, I'd like to go sooner rather than later. We need to check with the headmaster if you two can still come but I don't want to wait for your friends."

"That's fine," the two students blurted together.

"Is it?" Amy asked. Kylara could feel that the woman was suspicious. It was odd, given that the mage couldn't sense her aura at all. She tried to soothe her feelings but that only earned a glare. "I don't know which one of you is doing that but I work with Heartsbane on a daily basis so you'll have to be more subtle than that. And—by the way—nothing is more suspicious than a dragon trying to make you feel unsuspicious."

The young dragon mage tried to think of a more convincing lie but thankfully, she didn't have to. Amy truly was in a hurry. She marched toward Amythist's office and beckoned for the two of them to do the same.

A minute later—and with forty-nine minutes still on the clock —they were outside their destination. The mage knocked and pushed the door open without waiting for a response.

KEVIN MCLAUGHLIN & MICHAEL ANDERLE

Kylara knew instantly that something was wrong, even without her new aura power. A pale-faced Amythist was seated at her desk. Her eyes widened when she saw the two dragons and the mage standing at the door and she waved at them to enter as she finished her phone conversation. Dread, worry, and down-right terror dripped from the headmaster's aura and it seemed clear that this wasn't some kind of test, either. The ancient dragon hung up and gestured for them to close the door and have a seat.

"Let me fix some tea," she mumbled, more to herself than her guests—which was unusual—and tried to crush leaves to put into her teapot. Her hands shook so badly that she only succeeded in making a mess of crumbled tea.

"Here, Headmaster, allow me," Sam said politely and moved to take over from her. He didn't have heat powers like the head-master or Kylara, so they all had to listen to the kettle become increasingly louder as the water inside heated to boiling. Amythist said nothing while they waited—no niceties, no admonishments for being up so early, nothing.

The golden dragon poured the water over the crushed leaves and placed the teapot on the table for it to steep.

"Is everything all right, Lady Amythist?" Amy asked after a moment. "You look like you've seen a ghost."

"I fear a ghost is exactly the problem," the headmaster replied.

"What are you talking about?" The mage looked like she wanted to laugh but knew it wasn't a joke.

Kylara, however, knew what was wrong—or at least who must surely be to blame. She felt it in her gut.

"Tiamat has already struck," Amythist said and poured herself a cup of weak tea.

"She struck here, right?" Amy asked in clear confusion. "That's why I'm here."

The old dragon shook her head. "She struck at the Dragon

Council last night and used Kishar's ability on all of them. Kristen...that is, Lady Steel..."

The young dragon mage squared her jaw and finished the statement when her headmaster trailed off, unable to continue. "Kristen Hall is frozen in stone and I'm the only one who can turn her back."

CHAPTER SEVEN

"What are you talking about? Frozen in stone?" Amy demanded. She had begun to float out of her chair, as had some of the mess in the office.

"Kishar has a power that can petrify people," Kylara explained, her heart as heavy as rock. She felt nothing at all. While she knew she should feel fear, panic, or dread, all she felt was ice-cold resolution. Part of her insisted that she should have known this would happen.

"Tiamat must have used the ability to strike at the Dragon Council," Sam said. "That's why you haven't heard from them."

"She could not have frozen the entire Steel Guard." Amythist's aura said that she wanted to believe this but couldn't.

"No...I don't think so," Sam agreed. "But Kylara has the best idea about her. Do you think that's possible?"

The dragon mage shook her head. "No. I interned there all summer. It's a big place and Kishar's power doesn't have a huge range. Her aura, though? That's a whole other level of power."

"She must have used it on Brian," the old dragon said. The tea had brought some of the color back to her face. "He was always fairly susceptible to auras and he would have the knowledge to shut the electricity down."

The two students shared a look. Both doubted her assessment of someone's abilities when it came to tech. They both looked at Amy, who had elevated almost to the ceiling. She seemed to notice them staring at her and floated down. Her face was twisted in rage and her fists clenched with white knuckles.

"Amy, could Brian do that?"

"If this bitch hurt any of them, I swear on my magic that I will end her," the mage fumed. "Headmaster, I will need to leave these two with you. I need Sharra to drop the shield so I can port out of here and rip this Tiamat's head off her body."

"That would not be wise," Amythist said.

"I couldn't care less about wisdom right now. My best friend is trapped in stone and has been for possibly twelve hours. What kind of person am I if I don't even try?"

"A person who can help. You cannot rush in, Amy," the headmaster cautioned.

"The hell I can't. I have power this Timoot or whoever wouldn't dream of."

"Lady Amythist is right," Sam said. "Tiamat is much stronger than any dragon I've ever seen."

"So what?" Kylara said. "I'm with Amy. Let's drop the shields. I can portal in there, unfreeze the Dragon Council, and together, we can eliminate Tiamat for good."

"And if it's a trap?" he asked.

She had never had her opinion changed so quickly. He was right, of course. It irked her to concede but she knew he was right.

"Then we destroy it." Amy growled her rage and belligerence.

"No." The dragon mage shook her head. "I agree with Sam and the headmaster. It's probably a trap. Believe me, I'd love to rush in and start busting heads too, but Tiamat would have thought of that. If you haven't been able to contact them for a while, she probably hopes to lure us in immediately after our fight with her. We can't simply portal there and hope for the best, Amy."

The mage clenched her fists and the filing cabinet behind Amythist crumpled in on itself.

"Amy!" the headmaster chastised. "There were discipline records in there that I planned to pretend to update one day."

"Sorry," Amy said with no indication that she cared about either the records or the attempt to lighten the mood. "I tend to get pissed when a group of people who owe my best friend their lives decides not to save her."

"Excuse me?" Kylara demanded.

"You. Owe. Kristen. Your. Lives." The woman bit off every word for added emphasis.

"Absolutely. Why else do you think we need to be cautious?" she snapped. "If we rush in, we die and Kristen is frozen in stone forever."

"You don't know that."

"I know that Tiamat will expect us and I know the only way I was able to defeat her was with help."

"And we want to help," Sam added. He tried to soothe her with his aura and she seemed to calm. If nothing else, she stopped floating. "But first, we'll need more support. There's no way the four of us can fight both the cult and Tiamat."

"What about your friends? Can't we interrupt their beauty sleep?" Amy asked.

"Yeah, for sure," Sam said dismissively. "But first, Lady Amythist, who were you on the phone with?"

"Drew. I believe Kylara and he are well acquainted."

The dragon mage nodded. "Is he all right?"

Amythist sipped her tea again. "He's alive and seems to be in control of his will so I suppose we have to count that as a positive."

"How did he contact you?"

"You were correct to guess the city was without power," the headmaster said and fought to keep the emotion out of her voice. "He said something took everything down but that he found a payphone and was able to contact me."

"Did he give you a location?" Amy demanded and rose from her chair.

"I know we are all eager to help but this will go faster if you let me relay the information he gave me without interrupting," the old dragon said in her most matronly tone.

The mage scowled but she settled in her chair and folded her arms.

"He gave me an address and said they won't be there but will have the location under surveillance."

"Smart," Kylara said.

"Is he alone?" Sam asked.

Amythist gave the two of them stares that might have made rocks blush. "He has a small team of trusted operatives with him but he said most of the Steel Guard has fallen to Tiamat's powers, including Heartsbane."

"Heartsbane? No, not her." Amy looked like she understood the gravity of the threat for the first time.

CHAPTER EIGHT

Tanya, Galen, Karl, and Jasmine stood in the center of a beautiful meadow. That they had been here before in no way diminished how incredible this realm was. The field was filled with waist-high grasses that waved gracefully in a gentle breeze. Stands of wildflowers were speckled amongst the growth to add color and texture. A series of stone-lined pools were placed throughout. A stream entered the field at one end and ran from pool to pool. It splashed into each as a gently trickling waterfall and flowed out the other end and on to the next pool.

"What now, Galen?" Tanya asked after she drew a deep breath of the clean, fresh air.

"I...I'm not sure," he stammered. "Honestly, I didn't even get this far with my plan. I wasn't sure you would all agree."

"Why am I surprised." Karl scoffed.

"What is that supposed to mean?" she asked.

"It means that even if Kylara gets us back in an hour their time, it'll feel like days here because Galen is too stupid to have a plan."

Rather than defending himself, the other boy merely slumped. That would not do. Tanya had been bullied by Midnight before and was not about to stand idly by while he bullied someone else. "And do you have any idea how to fix someone who is trapped between their human and dragon form? Or are you simply talking crap to feel better about yourself for not being able to help the person who helped defeat Boneclaw?"

"I am not talking shit because I do have an idea," Karl retorted. "Anytime I've been here, soaking in these pools seems to boost my powers. We should start there and see if that can give him enough power to transform into either his human or dragon forms."

Tanya reddened. That was exactly like the shadow dragon. He talked like he was a jerk so he could make someone feel bad but he only did it when there was no fear of retribution. She had half a mind to change his mind about that.

"Honestly, that's a good idea," Jasmine said. "These ponds augment my powers too, plus this field is safe. We've only been attacked here once and that was at night. It's still dawn," she said and gestured at the closest pool.

"If all I have to do is soak in one of these, that would be great," Galen said and raised his head to meet Karl's eyes. "Thank you, Sir Midnight. You honor me."

"Yeah, whatever. Call me Karl, dork. I don't want to be all formal with a gargoyle."

Tanya wanted to tell him to cut it out but the other boy did not seem to mind. He seemed broken as if he had suffered so much since they had last seen him that a few names were not worth getting worked up over. She didn't see it like that, though. His tribulations meant they should be more kind to him, not less. How would Karl feel if someone constantly insulted him?

"Will you take your shirt off or are you worried the gentle pixie sun will give your pale shoulders a sunburn?" Jasmine asked.

In reply, Karl sneered and removed his shirt. "You called my freckles gross before. Well, they're about to have company."

The mage only smirked devilishly.

Tanya sighed. She supposed that to Karl's credit, he could roll with people making fun of him.

"Come on. Let's find a big one," she said.

The four of them wandered through the meadow and up a slight slope until they found one of the larger pools. Karl, already shirtless, stripped out of his black jeans and cannonballed into the water wearing nothing but boxers. Jasmine was able to get her robe off but before she could remove her undershirt, he caught her with a tendril of shadow and pulled her in after him.

She fell in with a splash. When she surfaced, she used her telekinesis to knock him over with a small wave. "Now my shirt is soaked, jerk."

"Off with it!" he said. "If it's not dry, you might catch hypothermia."

Jasmine snorted at this but sank under the water until only her chin was showing. A moment later, her arm pushed out of the water and tossed her soaked shirt at his face. It whacked him and wrapped around his head. She must have used telekinesis to make it thwack so effectively.

Galen shrugged out of the tattered jacket he wore. Honestly, it was little more than the remnants of a vest. The back was in shreds because of his wings and the sleeves had been ripped off long before. He kept his pants on, though. Tanya couldn't help thinking that there probably had not been much opportunity to acquire fresh pairs of underwear out in the desert.

That left her and fortunately, Karl was not the only one to remember the invigorating power of these pools. She used her plant powers to make a clump of nearby grass double in height so she could step behind it and emerged a moment later in a two-piece bikini.

"Hey, so I wasn't the only one who thought ahead." Karl smirked at her when she stepped out from behind the clump of grass. She had expected him to leer at her but he didn't seem to be acting especially uncouth. Although why would he? She couldn't see what was going on under the surface of the water, but Karl and Jasmine were seated close enough that almost anything could be.

"If you had an idea in mind, why did you ask Galen?" Tanya walked along the stacked stones and sank into the pool. The water was deliciously warm.

"I wanted to know if he had a plan besides this one," Karl replied.

"I wish I did," Galen said. His eyes were locked on hers. There was something in them besides fear or despondency. Gratitude? Relief? Between his half-dragon, half-human features and his muddy aura, it was hard to tell, but she thought that at the very least, he looked happier than she had seen him since she'd discovered that he was alive.

For a few blessed moments, the four of them sat in companionable silence and let the warmth of the water soak through their skin, their muscles, and into their bones.

That could not last, however, not with Karl in the pool.

"So, what's your endgame here, Galen?" The shadow dragon flipped his wet dark hair back so it hung behind him. "Do you hope to gain more power and become a super-jerk again or do you hope to be returned to your previously pathetic state?"

Jasmine laughed, although at least she had the decency to look ashamed about doing so.

"I don't want to be a freak anymore," Galen said. "I've thought about what form I would choose if I had to and honestly, I think I'd rather be a regular human than a dragon who can't transform at all."

Karl snorted at this. "Oh, come on. Do you seriously expect us to believe that crap? You were annoying when you were only a vanilla. I can't exactly see you moving to a small town and getting a job like a regular human. Be honest with us and tell us what power you want."

"I don't want any powers," the other boy insisted.

"Dude, can you even hear yourself? You got the ability to animate skeletons and used it to make an army. But now, we're supposed to think all that ambition is gone? Just because you're a powerless freak doesn't mean you have to be a liar too."

"Show some respect, Karl!" Tanya snapped.

"Oh, here we go," Midnight muttered but was silenced when Jasmine splashed him in the face.

"You don't know what it's like to grow up as a vanilla dragon," Tanya said. "Yes, we have more powers than humans, but dragons like you and your father never let us forget that we're still less than them. Galen and I were the first two—and are still some of the only—dragons to get powers in the pixie realm. I was lucky to get plant powers. His were something darker."

"Tanya, you don't have to defend me," Galen said. "I appreciate it, I truly do, but Karl's right."

"No, please don't encourage him," Jasmine said.

"He is, though," the boy insisted. "I was never a very kind person. My parents raised me to think I was both above the rest of the world because I was a Tempest and beneath them because I didn't have storm powers like my father and brother."

"Dude, my father raised me to think that Midnights were destined to rule as Followers of Tiamat and that a mage's place was beneath our talons. That did not stop Jasmine and me from showing him his rightful place."

"It took you some time to stand up to him, though," the mage pointed out. "You used to act like I didn't exist simply because I was a mage."

"And there's what you did to me our first semester," Tanya snapped.

"That was messed up of me," Karl said quickly. "Seriously, Tanya, using my powers on you and then getting the other guys to bind you like dragon slayers used to do… I don't know what I was thinking. Power is dangerous and it can do dangerous things to the mind. My father raised me to respect power above all other things. When I got to the Lumos School and realized for the first time in my life that I was one of the more powerful beings instead of the least, well...I didn't react well. I'm glad Kylara put me in my place."

"What, no apology for me?" Jasmine asked.

He snorted. "Are you serious? We're only together because you're, like, super-strong."

She used her powers to dunk him underwater. He resurfaced, laughing.

"I wish I had stood up to my father," Galen said mournfully. "When I had those skeletons, I could have easily made him show me some respect."

"Why didn't you?" the mage asked.

The boy shrugged and his wings ruffled and resettled as he did so. "Honestly? It never even occurred to me. When I got those powers, Kylara's aunt was still a huge threat. Compared to her ability to control elementals, my family didn't seem like that big a problem."

"Plus, your family never attacked the Lumos School," Tanya said.

"True. That's a distinction I alone hold." He nodded.

"Oh, not anymore, dude. That was so last year! So, what exactly did you hope to accomplish?" Karl asked.

"I know this will sound crazy, but I honestly thought that if I could raise enough skeletons, I could stop dragons, mages, and maybe even people from dying. Before I found out that those skeletons turned out to be connected to Boneclaw, I had hoped to use them to stop more wars. How could a horde of dragons stand against an army of their dead? An army that would not feel pain or suffer when burned? One that could use their injured to strengthen themselves and use their fallen enemies to join their ranks. It sounds so arrogant now, but I truly thought I could make the world a better place."

Tanya was speechless. She had powers unlike any other dragon but had never thought of anything so grandiose.

Karl—at least judging from his aura—was impressed. "You know what, Galen? I'm glad you told me that. Seizing the power of the dead to make the living stop fighting? That's simultaneously the biggest power grab and most altruistic thing at once. Looking back, it was insane but you couldn't have known that."

"I swear I didn't know anything about Boneclaw."

"Even if you did, Kylara says you helped beat him in the end," Jasmine added. "That's big of you."

Galen's aura was still hard to read, but Tanya sensed something besides misery in there—pride. She smiled, a little more confident in the situation. Okay, so maybe Karl wasn't that bad.

The sun had not yet moved an inch in the sky, so she knew they still had more than enough time. She leaned back and tried to relax while Karl and Jasmine—and after a while, Galen—began a debate about which powers could be used to make the world stop fighting.

She let the conversation wash over her and fuel her growing sense of contentment. The simple truth was that she had never dreamed of such power, not before receiving her plant powers or after. She realized she was the only one of them who had accepted her station in life. Her roots were in a middle-class dragon family—still enormously wealthy by human standards but unquestionably middle of the road by dragons' reckoning.

Her gaining an ability was a greater honor than she had ever dreamed of. She had already made her parents proud unlike Karl, who had fought against his dad, or Galen who couldn't face his, or even Jasmine, who navigated a world with entirely different socioeconomic politics than that in which her parents lived. Most importantly, she had the support of people who loved her. She decided that, more than anything else, made her rather privileged and hoped she could use that to help Galen.

The conversation turned to how he had survived—which, strangely enough, seemed to make Karl like him more.

"Are you telling me you hunted for your food?" Midnight asked as Tanya brought herself back to the conversation.

"Yeah, I did," Galen said with a slight smile. "Although most of my survival was gathering. You don't want to know how many different kinds of cactus I had to eat."

"And you'd cook them?" Jasmine asked.

"No, I don't have fire breath so the most I could do was blow smoke on them—like this," He inhaled and breathed out. Everyone—and perhaps no one more so than him—was surprised to see fire emerge from his jaws.

"Whoa, dude. Say it, don't spray it!" Karl joked. He had instinctively put a web of shadow tendrils between himself, Jasmine, and the flames.

"Galen, has that ever happened before?" Tanya asked eagerly.

"No! Never! I would have remembered if it had. I would have had an easier time out there for sure."

"Do you think you can transform?" she asked. She did not know how much time had passed in the warm, spring-fed pool, but the sun had moved from its place on the horizon to somewhere that suggested mid-morning. Of course, she reminded herself that the sun there had nothing to do with the sun in the real world. A minute could have passed over there, or thirty. The most likely way to get out of this realm was for them to complete the task that had brought them there. Intention was a powerful thing in the pixie realm.

Galen grinned, closed his eyes, nodded…and proceeded to sit there without changing his shape at all.

"Did it work?" he asked, opened his eyes, and held his hands out. His expression fell when he saw that it had not.

Jasmine nodded at this as if it were nothing surprising in the least. "I didn't think it would."

"But the fire—"

"Means that it still might," the mage said. "I spoke with Amy at length about how the Steel Dragon got her light powers in this place. It was a kind of quest—no, that's not right. More like a tribulation, I guess?"

"Right, now I get it perfectly," Karl said.

"Oh, shut up, Karl." Jasmine splashed him. "Amy said that Kristen's powers came after she endured things here—trials this realm seemed to create for her. She followed the stream for what felt like weeks and the creatures she had to face in order to earn the powers she needed manifested for her."

"Much like what Galen and I went through at that pond?" Tanya asked. "We were attacked by those skeletons and would have been killed or worse, but I manifested plant powers and Galen manifested his—"

"Creepy necromancer abilities?" Karl interjected.

"I only intended to say the last word, but yes, I suppose so," she replied.

Jasmine nodded. "I hadn't thought of that but yeah, it makes sense. I had hoped these hot springs would work, but I never thought they would. It's too easy. This realm doesn't give powers to those who lounge about soaking the magic up here. This meadow is more like a place to recharge or prepare for a trial than it is any kind of challenge."

They all sat in thought for a moment as each tried to find an answer. Galen spoke first. "So, where do you think we should go, then?"

"It was your idea to come here," Jasmine pointed out to him. "And this realm seems to have much to do with willpower and intention. Where do you think we should go?"

He looked from Jasmine, to Karl, to Tanya. He locked gazes with her and before he spoke, she knew what he would say.

"I think I have to go back there," he said. "To the place where my powers first appeared."

"No, Galen—" Tanya tried to protest.

"If this place manifests what I need, then I think I need to go there." His muddy aura had become increasingly clear. He didn't want this but he needed it. "I can't say I'll be able to transform there but something tells me I'll find at least a part of what I need."

"We'll come with you, of course," Tanya said.

"I think that would be wise," Jasmine said and glanced at the sky. The sun had moved overhead and made the meadow seem warmer—too warm, in fact. The pool they were in was no longer comfortable. Suddenly, the dark of the jungle at the edge of the meadow looked more inviting than it had previously. Tanya had tried to ignore the edge of the field in its entirety. Now, she felt like she could look nowhere else.

"What do you think, Midnight?" Galen asked.

Karl laughed bitterly. "You want to go back to the place where you were attacked by skeletons, had your powers taken from you, and where a crazy goddess was trapped. What could possibly go wrong?"

CHAPTER NINE

"All right, so we open a portal, go meet up with Drew, and take out Tiamat," Kylara said. "I'm sure they have dragon bullets. We merely need to engage her, hold her attention and stay out of range of her petrifying power, and get Drew in position to take a shot."

"It sounds good." Amy stood quickly and turned toward the door.

"You two truly are quite a pair." Amythist tutted and locked the door with her telekinesis so the woman couldn't walk out. "We cannot hope to rush in and defeat Tiamat as well as all the Steel Guard with only the four of us."

"It won't only be the four of us," the mage snapped. "Drew will have good people with him and Kylara's right. He'll be armed with munitions that are lethal to dragons. It's a good plan—the best we have."

"Excuse me, but with all due respect, it's not a good plan at all," Sam said hesitantly.

"It can work Sam. You don't know Drew like we do," Kylara insisted.

"You're forgetting that Tiamat has as many powers as you do

now," he pointed out. "What's to stop her from making a sphere of rock around herself or deflecting the bullets with her metal control?"

"Those bullets are made of bone," Amy interjected.

"Do you honestly think she doesn't know that?" he asked incredulously.

"She was gone for thousands of years," Amythist said, although Kylara could tell from the dragon's aura that she agreed with Sam. She was probably playing devil's advocate to better convince Amy. It was a subtle use of aura and one she realized had been lost to her when she had gone around in a bubble of magic that shielded her against them. She didn't quite know how she felt about it but decided it didn't matter. All the headmaster had done was make Sam elaborate, which he needed to do anyway.

"And she has an incredibly powerful aura," he said smoothly. "She could easily convince people to want to protect her. In which case, they would reveal the existence of the bullets and give her time to decide how to best defend against them."

"So what do you think we should do, Lumos?" Amy asked begrudgingly. "Leave one of our best people in the Motor City to be hunted like a rat?"

"No, not at all," he said. "I merely don't think we should rush in. We need intel. We barely freed Ky from Tiamat and only managed it because she wanted to be free. There's no guarantee that Kishar wants anything of the sort. She might be thrilled to have her goddess inhabiting her body, in which case, forcing Tiamat out will be next to impossible. We don't know any of her other weaknesses."

"Drew might," Kylara suggested.

"Totally," Sam agreed. "That's why I think we should go in and get him and anyone else he has with him out of there. He said he had people with him, right?"

"He said as much, yes," Amythist sipped her tea slowly.

"Then it's even more important that we get him out of there," Sam said. "If Drew is as competent as you two think he is, I'd be willing to bet he saved the best people he could. We'll need him and his team when we do move against Tiamat."

The mage nodded, although she didn't look particularly happy about it. "Fine. Let's drop the shield and I can portal us out of here."

"I think it would make more sense for us to use one of my pixie portals," Kylara said. "They're easier for me than portals are for mages."

"Amy, I'm afraid I must ask you a rather large favor that you will not like at all," the headmaster said.

"What is it?" Amy growled.

"Unfortunately, I have no doubt that Tiamat will move against this school again. Especially if Kylara and Sam intend to use subterfuge and craftiness to strike with Drew and his team, Tiamat will be left thinking they are here. While Professor Sharra and our security team's forces are strong, their efforts have been breached by the Followers of Tiamat before."

"No way," the woman said bluntly.

"I must insist, Amy. The lives of the students are at stake."

"I need to save Kristen."

"It would be foolish to think Tiamat will not strike at the mages. She is a goddess of dragons and there is no reason to think she will see the young mage students as anything more than vermin. Without you here to defend them, I fear there will be a tragic loss of life."

"You can't ask me to stay while my friend is in danger."

"I must ask you to stay. Kylara and Sam are not capable of defending the school. Neither of them has shield abilities. And Kylara is right. Her use of portals exceeds yours. You are needed here while she is needed there. That is the way of it, Amy."

The mage ground her teeth so loudly that Kylara worried she might crack a molar, but she finally conceded with marked resentment. "Fine. But I think these two should get their friends in case. I don't care if they are sleeping in. They're good in a fight."

Kylara clenched her teeth. Should she tell the headmaster? She didn't see how her friends could help in this situation. For now, she merely needed to get Drew and his people and bring them back. If they went to get Galen and the others early, would they even be able to find them? Even if they could, would the disfigured boy have finished his mission? The pixie realm was an odd place. If you said you would be there for an hour, the things that needed to be done there seemed to take an hour.

Still, she didn't want to lie. She was about to tell the headmaster everything when Sam spoke. "What about the campus, though? I mean no offense, Headmaster, but the last time the cultists attacked, our friends were in danger. Without Kylara here, they'll be needed more than ever."

"You make a fair point," the old dragon said. "And after everything that happened yesterday, a little rest would do them all—and the two of you, although you will have to forgo it—some good. They'll be here to help us, Amy will focus on defenses, and you two will go."

Everyone nodded.

"We're in agreement, then," Amythist said. "We must act quickly. Kylara, take this number. It's Drew's telephone." She relayed the number and the girl put it in her phone. "Sam, you will be..."

"Going with Kylara, of course."

"Very good," the headmaster said before the girl could voice her opinion. But it didn't matter. In the past, she might have argued for him to stay behind so he would not be in danger, but this was bigger than that and she had learned that she could not win fights like these by herself. Having Sam at her side would not only bolster her confidence but open up a different variety of tactics. Plus, the two of them both had light powers, which could heal. Hopefully, that particular ability would not be needed but it was better to have it and not need it than need it and not have it.

And then there were her feelings for him. Running off without him sounded painful. If she had to face Tiamat again, she wanted him there with her, no matter what the reason.

Amythist flicked her wrist and the door swung open. The four of them headed out to the U and Amy dropped the campus defenses. Kylara checked her phone. They still had thirty-nine minutes left until they had to retrieve Tanya and the others. It was more than enough time to portal to Detroit and back but way too long to sit around doing nothing while they waited for the clock to run out.

"Call or text the second you have them and I'll drop the defenses," Amy said.

"We will," Sam said as Kylara checked a map to confirm that the address Drew had given them was located in the Motor City. She opened a portal and the two students left the calm, serene morning of the desert for the underbelly of Detroit.

CHAPTER TEN

They stepped from the portal and into the streets of downtown Detroit. Kylara hadn't recognized the address right away but she did now. It was Buddy's Pizza, a favorite haunt of the Steel Dragon and her former SWAT buddies.

She had made them appear in the back of the parking lot between two huge SUVs and barely had time to shut the gateway before she heard the telltale cock of a shotgun.

"You're supposed to come in through the front gate," a man said. Despite having a weapon trained on her, his eyes looked sleepy but not exactly surprised. It was as if seeing two young people step through a portal and appear in his parking lot was to be expected.

"We only wanted a pepperoni and mushroom pizza," she blurted.

The guard looked at them for another minute, then nodded. "This way. Stay between the cars." He led them toward the restaurant—although, judging from the exterior, restaurant was a generous term. The pizza place was a small brick building in need of either a power washing or a fresh coat of paint.

It certainly was not as impressive to behold as the Chrome

Castle, the Steel Dragon's base north of there. That was a massive skyscraper, which in and of itself was not unusual, but at the very top, it did not feature a spire or a sky pool. Instead, a chunky European-style castle comprised the top five floors of the building, complete with multiple towers and a drawbridge.

That was where Kristen must be, frozen in stone along with the rest of the Council. It looked impregnable from there, which was why the Steel Dragon had built it, after all. She needed to have a base that only she understood to keep her and the Steel Guard safe from those who thought dragons, mages, and humans should not strive to live in equality.

The two young students followed the guard quickly through the parking lot. They noticed that the razor wire above the fence that ringed the parking lot wasn't all metal. Other whitish parts were mixed in.

"Are those dragon claws?" Kylara whispered to Sam and pointed at the fragments.

He paled when he saw them. She reminded herself that he hadn't spent a summer interning there, after all, so hadn't seen some of the things she had. "I thought the guard was foolish for pointing that gun at us but maybe there's something besides steel pellets in there."

She was not about to ask, though. They reached the door of the pizzeria and the guard let them in. The smells of tomato sauce seasoned with oregano and freshly baked bread enveloped them as a hostess led them past empty tables to a room in the back. "We'll get your pizza ready for delivery," the hostess said, left, and shut the door behind them.

They shared a look before the dragon mage took her phone out and called Drew. "Delivery, please," he answered and hung up.

After another blank look at one another, they settled in to wait. About fifteen minutes later—leaving only twenty-two minutes on their clock for Tanya—the hostess returned in with a stack of pizza boxes. "If you would come this way, please."

The students stood hastily and followed her to a different door than they had entered through. A van painted with a pizza on the side waited outside, its engine idling. That struck Kylara as odd. She had been here a few times with the team but had never gotten delivery.

The van looked well used. It had new tires with thick rubber tread on them, but every other part of it had seen better days. It was dented in a hundred places and patched in a hundred more. Stranger still, it seemed to have a fair number of bullet holes. She thought that maybe all of this could have been resolved if Buddy's had traded free pizza with a good mechanic and avoided doing deliveries in particularly rough neighborhoods.

Oddly enough, the paint seemed new. The exterior of the van was all white with red stripes at the top and bottom and the name *BUDDY'S!* across the top. A huge, Detroit-style pizza filled most of the door. The paint looked so fresh that she wondered if it would stick to her fingers if she touched it. Yet whoever had painted the van hadn't bothered to patch a half-dozen places on it.

The rear doors opened and her questions were immediately answered. The vehicle did not have insulated coolers for keeping pizza warm, nor was there anywhere to keep bottles of soda cold. Instead, hooks on the walls were loaded with weapons, bullet-proof armor, and what she assumed were explosives. A low bench ran along either wall—well, not so much a bench as sturdy plastic crates that looked heavy with cushions on top of them. Kristen's old SWAT team sat on those benches.

They wore camo gear instead of their usual black-and-silver uniforms and were all rather dirty. The smell of body odor that emanated from the back of the van was remarkable.

Drew leaned over from the front seat and gestured for the

students to get in. They complied, Hernandez shut the door behind them, and they accelerated away.

"Sorry for the subterfuge," Drew said once they were moving. "We don't want to risk using our cell phones much and staying put in any one place doesn't seem particularly wise right now. Thanks for coming to the party Ky-Lara."

He always said her name in his way. When she had met him, she had said her name was Lara in an effort to deceive him, not knowing at the time that he had been sent by the Steel Dragon to keep an eye on her. Although she had long since corrected the deceit, he still said her name with the odd emphasis. She didn't mind and it was like their inside joke.

"Is this everyone you got out?" Sam asked. Kylara hoped that none of them could read his aura as it felt strongly of disappointment.

"This is it," Butters said. "Allow me to introduce myself to your friend, Kylara. I'm Butters, the best shot you'll never see coming. They call me that on account of I think it tastes better on everything." He was a quite rotund gentleman with a warm, southern accent that made her want to attend a family barbecue with him one day.

"That's a bunch of bull. We call you Butters because you're as round as a thanksgiving turkey. Butterball is his full moniker. I'm Lynne Hernandez, by the way. Demolitions." The woman extended a hand for Sam to shake. The sides of her head were shaved close and the hair on top was pulled into a tight topknot. She had a new tattoo of a rose on the back of her hand to match the letters on her knuckles.

"A pleasure," Sam said and bowed slightly.

"It won't be," a tall thin man said with a hint of a British accent.

"Wow! Big words from Beanpole." Hernandez grinned.

The thin man—Beanpole—smiled placidly. Even though Kylara had spent an entire summer at the base and seen him on multiple occasions, she had never spoken to him much. From what she'd understood, he let his partner Butters do most of the talking.

"We've met briefly. I'm Brian Hall. Brother to the Steel Dragon." The young man proffered his hand to Sam. "You remember me. I'm something of a tech genius."

"Is that why the electrical grid went down?" the golden dragon asked.

Brian almost fell off his bench in embarrassment. "It seems I trained some of the recruits a little too well. I haven't been able to...uh, get all that working again—not remotely anyway." He blushed.

"This is Keith, the Rookie," Hernandez jerked a thumb at the man in question.

"I have been here longer than you," he replied quickly, although he didn't seem particularly annoyed by the nickname.

"And I am Erin Timeflash. I was a dear friend of your grandfather's, young Samuel. I was there in his last moments. He was a true hero, and not a day goes by when I do not try to live with the courage he displayed when he died."

"Thank you, ma'am," Sam said to the dark-haired woman who wore a purple pantsuit.

"So, how did you all get out?" Kylara asked when everyone had been introduced to Sam. "Was Hernandez so grumpy that Tiamat's aura didn't work?" She had been on a mission with the demolitions expert so felt comfortable joking with her. Plus, she knew the woman would trash-talk anyway so she might as well get in first.

But rather than responding with a joke, Hernandez looked pained. "I wish. Did you hear about Heartsbane?"

The students nodded. "We did."

"If she couldn't resist, I wouldn't have stood a chance," the woman admitted.

"But how did you escape?" Kylara asked.

"We didn't," Drew interjected. "We were on our way back from an airsoft session when Timeflash arrived to warn us about the attack on the base. By the time we were geared up and close enough to strike, it was too late."

"That false goddess had already moved the Council onto the drawbridge," Butters said. "I saw them out there through my scope—not Kristen, though. If that platform breaks, they will all tumble below and the stone they're made of doesn't look exactly sturdy."

"I wanted to go in anyway," Hernandez said.

"But cooler heads prevailed," Beanpole added.

"If Heartsbane could not resist her aura, none of us could have," Timeflash said. "Speaking of which, Kylara, your aura feels…different."

"That's because you're feeling my aura now." She moved her hand reflexively to where the pendant had rested on her chest for her entire life. "Before, I had…protection."

"I see," the dragon said and she could sense worry coming from her aura.

"Where are we headed?" Sam asked.

"To our hideout. We have maps and plans worked out. We'll show them to you when we get to the pawnshop."

"But after we eat!" Butters added.

"A hideout?" Kylara asked and glanced at Sam. "I think it might be better if we get out of here. Amy is at the Lumos School. Our plan was to call her, have her drop the shield around the school, and get you all out of here."

"That sounds great." The Rookie grinned.

"Let's stop and get some of our maps," Drew said as he pulled into the front of a run-down pawnshop. "Then you can take us out of here. Go ahead and call Amy. We only need a minute."

"But the pizza!" Butters protested.

"Can wait. Fifty seconds. Let's go," Drew said as he stepped from the van.

Even though they had all been joking a moment before, the team sprang into action and streamed into the premises like ants invading a picnic. Rather than be the gear that slowed the machine, Kylara took her phone out and dialed Amy.

She was about to bring the device to her ear when a bolt of electricity streaked from the sky and exploded it in her hand.

"We have company!" Sam said and pointed in the direction the lightning bolt had originated from. A wing of dragons mounted by mages soared toward them.

"How did they find us? No way could they have a bead on Kylara's phone." Brian said.

"It's her aura," Timeflash said and gestured at the girl before she took her dragon form. "You need to get that under control, Kylara."

"I think it can wait," Hernandez said. "Right now, I hope you can do the shadow, light, thunderstorm thingy to stop us from getting incinerated."

The students transformed into their dragon forms.

"We'll do our best!" the dragon mage roared and took to the air. Her diamond scales covered her body and protected her as the first blast of fire caught her. She lashed out with shadow tendrils, caught hold of the dragon, and swung it to hurl it earthward, where Drew and his team used a few rounds in a few choice places to incapacitate it. She noticed that they didn't kill it, but why would they? This was one of their coworkers, someone who had fought for equality. Not an enemy, merely someone being controlled by one.

This fight would be a tough one, but without anywhere to go, she saw no easy way out. They had to stop the mages so they could reach Amy, which meant she had some fighting to do.

CHAPTER ELEVEN

Tanya had led Galen, Karl, and Jasmine through the swamp for what felt like hours. Despite being able to communicate with the huge cypress trees, vines, and flowering plants growing amongst the knobby roots of the huge trees, the going was not easy.

At first, she tried to make the trees move their roots to provide a bridge through the swamp for the four of them but it had been less than successful. Their width was limited and while they seemed to self-stabilize to keep her from falling into the muddy water, they were not so accommodating to the other three. Galen had already fallen in the muck twice. Karl had fallen only once, although he was far more vocal in his complaints. Jasmine would have tumbled but had managed to stop herself with her telekinesis.

They had given up on that method and now tried to walk on the muddy banks, holding onto branches and tree trunks more often than not. The sneakers and jeans Tanya had borrowed from Kylara were already a muddy mess. It was a good thing they were so ugly to begin with. It wasn't like this could ruin them or anything.

"How much farther?" Karl whined. He had complained about

the walk every few minutes. She had already tried to make the branch of a tree knock him into the murky water but his reflexes with his shadow powers were sharp and he had dodged her clandestine shove easily.

"I don't know," Galen said. He was directly behind Tanya and the most comfortable in the environment. Tanya decided that made sense. He'd lived in the wild for months. A little mud was probably a welcome change from the desert. "All of this looks the same to me."

"The blind leading the blind," Jasmine muttered.

"We started in the right direction," Tanya said, trying to be helpful. "We simply need to press on. I know it feels like we've been at it for hours but I'm sure there's still enough time on the other side."

"Because of intention?" Karl asked with derision. "What if Kylara wanted us out of the way? What if Galen wanted to feed us to a pixie 'gator? Face it, you know as little about this place as anyone else."

"Maybe we should turn around," Galen said. "I wouldn't want all of you to be stuck here on my account."

"It's too late for that," Jasmine said.

"No, it's not. We, you know, turn around," Karl made a little circle with his finger to illustrate the eloquence of his plan.

"I'm not so sure those guys will be okay with it," Jasmine said and pointed into the swamp.

Tanya had asked the plants for warnings about exactly this kind of thing, but there were so many living beings in the swamp that the plants told her constantly about creatures climbing over them. She had wearied of repeated false alarms and barely paid them any attention. As a result, the pack of skeletal dragons caught the group off guard and she couldn't be sure if the vegetation had warned her or not.

"No!" Galen screamed, raised his claws in front of his face, and flapped his wings to fly back and away from the group of dog-sized creatures.

"Finally!" Karl grinned and raised his fists. Ropes of inky shadow extended from his knuckles and raced across the muddy surface of the swamp. He caught one of the skeletons with a tendril. As soon as the shadow touched it, the other filaments puffed to nothing while the one on the dragon grew thicker, branched into a hundred strands that bound the bones, and pulled it into the mud. "Tanya!"

"On it!" she replied and called on the roots of the nearest tree to bury the dragon. A thousand tiny rootlets erupted from the ground, surrounded the monster, covered it, and dragged it into the muck. It struggled until about half its bulk was beneath the mud and finally went limp, animated no longer and seemingly at peace.

Jasmine also swung into action and created a sphere of shielding energy around one of the dragons that came from above. As soon as it leapt from one tree to another, she snagged it and flung it into the mud. She released the sphere as Tanya ordered more roots to bury it.

"There are too many to do this one at a time!" Karl shouted and used ropes of shadow to keep three of the skeletons at bay. More approached through the swamp. They swam in the water, scurried across the mud, or jumped from tree to tree. "Galen, can you do something about this?"

"No...no, I can't!" The disfigured boy was the only one of them not fighting. His face was a mask of panic and his motions uncontrolled. He flinched whenever a skeleton came too close to him. His wings magnified his movements and sometimes, they caught the air unintentionally and pulled him back.

"Galen, you have to face your fears," Tanya shouted as she tried and failed to drag another of the skeletons below the surface of the mud. It was so odd fighting the aberrations. They fought tooth and nail to not be buried, but as soon as most of their body was submerged, they seemed to go willingly as if they were falling asleep.

"I don't think I should," he said and stumbled away until his back met a tree trunk and forced him to stop.

"Can you feel any powers?" Jasmine shouted through clenched teeth as she caught two of the skeletons and hurled them into each other with enough force to scatter the pieces of their fleshless bodies into a bony mess. Rather than defeating them, this simply inspired them to try a new attack. The two dog-sized creatures combined. Now, instead of two four-legged dragons, they were one long, sinuous monster with four legs on each side, two heads at the front, and one extremely long tail. She threw a shield up to stop it from plowing into her.

"Galen, we need your help!" Tanya shouted and tried to use the branch of a tree to knock the skeleton attacking Jasmine into the mud so she could bind it beneath the surface.

"I...I feel something," Galen blurted from where he had sagged against the tree. "I can sense their presence like I could before."

"Then tell them to cut it out!" Karl roared. He had created a shield of shadow all around his body so it seemed like a monster of pure darkness fought alongside the two girls. The skeletons did not seem at all frightened by his bizarre appearance, though.

"Okay... Okay, I'll try," Galen said and pushed hesitantly away from the trunk. He extended both hands, took a deep breath, and said in a strong, clear voice, "Stop!"

All the dragons—about a dozen of them were in fighting range at this point—froze. Each and every head—and in one case both heads—stared at him.

Tanya felt victory start to bloom in her chest but only for a second before all twelve monsters attacked Galen.

"Ahhh!" He screamed as the creatures swept past his three companions. In an instant, he was enveloped in a swirling mass of bone and claw. They screeched as they tore at his wings with their claws. One of them bit his forearm and drew a pained shriek from him. Tanya thought his bones might have broken if not for the dragon scales that still offered him some protection.

"Tell them to cut it out!" Karl repeated, snatched the beast with two heads from behind, and yanked it to the dirt with a rope made of shadow. Tanya seized it with roots and drew it into the mud like the earth was eating the world's most unsettling noodle.

"I tried that!" Galen shouted from inside the swirling mess of bones.

It hadn't worked the first time and probably wouldn't if he tried again. "Galen, I have an idea. I need you to run away from us, all right?" the plant dragon said.

"I don't want to be left alone!" he screamed, his voice rich with terror.

"You won't be. But I need you to run."

The boy screamed but he managed to break free from the dragon skeletons that harried him. He spun around the tree trunk he had been backed up against and blundered through the swamp. His attempt to run was little more than him stumbling on human legs with dragon talons while he flapped wings with bloody holes in them that hardly increased his pace at all.

Tanya called on the tree he had leaned against. It was old and venerable with many seedlings living throughout the swamp. She reminded it that it would live on and that by doing as she asked, its offspring would survive there for eons. It was enough to convince the tree, although she also knew the dragon creatures played their role. The plants that grew there did not like them.

Her encouragement and its natural dislike of revenants were enough that it wished to stop the monsters badly enough to rip half its roots from the ground. She stood back as the tree started to lean toward Galen.

"Faster, Galen!" Jasmine shouted when she realized what was going on.

He tried to accelerate clumsily but was not able to get

completely clear. When the crown of the tree descended and crushed the dragon skeletons beneath its multitude of branches and twigs, he was knocked down too. But while the tree immediately went to work turning its branches into roots that grew around and through the skeletons to drag them ever deeper into the mud, it left Galen alone.

The half-boy, half-dragon's eyes widened as he watched the skeletons that had torn and bit at his flesh being pulled into the mud. A moment later, the fight was over. He was on a tiny island of mud and branches with a tree trunk pointing directly at him. The skeletons were gone, all buried by Tanya and the willow.

Except they weren't all gone. She could feel them now that she had fought them. The trees had not considered them a threat to the person who could give them energy before, but since she had asked them to bury the beasts in the muck, they knew what to look for. There were dozens more in the swamp. Some of them clung to tree trunks and peered around so only the tips of their bony noses could be seen. Others waited beneath the surface of the water, where they tried to avoid touching the roots but didn't quite succeed.

"We're being watched," Tanya said.

Karl looked around. "I see them too."

"What are they waiting for?" Jasmine asked.

"I think they're waiting to see what Galen will do," Tanya said. Then, a moment later, "Galen? What will you do?"

"I don't think I should try to control them anymore," he said quickly. "I think they're angry that I tried as I've lost the power. They attacked because I tried to use it again. They're guardians of this place and I have no right to interfere with them." He dragged in a breath and spoke louder. "I'm sorry. Okay?"

Somehow, apologizing to the brainless bone creatures worked. Through the tree roots, Tanya felt them slip away deeper into the swamp to continue their ceaseless vigil.

"Okay, before anyone starts talking trash, my bad on thinking that Galen could control those little bastards," Karl said.

"You can say that again," Jasmine said.

"What do we do now?" Tanya asked. "Should we keep going or turn back?"

"We can't turn around, not after we've come this far," the other girl said.

"But if we keep going, we might be attacked by those freaks again," he complained.

"They didn't attack us," Jasmine pointed out. "You attacked them."

"I did not!" Midnight protested although his aura made it clear that he was unsure.

"You were excited when they appeared," Tanya said. "If this realm relies on intention, you essentially brought them down on us."

Karl's pale face reddened and his aura flushed with regret. "I...had not thought of that."

"I wonder what would have happened if we had simply ignored them," Jasmine said almost to herself.

"Do you think they would have let us through?" Galen asked.

"I think it's possible. They were never part of our mission but seem to have a place here. Maybe if Karl had been less... exuberant when we met them, they would have let us through."

"What do you mean they're not part of our mission? They're the entire reason we're here," Karl said.

"No, they're not," Galen said, his voice surprisingly firm. "Boneclaw took my power to control them away from me and that's fine. I don't want to be able to control the dead. Losing that power was a relief. I know that may come as a shock to you, Karl, or you don't believe me or whatever, but it's the truth. I don't want to carry that burden."

"What do you want?" Jasmine asked.

"I don't want to look like this anymore," the boy said. "I simply want to be normal. Being a dragon again would be great, but even a human would be better than this monster." He hung his head, reminded again about what Boneclaw had turned him into.

"I think we should press on to the pond," Jasmine said. "That was where Boneclaw did this to you, correct?"

Galen nodded.

"Then I think that's where this could be undone—if it can be undone at all."

"That makes sense to me," he said although he didn't look at all excited about going deeper into the swamp.

"Well, that's all fine and good, but how are we supposed to find it?" Karl asked.

"I...I think I can feel it," Tanya said. "It's far—like, very far—but there's a place ahead without any tree roots. I can feel the edges all around it but not the center or the bottom."

"That's where we need to go," Jasmine said.

The disfigured boy grimaced and shrugged. "I agree. I don't want to but it feels right."

"Then what are we waiting for?" Karl asked. "Let's go find Tiamat's resting place."

CHAPTER TWELVE

Kylara took to the air and dodged blasts of a dozen different kinds of energy as she rose above the members of the Steel Guard who tried to load the van with the documents and weapons they had stored in the pawn shop.

Sam followed her, as did Timeflash. It was already clear that they were hopelessly outnumbered but they only had to hold the dragons off long enough to let the team finish their work.

One pounded into her back and forced her to lose elevation. She called on one of her new powers—the ability to control metal—and ripped a stop sign out of the ground. It launched like a spear and stabbed her attacker through the shoulder. The huge claws went slack and released her as he tried to fly safely to the ground.

Another came from above and tried to force her to land but she had more than only the metal power. She made a pillar of stone surge out of the ground directly in her opponent's path. Unable to stop or swerve, the dragon drove into it and the impact flung the mage from his back.

Kylara took a brief look at Sam and Timeflash. He fought defensively and focused on beams of light to blind his opponents and leave them unable to fight for a few moments. This worked fairly effectively—especially since they only needed to make this fight last long enough to get the team out—but it wasn't a flawless strategy. He aimed at the dragons' faces, which often meant their frills and horns blocked the light from hitting the mages. So, while the dragons wheeled upward and waited for their vision to return, the mages on their backs still fired their blasts of magic onto the battlefield below.

Still, despite his less than perfect strategy, he was doing better than Timeflash. Kylara had worked with her a fair amount during the last summer when she had interned, mainly because she spent much more time at the base than many of the other dragons. Her powers were incredibly valuable but not particularly useful for combat. She held her own, though, as she slashed and snapped at a dragon with her talons and jaws, but another approached her. The dragon mage had no delusions about how the fight would go.

She raced toward the duel and used a gust of wind to boost her speed. Seconds before she slammed into the dragon sneaking up on her ally, she exhaled a blast of ice to freeze him into a block, the mage on his back included. She let them fall almost to the earth before she caught them with a net of shadow. This was both to save the mage from dying on impact and also to keep the dragon frozen in the block of ice.

Satisfied, she turned to Timeflash, who had managed to untangle herself from the other dragon. Kylara used the temporary separation to spray him with acid. He screamed as the caustic liquid burned holes in its wings and he plummeted toward the earth while the mage on his back tried desperately to slow their fall with wind. She decided the mage had it under control and turned her attention to the team on the ground.

"Drew, are we ready?" Kylara yelled.

"I was about to make the call," he replied and gestured with his free hand for everyone to scramble into the back of the van.

No sooner did he lift his phone than a bolt of electricity shattered it.

"Damn it!" he shouted to no one in particular. It seemed the dragon with the lightning-blasting mage mounted on her back took umbrage at this as she tucked her wings and dove at the vehicle.

"Drive, damn it. Drive!" Hernandez shouted from the back and fired a couple of rounds at the dragon. That the bullets were the dragon-slaying variety was immediately clear. They tore through the scales on the dragon's torso and the great beast crumpled and fell. Kylara could feel from its aura that it was still alive but it would not fight anymore that day.

The van's front wheels screeched as Drew urged the disguised vehicle to move.

She descended sharply and matched speed with the van so she could spread her wings wide to provide cover. "You have to get a gate open for us!" Drew shouted. "You're the only one who can get us out of here."

"I can't get us to the Lumos School, though. The shields are up." She could punch a hole through the shield with a portal but it would hurt badly enough to hold it open for the van that she wasn't sure she'd have anything left thereafter.

"We'll do our damnedest to get through but it doesn't matter if this van gets fried," Drew shouted in return. "In a storm, all ports are safe ports."

"I'll open one at the end of the street."

"Great!" The vehicle increased in speed when the portal blazed into life a block ahead.

But before the van could make it through, a dragon barreled into Kylara. This alone might not have been enough to stop the diamond-scaled dragon, but the mage on the back of her attacker wrapped her head in a sphere of shielding magic to cut her supply of oxygen off.

She gasped and tried to breathe but there was nothing there.

The portal flickered out as the team would have driven through it.

Her vision began to close in and she still couldn't breathe. The dragon landed in front of her. He was so very close, as was the mage on his back. The dragon mage reached inside for her arsenal of magic. One power, she knew, would undoubtedly work. She could send out the petrification mist and freeze the two of them in stone. Somehow, she knew the strange, heavy mist would ignore the shield in the same way that it ignored wind. She could do it easily but she would not. It felt wrong, even with her struggling to breathe.

Fortunately, before she collapsed, Sam plucked the mage from the dragon's back. Immediately, the shield cutting her air off was gone. She sucked in a breath and her dragon healing banished both her headache and tunnel vision instantly.

So it was with crystal clarity that Kylara saw the dragon Sam had been fighting swoop down and sink its claws into the van. It pumped its wings and lifted it from the ground.

"Get out of there!" Timeflash screamed from somewhere up above.

Drew and his team did not need to be told twice. They bailed out of every door the vehicle had, landed hard, and rolled—or, in Butters' case, screamed in pain when he broke an ankle.

The dragon was not able to get the van very high into the air before he dropped it. Still, twenty feet was twenty feet. It plummeted nose first, crumpled impressively, and fell forward onto its roof.

Kylara stared. It had not exploded so she could still get everyone, their intel, and their weapons out of there. She also knew she had to because without a doubt, one of the mages she was currently fighting had already contacted the rest of Tiamat's aura-controlled henchmen. It was only a matter of time before they—or the self-declared Mother of All Dragons—arrived. She had to be long gone before that happened.

"Can you open a portal beneath the van?" Drew shouted.

"I can," she replied.

"Do it now. We'll cover you."

But she wasn't fast enough. The dragon who had lifted it exhaled a massive inferno that instantly engulfed the vehicle. Through the open doors, she could see the seat cushions—and all the rolls of paper on them—turn to black ash before the force from the fire breath forced the ash to scatter to the wind. The racks of weapons and armor melted. The dull popping of well-packed ammunition detonating could be heard from the back as well. By some miracle, Hernandez's supply didn't explode but it didn't matter. The van was ruined.

"The portal!" Drew yelled. "Kylara, open the portal beneath the van!"

He and his team continued to fire at the dragon as if they still needed to protect the burned husk. The joint on the dragon's wing exploded with blood and he screeched and shook the asphalt with his impact. The SWAT team drove him back with a storm of bullets.

"Kylara, *now!*" the team leader shouted again.

She nodded and opened a portal on the street. The van, denied the surface it had rested on, fell through and vanished.

"Butters, you're next!" Drew shouted as he fired at an approaching dragon.

Beanpole and the Rookie each threw an arm around the rotund gentleman to try to keep his weight off his broken ankle. Still, he yelped in pain until Brian joined them in the effort. The four of them toppled through the glowing pit and vanished from the fight.

"Hernandez, Timeflash!"

The dragon was flying overhead but at his order, she blasted her opponent with fire to create distance, tucked her wings, and streaked toward the portal as if it were a diving well instead of a hole in the street. No sooner had she vanished than Hernandez sprinted toward the gate and jumped through.

"Let's go, Ky!" Sam shouted, transformed into his human form, and flung himself into the glowing aperture.

"Come on, kid," Drew said, gestured at the portal, and fired a few rounds to keep the dragons at bay.

"But the intelligence—maybe you and I can get more?"

"No need. Come on. We can't lose you."

Kylara nodded—even though she hated being the only person who could open portals—and leapt through with Drew.

They fell perhaps five feet through the pixie realm before they emerged through another portal in the desert outside the Lumos School.

They would have fallen another ten feet—she was not the best at vertical portals—but the charred van was there to break their fall. Fortunately, Brian, Keith, and Beanpole had already helped Butters off the roof. He sat on the ground nearby and clutched his ankle that had swelled to the size of a cantaloupe.

Much to Kylara's confusion, Hernandez and Timeflash tried to push the van from its side onto its wheels as if they intended to drive it out of there.

"We should get inside the school grounds," Sam said. "It's only a couple of minutes' walk."

"Or—and hear me out here—you could stop standing around keeping your hands clean and give us some help to get this van on its wheels." Hernandez grunted as she threw a shoulder into the side of the van.

"But...it's ruined," the golden dragon said. "It would make more sense for Kylara to simply bury it so if they track us here—which seems very likely to me, by the way—they don't have a clue."

"And leave all my toys behind?" Drew asked. "No way."

Confused but not about to argue the point, Kylara walked closer, activated her momentum power that made her almost unstoppable when she was moving, and threw her shoulder lightly into the vehicle. It tipped from its side onto its four wheels. The only one that had still held air hit a sharp rock and deflated as the van settled.

"Thanks, Kylara." Hernandez stuck her tongue out at Sam.

"That doesn't change anything," he said. "I know I'm a dragon and don't know much about machines or whatever, but even I know you can't drop a van on its engine and expect it to run."

"Yeah, if only that had never happened," Keith said and his grin made it obvious why everyone called him the Rookie.

"You're not making any sense," Kylara said. "Sam's right. We need to go."

"Can you level the surface between the van and the school?" Drew asked.

"Yeah, sure, but why bother?"

"It is not human powers you are underestimating, young Lumos, but the abilities of dragons," Timeflash said and stepped in front of the van.

The SWAT team all grinned and took a few steps back as she raised her hands and a purplish mist flowed from them to enshroud the vehicle.

From her vantage point at the rear, the first thing Kylara noticed was that the racks of weapons seemed to melt into their proper shapes. One of the crates under the bench seats straightened and pieces of shrapnel withdrew inside it in the process. Next, one of the cushions reformed, then another.

She gasped as the blackened exterior of the van un-blistered. The paint had been burned and cracked into an ugly web but now, those filaments extended into white and red paint and even rewrote *BUDDY'S* and the image of the pizza on the side. The tires repaired themselves and reinflated. The front of the van stretched to assume its original shape and the engine sounded as if it were putting itself back together under the hood.

Finally, the holes on the two sides of the van—the first damage that had been done to it in the battle—sealed themselves.

In mere moments, the vehicle was in the same shape it had been in at the start of the fight. It had not been fully restored, however. The bullet holes and patches from combat in the past were all still there, but all the damage that had been inflicted in the last five minutes or so was gone.

Timeflash exhaled a sharp breath of air and almost fell back. Sam raced to her and caught her before she landed. He infused her with light and she inhaled and smiled. There was something incredibly comforting about having a dragon on the team who could heal others.

"Are you all right, Timeflash?" Brian asked. "I wouldn't have thought a van would have tired you out so much."

"I'm fine, thanks to young Lumos," She nodded at Sam. "It is not the size of the object that gives me trouble but the particulars. Fixing the engine, axles, and everything else would have been all right, but repairing all the guns was a little more than I anticipated."

"They look good, though," Drew said. He had already broken down an assault rifle into its constituent components and now worked to reassemble it. His motions were so fluid and practiced, it was almost as mesmerizing to watch as Timeflash's magic had been. "Thank you."

"Not to be a party pooper, but were you able to get the blueprints for the Chrome Castle back?" Keith asked.

Timeflash shook her head. "I reconstructed everything that was inside. The ash from the plans must have blown out of the van. If we went back—"

"That's not an option," Drew said. "You did good, Timeflash. This should be enough to do some damage."

Beanpole peered into one of the crates of ammunition. "I hate to be a bearer of bad news but—"

"Oh, come on, Beanpole, when have you ever said anything cheerful?" Hernandez snapped.

"The ammunition doesn't look great," he finished lamely.

"Doesn't look good?" Hernandez asked and pushed him aside to look inside the crate. "It looks like rats chewed through our bullets."

Timeflash nodded. "I'm sorry. Some of them must have detonated from the heat of the flames. Any pieces that didn't go through the portal are beyond the reach of my powers. There's nothing I can do."

"We're all alive and that's what's most important," Drew said and sounded sincere. "We'll go through the rest of the ammunition once we're somewhere safe. Kylara, the road?" He climbed into the cab of the van and turned the key in the ignition. It took a moment for the engine to turn over but despite it being incinerated minutes earlier, it started without issue.

Kylara turned toward the school and made the ground in front of the vehicle flatten enough to be driven on.

They all piled in and crossed onto the Lumos School grounds. She was worried that the statue guardians might try to stop them but instead, they saluted. After all, these were old friends of Amythist's.

She only wished the reunion could have come under more pleasant circumstances.

CHAPTER THIRTEEN

They drove through the woods, across the dueling fields, and into the U of the Lumos School. Kylara, Sam, and Timeflash flew overhead to keep an eye on the sky in case Tiamat arrived via a mage's portal. None of them thought they would have much time so it meant every second counted.

"I want that building secured!" Drew yelled as his team scrambled out. "We don't have dragon bullets, but if Tiamat and her dragons attack, they don't need to know that. Butters—"

"I won't be able to get on the roof, sir," the marksman said and pointed to his ankle.

"I think we can do something about that," Sam told him. He placed his hands on the injured joint. The big man winced but sighed with immediate relief as power flooded the limb and began the process of knitting damaged bone together. "It's not perfect, so take it easy. You don't have dragon healing to finish the job but it should be better than it was."

"It is, thanks," Butters replied and flashed him a big smile. "I'll take it as easy as Tiamat will allow."

"Stay in the van, then. You'll be the only one with dragon bullets. I need you to hit one of them early so they know we're a threat. That might make the rest of our ammunition worth something."

"Yes, sir," Butters said and hobbled toward the back of the van, leaning on Beanpole to keep his weight off his ankle.

"Everyone else, you all know the drill. I need to talk to Amythist."

Drew joined Kylara, Sam, and Timeflash as they entered the building and headed directly to the headmaster's office.

Before they could knock on the door, it swung open.

"Drew!" Amy said. "Thank God you're all right! Is your team…"

"They're all fine, thanks to Kylara," he said. "But we most likely don't have much time."

"You were seen, then?" the old dragon asked.

"That's putting it mildly." Timeflash smirked. "We managed to get into a full battle with some of the Steel Guard before we left."

Sam clenched his teeth "Kylara portaled us out of there but—"

"There are precious few safe locations for her to take all of you to hide out, yes." Amythist nodded. "It is good you came here instead of taking them to your home, Kylara."

"Oh no, you don't think—" The dragon mage reached for her phone and grimaced immediately when she recalled the sensation of having it blasted out of her hand by a bolt of lightning. "Tiamat was in my head. She'll know that I either came here or went to my mom's house. I have to call her."

Amy put her phone in Kylara's hand. She dialed her mom but there was no answer. Her mind raced. Did that mean Hester Diamantine was outside? Or had she already been caught? She hung up and returned the device. "I have to make sure she's all right. I'll be right back."

"No, Kylara, that would not be wise," Amythist said.

"We can't always be cautious, Headmaster." She started toward the door.

"Lady Amythist is right, Kylara," Amy said, which surprised

her. She had wanted to rush off to save the Steel Dragon, risks be damned. "Currently, we're outmatched. I hate it but it's the truth. I know I wanted to save Kristen, but can you imagine what would have happened if we had gone into that complex?"

Drew shook his head. "You wouldn't have made it. Her aura... it's something else. She has some of Kristen's most loyal people working for her."

"She had Heartsbane." Timeflash said the words as if it pained her to speak them aloud.

"This is different!" Kylara protested.

"This is the same thing, Ky," Amy said. "Your mom didn't answer. I know that's worrying but that doesn't mean she's been captured. If she has, we'll rescue her when we have a decent plan but right now, we have to focus on the people we have at hand, not the people we care about."

"Speaking of people, we care about...Samuel, where are the rest of your little band of troublemakers?" Amythist asked.

Kylara and Sam shared a look.

"Come now, children, we have no time to keep secrets. I promise I won't give you detention unless we fail to stop the evil dragon goddess. Now, where are they?" The headmaster flexed her aura to let them know she was serious, but the dragon mage didn't mind for once.

Sam shrugged as if to say "you tell them," so she did.

"Headmaster, do you remember Galen Stormwing?" she asked.

"We have no time for such questions, Kylara. Of course I remember the boy who brought an army of dragon skeletons to attack the school. He's gone, though. You told me he had perished fighting Lord Boneclaw."

"I lied, ma'am," she admitted. "He became trapped between his human and dragon forms and has been living out in the desert. He contacted us last night and asked for help."

"Oh, child. Please don't tell me you said yes."

"Tanya thought she could help him and I agreed," Kylara said. "Right now, Tanya, Karl, and Jasmine are in the pixie realm trying to get him to transform. And...uh, I should peek in on them."

The headmaster snorted in displeasure but nodded. "Amy, the shields. Quickly now, Kylara."

Amy raised her hands and closed her eyes and Kylara was able to feel the magic shield drop. Immediately, she opened a portal to the meadow in the pixie realm. Her friends were nowhere in sight. "They aren't there, ma'am."

"You foolish children could not have picked a worse time for such a jaunt," Amythist snapped, although her aura made it clear that she also understood why they would want to help a friend, especially someone who had been through as much as Galen had.

Drew cleared his throat. "Not to say I don't trust the kid, but this is all a little convenient, isn't it? This crazy dragon goddess appears and turns everyone to stone and at the same time, this kid with a questionable past comes out of the desert asking for help?"

Kylara was about to defend Galen but Amythist waved Drew off before she could. "I suppose technically, it is possible that he is somehow involved with the cult, but I find it highly unlikely. The Followers of Tiamat—and I would assume Tiamat herself—prize dragon powers highly. Galen's father was always dismissive of his second-born who lacked powers, and if he is now trapped between the two forms, I doubt Tiamat would look at him as an ally."

"I agree, ma'am," Kylara said. "She wants everyone to know she's a goddess and goddesses don't need students to help them. This doesn't feel like the kind of thing she would do."

"Fireball!" Amy's eyes widened in shock. A moment later, the sound of a fireball as it streaked into the school's magical shield could be heard echoing across the campus.

Amythist smiled tightly. "Now that feels more like the kind of thing Tiamat would do."

CHAPTER FOURTEEN

It felt like they had slogged through the swamp for days, but Galen didn't mind. Compared to trying to survive in the desert, subsisting off of what stringy animals he could find and cactus pads he could only sear with smoke, not cook, this was like heaven. They hadn't eaten anything there—although they felt no hunger in this strange realm—nor had they rested, yet he felt energized in ways he had not felt since being effectively exiled.

He didn't even mind Karl Midnight constantly talking trash.

"I don't see why you don't want to be king of the Gila Monsters. Think about it—you, looking like a big ol' deformed one of them—asking for bugs or whatever you ate out there. It sounds better than this to me." The shadow dragon wrinkled his nose as he put his foot into a particularly clinging puddle of muck.

"Oh, hush, Karl. You wouldn't have lasted twenty-four hours out there," Tanya said. Galen did not know why she was always so quick to defend him but he was not about to complain about it.

"I could have. I would have made shade to protect me from the sun."

"And at night when the temperature plummets more than fifty degrees?" Jasmine asked pointedly.

Karl grinned. "Yeah, you're right. I would have gone to my parents' house. Oh. Right. Sorry, Galen."

The other boy only smiled and decided he deserved worse than someone teasing him. He had desecrated the bodies of dragon heroes and his actions had caused a school to be attacked. What he deserved was to be left out in the desert until he became nothing but desiccated remains. But he had asked for help and somehow, these amazing people had rallied around him.

Even Karl had agreed to help. That meant far more to Galen than a few complaints. Plus, he had known him when he was friends with his older brother. The Midnight son could be far crueler than he had been. He would walk another week with these people merely so he could hear their voices, converse with them, or be in their presence.

But it looked like he wouldn't have to.

"Are you all right there, Galen?" Midnight asked. "Did you remember where you left some cactus pads or something?"

"No." Galen's mouth felt drier than it ever had in the desert.

"Oh, you forget where the pads were?"

"Will you shut up, Karl? This is the pond. This is the pond where…"

"Where Boneclaw took my powers," Galen finished for Tanya.

Jasmine raised her hands to her temples. "I can feel something here—power deep down in there."

"It's not a dragon," Karl said prosaically. "I can't feel any kind of aura."

"Me neither," Tanya agreed. "But the poor plants. They've been completely neglected." She settled her feet in the mud and raised her arms. Galen was amazed by her power every single time she used it.

Tree trunks with burn marks sloughed bark off until they looked as if they had never been touched by dragon fire at all.

Branches as thick as his legs mended themselves. Vines withered and died to become part of the soil as they regrew from their roots and spread around the pond before they bloomed with white flowers tinged with pink. The smell of jasmine drifted through the air, a pleasantly saccharine scent compared to the stench of decay they had endured.

Galen sometimes wondered what his life might have been like if he had earned the power to control plants like she had instead of the power to raise the dead. At first, he had thought her ability foolish and weak, then he had become jealous when he had lost control of his power. Now, he simply accepted it as the way of things. She understood the nuances involved so it was right that she had it and not him.

She exhaled and opened her eyes. "That's better, isn't it?" she said quietly, although the disfigured boy did not know if she was talking to them or the plants.

"Thank you all for helping me get here." He took a step toward the pond and could still see the imprints in the mud where Boneclaw had taken his powers from him. With a shudder, he took another step toward them, drawn to them like a moth to flame. "I don't know what will happen to me but I welcome whatever it may be. If I don't come out of there... Well, please tell Kylara thanks for me as well."

"It's a little melodramatic, huh?" Karl whispered to Jasmine but otherwise, the three of them were silent.

Galen stepped into the pool, past the signs of his struggle on the shore, and into the muck itself. He closed his eyes and felt the still, cool water against his legs. How long had he dreamed of this moment? How many times had he thirsted for the water he now stood in and yet had always been terrified by the prospect?

The other boy cleared his throat. "So, will you do something or..."

"He's trying," Tanya snapped.

"Maybe you should try something else," Jasmine said and tried to sound helpful.

They were right. Nothing was happening. Galen dropped to his knees and the water now came past his waist. He swooshed his tail from side to side, kicked mud up, and buried it beneath the muck. He bent back and dipped his stumpy wings in the water. Still, nothing happened.

"Have you tried thinking about what you want to happen? That's assuming you don't want to be covered in mud for your super-dry scaly skin." Karl couldn't hide a smirk.

The deformed boy said nothing. He merely closed his eyes again and tried to make his intentions clear. He had told himself for so long that all he wanted was to be in one form or the other and that he would accept being a human or a dragon, as long as he didn't have to be both at the same time any longer. But now, as he stood in this pond, that seemed fake.

He had told himself that he wanted so little for so long because there had been no reason to hope for more. But now, he felt he needed to be honest above all things.

"Please..." he whispered to the surface of the water. "Please let me be a dragon again as I once was. Please, let me be like I once was." He dipped his face in the cool water and held his breath for a minute...two...five before he lifted it out of the water.

"Dang, nice trick—dead man's kneel and all that. Did you wish to be able to hold your breath as long as a dolphin or something? I have to say, I had my money on you becoming normal again but you do you," Karl said.

Galen stood. He was as he had been when he walked into the pond with the same mess of human skin and dragon scales and the same elongated face and jagged mess of teeth. He touched his head to find he still had wisps of hair hanging limply between patches of scales. It had not worked at all. "I'm so sorry for wasting your time," he said, unable to turn and face the three who had come so far through the swamp with him and who had risked their lives to fight beasts who by rights should have ended him.

"Galen, you don't need to apologize. We'll think of something," Tanya said.

"Tanya's right, man. This only cost us like an hour in the real world. No worries."

He sighed, took a deep breath, and tried to harden himself for when he faced them.

But before he could turn, Jasmine waded out into the pond. "What's that?" she said and pointed toward the center. It was odd to see her splash through the water. The surface formed waves and droplets as she moved through it but no ripples spread from her movements. The pond swallowed them and remained completely still except for where she was. "Do you see that? There's something down there."

"I don't see anything..." Tanya said but sounded hopeful. Galen wondered if her aura might be betraying her. He hadn't been able to properly sense an aura since his transformation. Everything was muddled like looking at the sunrise through a curtain.

"Look toward the bottom," Jasmine said and pointed again. "There's a light down there but it looks deep. Too deep."

"I see it too," Galen said, shocked that he could. He had looked too close to the surface. Something glimmered but it looked impossibly deep—deeper than a pond could be. "But I never went that far. I don't see how it could have anything to do with me."

"Not to be rude, dude, but what if it's bigger than that?" Karl asked. "What if it's connected to Tiamat somehow?"

"That makes sense," Jasmine said. "That's why Boneclaw brought you here, after all, because it was where Tiamat was sleeping. I think we need to investigate."

"I agree," Tanya said. "It might be the key to healing Galen, but even if it's not and it has something to do with Tiamat, we owe it to Kylara to investigate."

"So we need to get down there?" Karl asked and grinned despite the arduousness and possible danger of the task.

"I guess so," Galen said. He wasn't sure exactly what he had agreed to but knew he would do anything for these people who had helped him, even if it had all been for nothing.

CHAPTER FIFTEEN

"Come. Follow me to the second floor," Amythist said and led everyone out of her office.

Kylara, Sam, Timeflash, Drew, and Amy followed the headmaster out of her office and up to the second floor of the building. They entered a large room—a library of some kind, perhaps, although Kylara had never been in it before—and approached a wall of windows.

A portal was open halfway up one of the mountainous slopes that framed the Lumos School. From it poured a small army of humans, mages, and dragons. They assembled into ranks as they came down the hill.

A group of mages stood off to one side, working together to make a massive fireball. Together, they hurled it against the shield protecting the school. Huge chunks fell from the sky and evaporated to nothing as they plummeted toward the ground.

"I can't hold them for long." Amy grunted. "Those are my mages. I've trained them how to make defensive shields—and how to break them. I'm stronger than any one of them but together, they will overwhelm me."

"Keep the shield up as long as you can," Amythist said and

snatched a glass sphere balanced on a pedestal. "Teachers," she said into the orb, "we are under attack. I want every single one of you to take our students and evacuate. I repeat, evacuate now. Get past the gargoyles and get out of here."

Voices replied from the orb—acknowledgments and wishes for good luck. Kylara noted that no one complained, argued, or questioned. They simply obeyed.

The mages threw another fireball against the shield and more massive pieces of energy given solid form fell from the sky, although these did not evaporate quite as quickly. One of them pounded into the center of the U and became a great shower of blue sparks as it vanished.

"One more strike and it's gone." Amy groaned.

"Drop it now. We'll need your strength," Amythist said.

"But—"

"Drop it now!"

The mage obeyed and the shimmering light in the sky vanished.

In that moment, Tiamat stepped through the portal.

Already, Kylara could feel her aura. It radiated from her like energy from the sun. It made her want to feel calm, to sit, and to relax...or else.

The goddess dragon pumped her diamond-crusted wings and took to the air. Something about seeing the enemy with her diamond scales pissed the girl off. It seemed like she must have maintained all the powers she'd held while residing in her body. Tiamat flew effortlessly down the hillside, buffeted by winds she created. Her diamond scales sparkled in the desert sun and reflected a thousand different shades.

"Greetings, students and teachers of this...*school*." She sneered the word as if it could be more accurately described as a prison. "I come to you as your rightful leader, mother, and goddess. It is good of you to welcome us by dropping your shield. All I require is for you all to come out and kneel."

No one moved.

"It is not by decree that I command this but by right," the dragon continued and her aura made it seem as if it were perfectly natural to be unsure about bowing to her. At the same time, it made it very clear that if they did, they would feel so much better. "I have defeated the old Dragon Council—every single one of them. By dragon law, I am the Council now."

"She's insane if she thinks that's how it works," Timeflash muttered.

"She's trying to bait someone into saying exactly that out loud," Amythist warned.

"Hold steady, team," Drew said into his walkie-talkie. "This is not the time to get into dragon bureaucracy with the enemy."

While Tiamat had been speaking, her force approached. They fanned out and now stood along one edge of the school a little beyond the line of statues that guarded the perimeter of the property.

The glass sphere that Amythist had given orders into flashed green. Relief came from the old dragon's aura—although it was almost hard to sense compared to the overwhelming desire to surrender that emanated from the usurper. But Kylara was certain that she had sensed it. As soon as the sphere flashed green, the headmaster shattered the window in front of her with a blast of telekinetic energy.

She jumped through and her dragon strength made the tiny, frail frame of the old woman look like an Olympic gymnast until she transformed into her dragon body. She soared across her campus to land between the building Kylara was still in and the wall of enemies that remained in position off-campus.

"This is my school, Kishar. I will not allow anyone—not even a religious zealot who has become carried away with herself—to come here and threaten the people in my care."

"You speak to the vessel when you should address the spirit," Tiamat rumbled. The dragon mage wondered if Kishar was even

KEVIN MCLAUGHLIN & MICHAEL ANDERLE

conscious inside the dragon. When the Mother of All Dragons had taken her body, she had not even let her see the outside world. Would she give Kishar more freedom since she had been the First Walker of the Followers of Tiamat?

"I speak to whoever thinks she may come bearing nothing but threats."

The black rainbow dragon laughed. "Threats? I have made none. I am here to spread the good news of my return, not send threats."

Amythist snorted as if her adversary were nothing more than a student who had snuck off campus. "If you do not threaten, what was that fireball?"

"Oh, that." Tiamat waved her claws at the complaint. "That was simply to get your attention. I would not have dragons bowing to anyone who flies around, even if they do have mages obeying them and making portals. The fireball was to give you a glimpse of what power your goddess now commands so when you kneel, it feels right. Consider it a kindness."

"You will not enter these grounds, Kishar, or Tiamat, or whatever you want to call yourself," the headmaster said.

Tiamat smiled warmly. "As you wish, Lady Amythist. I will respect you exactly as you will respect the wishes of those around you to worship as they see fit."

She extended her aura fully and Kylara no longer understood why she had ever bothered to resist this one true goddess of dragon kind. She jumped from the window—Sam and Timeflash at her heels—and coasted to the ground after she transformed into her dragon form in mid-leap.

Out of the corner of her eye, she saw that Drew's team on the roof of the school were no more foolish than they were. They raced inside, down the stairs, and came out across the U. Even Butters, whose ankle had not healed fully yet, hobbled from the van. He grunted when he stepped on the ankle but he probably understood—exactly like she did—that being with their goddess was worth any discomfort.

Part of her tried to say that this was wrong, that mere moments before, she had not felt this way at all. But it was a tiny voice compared to the symphony of emotion that radiated from the black dragon and urged her to go closer, to join the goddess, and to follow her to the ends of the earth.

The only person, dragon, or mage who didn't approach was Amythist. She had transformed into her frail human body and stood ahead of Kylara, Sam, and the humans. She clapped slowly, loudly, and disrespectfully.

"I applaud your effort to change my feelings," the headmaster shouted at Tiamat. "With a little more refinement of your technique, you might have been able to do so. Your power is impressive but it lacks finesse—like using a Ferrari to take the kids to school."

"What?" Tiamat growled and flexed her aura. Kylara felt her love for Tiamat even more keenly now. How did Amythist not feel what she knew to be true?

"Oh, sorry. I forgot you were buried in muck for a few millennia. Your technique is like using a sword to chop a carrot. It might work and when it does, I'm sure it feels impressive but ultimately, it's a waste of everything."

"Perhaps I am a little rusty," the black dragon snapped and narrowed her eyes at the old woman.

Kylara had expected the goddess—her goddess—to defeat the headmaster in seconds. After all, she could breathe fire or ice. She could turn Amythist to stone if she wished or open the ground beneath her and make the earth itself swallow the tiny woman.

But she didn't seem capable of changing her mind.

And why would she be able to?

The young dragon mage stopped walking toward Tiamat. She had been duped by her aura along with everyone else. But now that the goddess had focused her efforts on Amythist, she found her emotions were hers again. She knew she only had moments to act. If the black dragon could not overpower the headmaster's aura, she would simply attack—she would be a fool not to, and she was no fool. That meant she had to do something now. But what?

She didn't think four dragons, a mage, and a handful of humans with hardly any dragon bullets stood much chance against a force like this. Even if they could, none of them would as long as they were under Tiamat's aural control. And if they weren't free now, there was no reason to think they would break free as long as the enemy was here.

Although, if the team went somewhere else, that might accomplish the same thing.

Knowing that time was of the essence, Kylara opened a portal on the ground in front of the humans who exited the building. Before any of them could notice it, they all toppled through the hole in the earth and were transported to a different place.

She opened a portal in front of Amy next. The mage flew her skateboard into it.

The gates in front of Timeflash and Sam didn't work on the first attempt but on her second, she used whips of shadow to catch each of them by a horn and guide them through.

All that was left was the headmaster. "Lady Amythist, come with us!"

"I cannot!" the old dragon replied through gritted teeth. "The rest of the students need time to escape. The guardian statues will fight more fiercely if I'm here to fight with them."

"I'll go get them," Kylara replied.

"No, Kylara, you know what must be done. The Dragon Council must be unpetrified and you are the only one who can help. Go now, and don't worry about me. I've waited a long time for a rematch with Kishar."

On Amythist's use of Tiamat's body's name, the dragon goddess roared in fury. Her army of mages, humans, and dragons rushed onto the school grounds and promptly discovered that the statues of mythological beasts weren't simply decorative. Centaurs, chimeras, and gargoyles came to life and joined the battle against the invading force.

The girl didn't want to leave her mentor but she did as she was told and escaped through the portal.

CHAPTER SIXTEEN

Kylara reappeared a split second later at her mother's property in the mountains of New Mexico.

"Kylara, you're all right!"

She grinned and wrapped her mom in a hug augmented with dragon strength. "I was worried about you too."

"Me?" Hester asked. "I'm not the one who pissed a goddess off."

The dragon mage swallowed and wished she could laugh at the joke. "Is everyone all right?"

"Yes, ma'am," Drew said and sounded for all the world like Kylara was his boss. "We all made it through without injuries—well, except for Butters who walked on his ankle."

"I'm so sorry," the rotund marksman said and his southern accent came through more strongly than usual in his stress. "I felt like that dragon was...I don't even know. The preacher from the church where I grew up mixed with the best chicken fried steak I ever smelled. I couldn't resist her."

"I couldn't either," Brian said. "I felt like if I went to her, I would get a new game system or whatever. I don't think I could have stopped myself."

Beanpole, Keith, and Hernandez all nodded as well and seemed extremely freaked out.

"None of them could," Amy said. She held her hands a few inches away from Butters' swollen joint. A white mist flowed from her fingers to his ankle. Slowly but surely, the swelling receded again. "This would be much easier if you had dragon healing powers," she muttered. "Next time, listen to the healer and stay off it for a while?"

"How did you even get us out of there, Diamantine?" Hernandez asked.

"It was Lady Amythist," Kylara said. "She knew how to resist and that distracted Tiamat long enough for me to open portals."

"But why didn't any of us feel her influence lessen?" Sam asked. His aura was morose.

"Perhaps it had something to do with Kylara being the Sum of All Dragons?" Timeflash suggested.

"Maybe," she acknowledged. "But we can't pretend that will work again. If Amythist hadn't been there, I don't know what would have happened."

"We won't need to guess," Drew said. "We need to assume that she'll come here."

"How could she possibly know where we went?" Keith asked and sounded for all the world like a rookie.

"She was in my head," Kylara said. "When I escaped, I fought her inside my memories of this land. This will be one of the first places she checks."

"Which means we need to get out of here," Hester said.

"We?" Kylara asked. "Mom, you don't have to come with us."

Her mother raised an eyebrow so sharply she wondered if it could cut her. "My daughter is being pursued by a ghost calling herself Tiamat and a horde of cultists and you want me to stay here? And I thought I raised you right."

"That's not what I meant—"

"Kylara, even if there was some reason for me to stay behind, it wouldn't do any good," Hester said. "I've never been terribly skilled with my aura. If Tiamat's is strong enough to make all of you feel like she truly was the Mother of All Dragons, I'm sure it would work on me too. Besides, you'll eventually need to bring the fight to her. I'd like to be there for that."

"It sounds good to me," Drew interjected before the girl could ask her mom to go somewhere else instead of going with them. "We'll need allies."

"The more the merrier." Keith grinned.

"Yeah, and even if your aura sucks, your diamond skin should help," Hernandez said. "Maybe that'll help you resist."

"Resist—hey, that gives me an idea," Drew said.

All eyes turned to him.

He wiped the excitement off his face before he spoke. "The pixies are fond of Kylara, right?"

Sam nodded. "That's an understatement. They call her the Big Pixie, after all."

"Right, well...what if we hide out with some pixies? Kylara, do you remember those who live with Atramento in the Rocky Mountains? It's an out-of-the-way location. Maybe that can buy us some time to think of a way to free the Dragon Council."

"I hate to be negative but...well, Tiamat was in my head. She knows I went there," Kylara said. "I think it would make more sense to go somewhere random."

"No, I don't think so," Amy said. "Remember, pixies were created as a weapon against dragons. They're naturally resistant to dragon auras. It might not be enough but if anything can stand against her, it might be them. Plus, if we second-guess your instincts, why would we think Tiamat won't be able to follow those same instincts?"

"Where would we go, anyway?" Sam asked. "The Prairie King's castle where we went on that field trip?"

Kylara felt her face flush and her aura reveal her embarrassment. That was exactly where she had thought they should go.

But if Sam had thought of it, their enemy might too. "All right, I think you're right. Let's go to Atramento's. It's better if it's Drew's idea. Tiamat might be able to guess my mind but not his."

"Speaking of allies, where are your other friends?" Hester asked.

"It's a long story, Mom, but they're in the pixie realm right now," Kylara reached for her phone to check the time, only to be reminded again that it had been destroyed. "I should go check on them."

"They can wait until we get to the mountains," Drew said. "Do you have the energy to take us there now, Kylara?"

"Sure."

"Wait a minute, Kylara...you're not wearing your amulet?"

"No. It was broken by Tiamat. She crushed it."

"That's great!" Hester exclaimed. "I'll be right back." She ran toward her house.

"Do you have any idea what the hell that was about?" Hernandez asked.

"My birth mother gave me an amulet when I was a baby that protected me from dragon auras. It even helped against Tiamat before she came fully awake but then she destroyed it."

"Isn't that bad news?" the woman asked.

"I have worse," Timeflash pointed east to the horizon.

It was hard to see in the glare of the sun off the sand and rocks of the desert but after a moment, Kylara discerned winged shapes growing in size as they approached. Already. they were too big and too spiky to be birds.

"There are so many," Beanpole muttered.

"I don't get it. Why didn't she simply port here?" Keith asked.

Amy stood from healing Butters. "Opening portals is difficult for mages. She must have wanted them to have as much strength as possible when they found us."

Kylara nodded. "We'll definitely go with Drew's plan. She knew where I'd try to run to. She'll probably anticipate whatever else I thought of too." It was a horrible idea that her memories could no longer be trusted but she was confronted with the reality of it right now.

"You have enough to open portals, though, right?" Butters chuckled. She could read his emotional state with her aura and could see that the chuckle was false bravado. Wisely, she did not bother to say anything to the humans who could not read auras.

"All right, ready!" Hester rushed out and a replica of the amulet dangled from a chain she held in her hands. She pushed it into her daughter's hands. "Put it on."

The dragon mage complied and immediately felt more comfortable. No longer could she feel Timeflash's anxiety, or Sam's concern for her, or her mom's grim determination. She could only feel herself. She had spent most of her life being protected by this very same amulet. It was good to put it on, even if she was confused by its existence. "But...Tiamat destroyed it."

"She destroyed your mother's, yes, but this is your Aunt Cassandra's."

"But how?"

"I took it from her body after she died. I didn't know why I did it at the time but now, it seems obvious. Your grandfather made this for his daughters and their children, Kylara. He made it for you. It has as much power as its twin did. I had hoped you wouldn't need it but...well..."

"Thanks, Mom." She hugged Hester.

"So great, the family memento was returned. Now, if it's not too much to ask, can we get the hell out of here?" Hernandez asked.

Kylara nodded, opened a portal to the pixie house in the Rocky Mountains, and they fled before they were overpowered by the enemy.

CHAPTER SEVENTEEN

Jasmine honestly had no idea what lurked at the bottom of the pool. All she knew was that they were in the pixie realm, Tiamat had once been trapped down there, and that lights did not generally shine from the bottom of normal bodies of water. All these truths made her curious and she decided to investigate.

She stepped a little deeper into the pond so the water came up to her waist. Even at this depth, she did not make any ripples whatsoever. It was odd because she felt the water moving around her legs. It wasn't as if this was an illusion of a pool that was solid or even like it was a different material than water. The surface simply did not behave as it should have. The mage guessed that this had something to do with whatever was glowing down there.

After a deep breath, she extended her hands and released a string of telekinetic energy from each fingertip. Cautiously, she sent the telekinetic tip of each finger into the pool. The water puckered where her energy pushed through but it did not ripple any more than when she splashed through it.

"What's down there?" Karl asked from the edge of the pond.

"I've reached down maybe four feet and so far, nothing,"

Jasmine replied and extended her search even more. It was hard to judge distance with her telekinesis. Her powers weakened over distance but she had learned how to make them work up to a few hundred yards. Although the pond was deep it wasn't that deep, which left her unsure of its dimensions.

Eventually, though, she felt the bottom. First, one telekinetic finger found it, then another, followed by a third. All ten fingers probed through the muck and checked at the edges for traps or more of the buried skeletons that had attacked them. She found nothing so she worked inward until one finger felt something hard and she paused to explore it carefully.

It was hard to tell texture with her telekinetic probing, but Jasmine got the sense that it was rough like beams of wood.

"What's down there?" Tanya asked. The mage had kicked up a little muck with her search but everyone else could tell that she had reached the bottom because the light was now flickering, obscured as it was by the mud.

"There's like a pit or a hole…framed in wood, I think. The light comes from below it," she explained.

"Can you reach inside?" Karl asked.

She released her telekinetic tendrils and shook her head. "I've never practiced using my abilities under water. The pressure combined with the distance makes it difficult."

"Well…it was a good effort," Galen said and wiped his eyes with the back of the dragon talons that grew from his hands.

"We won't give up," Tanya said.

"But Jasmine said she can't reach—"

"I can reach." The mage cut Galen off. "But not like this. I think if I make a sphere around me, I can descend and the distance won't be a factor."

"Are you sure you want to do that?" Karl asked. "Go down there alone, I mean."

"I'll be wrapped in a shield that can protect me from dragon fire. I'll be fine," she said, lifted herself out of the pond with her powers, and wrapped a shimmering blue shield of energy around her body. She plunged into the pond but only sank a couple of feet below the surface before she popped up.

"That was quick." Midnight grinned.

"The air is making me too buoyant, you dolt. I didn't get down all the way," Jasmine said.

Karl only grinned wider at the insult. Jasmine loved how they could tease each other. Most people thought she was mean but she merely had a prickly sense of humor.

"You need a weight," Galen said.

"So, we need to find a rock for you or something, right?" Karl poked around on the shore. "Wood floats or we could simply knock a tree down."

"Hmm...let's think about this... I need something that is dense, stubborn, and a real downer. I know just the thing!" The mage caught him with a hand made of force and yanked him into the pond.

He yelped when he splashed into the water but emerged smiling. When he trudged toward her, no ripples followed him although he moved far more forcefully than she had.

"Your head has to be the densest thing around," Jasmine said sweetly.

"And if we need something sharp to get into whatever's down there, we have your tongue. We're a perfect team." He nodded.

She grabbed him by the arm and pulled him close.

His eyebrows rose in surprise at exactly how close but he put an arm around her and licked his lips devilishly. "I want you to know that if I run out of air, I fully expect mouth to mouth resuscitation."

"I know we have way more time here than in our realm, but that doesn't mean we want to spend it watching the two of you flirt," Tanya shouted from the shore.

The mage ignored her and wrapped a force shield around her

and Karl. She moved them farther into the pond, then stopped supporting them and they sank.

Karl's weight did indeed help. It only took a little extra energy to keep them moving downward.

"So…" he said and grinned like a devil as his face was mere inches away from hers. "Do you like it here?"

"Do you mean deep inside mysterious ponds that might be magical prisons?" she asked.

"By here I meant in my arms."

"Technically, you're in mine."

"You know, I'm all right with that."

"Are you? I thought your dragon honor meant you couldn't date a lowly mage like me."

Karl smiled and his eyes smoldered. "There is absolutely nothing lowly about you, Jasmine Patel. You're smart as hell, super-powerful, and beautiful too."

She blushed although Karl couldn't see it in the dim light filtering from both above and below in the murky pond. He could feel it in her aura, however, as he pulled even closer.

"There's no need to be shy, Jasmine. I…I think I love you."

"I…I might feel the same," she replied breathlessly. "But your father—"

"Had his ass kicked thanks to your help. I know you might not believe me but when all this crazy Tiamat stuff is over, he'll look at you differently. And if he doesn't…well, we'll have to kick his ass again."

"He might throw you out."

"That would free up even more time to be with you, so I don't see the problem," Karl said.

Jasmine's face grew hot and her breathing became more labored. Why had he never talked to her like this before? Why had he never been so overt about his feelings? Why had she never felt like this?

"We're running out of air," she realized belatedly and said it aloud.

"Huh?" Karl's speech was slightly slurred.

She looked down. They were only a few feet above the bottom of the pond. She ignited a small ball of light and saw that there was a construction there—a frame of wood in the shape of a square. From the surface, she had thought that whatever was glowing at the bottom of the pond had to be inside this frame but she saw now that the wood served as more of a gate. The pool seemed to go on for at least another fifty feet past it before they would reach whatever was down there.

The mage didn't have the air for that.

"We have to surface," she said. Her words came out like there were marbles in her mouth.

"Tanya was right, we shouldn't have been flirting." Karl grinned although it lacked the mischievous quality she liked so much. His eyes looked duller due to lack of oxygen.

Jasmine had to get them back to the surface.

She pushed on the bottom of their bubble and forced them to rise but it didn't work. Distracted by Karl and by their quest, she had not paid enough attention to the pressure building all around them. It took almost all her strength to keep fifty feet of water above their heads from crushing them. That pressure, combined with their diminishing air supply, left her drained.

The harsh reality was that she didn't have enough to get them to the surface. Worse, she could feel the bubble around them weakening and soon, the water would burst through.

Their magical sphere settled on top of the wooden gate. It took all her strength to stop it from popping. They were stuck above some kind of magical prison without enough energy to get them to the surface and barely enough air to keep them alive for another minute.

The mage sighed. At least she had Karl with her. It was better than dying alone, she decided although frankly, she thought the whole tragic teenage love motif was stupid.

That only made their increasingly dire situation ironic, however. "I can't believe I'll die down here with you," she said and her breath felt too hot as it left her.

Karl smirked. "You wish," he said and pushed out of their bubble and into the crushing depths of the cursed pond.

CHAPTER EIGHTEEN

Kylara stepped out of her portal and into a clearing in a forest.

"Where is this place?" Timeflash asked and sniffed the air. "It doesn't smell quite right."

"Look at the sky," Hester's mom said and pointed to the patch of rich purplish-blue above their heads. "I've never seen a color like that on earth."

"That's because we're not on earth," she explained. For her portals to transport her somewhere in the real world, she needed to open one to the pixie realm, then another out of there and into a new location. She had become quite adept at making the two gates appear extremely close to each other in the pixie realm so her portals seemed to function the same way as the mage ones did. There were times, however, when there was a real benefit to going through the pixie realm.

Like when she had friends who had been trapped there for hours.

"That does explain the pixies," Keith said and waved to two of the little creatures who diligently sniffed flowers. When they noticed that Keith had acknowledged their existence, they darted to another patch of flowers deeper in the woods.

"There are time distortion effects here, right?" Brian asked.

Kylara nodded.

He grimaced. "Then we can't stay long. I don't trust Tiamat to not shatter my sister into a thousand pieces and claim it as her divine right to do so."

"We won't be long but I want to find my friends if we can," Kylara said. "Tanya!" she cried. "Jasmine! Kaaaarl! Galen!"

There was no answer so she shouted their names again even louder.

"Is that seriously your plan?" Hernandez sneered.

"Well, I had hoped that you would all help me look." She returned the scornful look.

"Well, yelling is all right but why not try something a little more visible?" The woman took what looked like a gun from her belt, aimed it at the sky, and fired. A streak of red light arced and ignited to burn even brighter.

"A signal flare—nice," Drew said.

"Is it, though?" Sam asked and pointed at the flare. Three pixies raced after it, throwing off light and sparks of their own.

"I don't think anyone would be able to tell that it's any different than whatever this place is." Butters frowned at the muddy earth.

"Ky, what about your new powers?" Sam asked.

"Good idea." Kylara transformed into her dragon form and reached into her inner magic for one of the many powers she had been given when the Followers of Tiamat had beaten them into her. She wished she had more time to practice. There were powers she hadn't even used yet, and her experience with her ability to control shadows and light proved that there were often novel applications to even seemingly straightforward abilities.

But for the moment, she knew one that might work. She drew on her inner magic and felt the skin of her throat change slightly in composition. A moment later, she inhaled to fill a massive sack of air that simply hadn't existed before she had magically created it.

"You might want to cover your ears," Sam said casually before he plugged his.

"Tanya! Jasmine! Kaaaaaarl! Galen!" she roared so loudly that leaves fell from the trees, insects launched from the forest floor, and the sky filled with birds in colors for which there were no names on earth.

But there was no sign of Tanya, Galen, or any of her friends.

"Damn, girl, I should have listened to you. That was awesome." Hernandez grinned although she looked as if the sound had disoriented her.

"I'm not so sure," Sam said and pointed through the woods.

Kylara cursed when she saw what he was pointing at. Glowing balls floated toward them. There were only a few at the moment but she knew that if they waited long enough for the balls of energy to get close enough to reveal their true form— jellyfish-like motes of light armed with shocking tentacles—it would be too late. These strange creatures traveled in huge groups that could either stay dark or come out of some other dimension entirely at the last moment. They would be surrounded in minutes.

"What do we do?" Drew said. "We can try to make a barricade with some of these trees but I can't tell how many of those are out there. Can we hold against them while we find your friends?"

The dragon mage bit the inside of her cheek. "No...no, we can't. If we start to fight them, more will come."

"What are they?" Keith asked.

"I don't know, exactly, but I've seen them before. They aren't the kind of thing we can fight. It'd be like battling with a hornet's nest. Even if we win, we'll lose," she said. "We have to get out of here."

"What about your friends?" Drew asked.

"They aren't near us," Kylara said reluctantly. "Which means we can't get to them, not with these will-o-wisps in our way. Maybe they heard me and we can buy them some more time." *And maybe they've already been killed by these damn zapping things in which case, none of this matters,* she thought but did not say aloud.

Instead, she opened a portal to the mountain pixies' home. "Come on. Let's get through and out of these woods. I've never seen these will-o-wisps go after pixies so maybe some of them can help." She was thankful to have the magic-dampening amulet on as it made it easier to sell the lie. In all honesty, she was terrified that they were far too late but saw no point in telling anyone that.

"That's a good plan, Ky," Sam said.

Kylara nodded and tried to make herself believe it. She and Drew went through first as they were the only two who had been there before. As he directed each new arrival to the field to form a perimeter around the portal, she looked around.

Where was everyone?

She didn't see Atramento, nor did she see any pixies—not the Hound, Oda, Mari, or... "Rider?"

The dragon mage raised her arms to protect herself as a great horned owl swooped at her.

"Back to the nether realm with ye, foul beast! Back, I say!" screamed a tiny pixie from the owl's back. Rider had big eyes, antennae, something like a beetle's chunky wings on his back, and was about a foot tall. He held onto the owl's two ear tufts with every ounce of strength he had. "No mages come here without Atramento's blessing and blessed ye have not been!"

The owl—goaded by its tiny rider—clawed at Kylara but she turned her skin to diamond so its talons did nothing to her.

"Rider, it's me—Kylara."

"I know no woman of such a name! Be gone with ye!"

She sighed as the poor owl tried and failed to savage her arm. "It's me. You know. The Big Pixie?"

"Ack! The Big Pixie! Well, why didn't ye proclaim it when you had the chance?" Rider yanked on the owl's ear tufts and the poor creature flew to a nearby pine tree to roost.

Once it landed, he hopped off and flew toward Kylara. Someone else might have thought it odd that a being who could fly would ride anything, but she was a skilled enough flyer to recognize how clunky Rider was in flight.

"Hi, Rider. Do you remember me? Drew?" The man held a hand out for the pixie to shake.

"Ack! Aye! I mean I do!" the pixie replied, grasped one of Drew's fingers, then wound the rest of his hand in tight bands of glowing golden sparks. He grimaced as the tiny being squeezed his hand.

"I don't seem to remember your accent being quite so Scottish," Drew grunted.

"I told you that you weren't allowed to watch Braveheart again, you little rat!" Atramento emerged from the house. As usual, his hair was shaved into elaborate geometric patterns that matched the tattoos on his hands and fingers. He wore a ceremonial robe and seemed to be trying to catch Rider in a net of telekinetic energy.

"Ye can take our lives, but ye'll never take our freeeeeeedom!" Rider roared when Atramento finally nabbed the little guy and dragged him off Drew with a length of invisible rope.

"Kylara, it's very nice to see you," the mage said and bowed formally. "Lady Timeflash, Lady Diamantine, Lord Lumos, you honor us with your visit."

"What? No bow for me?" Hernandez grinned.

"You are lucky I have not wrapped you up like I did him." He gestured at Rider, who had broken free and now rode a rabbit around the meadow.

"You're still mad about that ink bomb, huh?"

"You cost us weeks of paperwork." Atramento growled.

"It's a good thing you like it so much!" Butters grinned as he approached the man and wrapped him in a bear hug. "Long time no see, Atramento. Are you doing all right?"

"I am, thank you, Butters. Although I have a feeling you are not all here because you have good news to share."

"I wish I could say you're wrong but—"

The man waved Drew's explanation away before he could go on. "Come inside, come inside. Mari and Oda put tea on and are quite excited to have visitors. Whatever bad news you have had better be shared with them as well or else they'll simply make you repeat it."

He led them inside as Kylara kept her eyes on the horizon and wondered how good a hiding place this truly was.

CHAPTER NINETEEN

The tea was barely poured before Drew started talking plans. "With Kristen and the Council out of commission, I'm concerned that we won't be able to rally enough dragons to our side to fight against Tiamat."

"I don't know if rallying dragons is a good idea," Timeflash said. "If she can overwhelm Heartsbane, could anyone stand against her? Those we get to join our side might simply be converted to hers."

Kylara tried to focus on the conversation but she found it difficult. She couldn't stop thinking about Galen and her friends. Where had they been? She knew from Amy that when Kristen went to the pixie realm to try to earn more powers, she had only been gone a short while from the material world, even though weeks had seemed to pass for her there. How long had it been for Galen and the others when it had been hours here?

"Ky?"

"Huh?"

"What about your pendant?" Sam said. "Do you think it would be strong enough to resist Tiamat?"

"I...I don't know. It helped before when she was still in the pond. But now that she's free, I can't be sure. She feels so much stronger now."

"We've been discussing it for the last few minutes," Amy snapped. "Is there something more pressing than defeating a false goddess?"

"No… No, I guess not…only…"

"Only what?" Drew demanded. All eyes turned to her and no one spoke. They all wanted to hear what she had to say.

"Only I still have friends in the swamp in the pixie realm. I know we have bigger fish to fry or whatever, but I've never won a fight without their help. I can't simply abandon them there. If something happens to me, I'm the only one who can get them back."

"Something happening to you is why we can't allow you to go to the pixie realm," Amy said. "You're the only person who can undo Tiamat's petrification process. We need you here, Kylara. I'm sorry, but your friends will have to wait."

"Oh, but we need to race off after yours?" the girl snapped.

The mage said nothing and merely grimaced. Everyone else at the table looked uncomfortable as well. Of course they were. They had all been Kristen's friends long before she became the head of the Dragon Council. They were rescuing a friend and it just so happened that doing so was a tactically wise plan if it could be accomplished.

"You're not the only one who can go to the pixie realm, Big Pixie," Mari said, fluttered her butterfly wings, and landed on the table in the center of the discussion so she didn't have to raise her frail voice. "A pixie can retrieve your friends, although I'm not sure if any of those here would be brave enough."

"Brave enough?" Rider demanded, hopped up on the table, and upended Beanpole's cup of tea. "Have you forgotten that Rider walks among you? If there is a mission in need of bravery, I am the pixie for it."

"But it will be difficult," Oda, the other elder pixie, said cautiously.

"I eat danger for breakfast!" Rider boasted.

"Time will be of the essence," Mari added.

"Let me summon my peregrine and teach you all the meaning of speed!" the pixie shouted and augmented his voice with magic so it echoed off the ceiling. He raced from the room.

"Can we return to the discussion at hand?" Drew asked. "I know you're worried about your friends, Kylara, but time is of the essence. I hope we have some breathing space here but we can't bank on that."

"We'll be all right," Hernandez said with bravado. "She's probably scanning every place she can think of right now—a waste of time and energy."

"She'll think of this place eventually," Kylara said. "She's seen my memories. I think we'll have a little more time because it was Drew's idea to come here and not mine, but he's right. We can't linger here."

Something slammed into the door and Brian went to open it. No one was there but a moment later, a squawk made him look down to see a peregrine falcon wearing a saddle and with Rider on its back.

"You couldn't get the door open, huh?" he asked.

"Cursed doorknobs!" the pixie screamed.

"I don't know… I appreciate the offer but can Rider truly find them?" Ky asked.

"I know his methods are unorthodox in this land," Mari explained, "but in the pixie realm, there is not a trail that he cannot follow. He has tracked beasts the rest of us thought were nothing but myth. He will find your friends, I assure you."

Kylara nodded and let the pixie go. He opened a portal and charged through to another dimension with a warrior's yell.

"All right," Drew said, smacked the table a little too hard, and

KEVIN MCLAUGHLIN & MICHAEL ANDERLE

made everyone's teacups rattle on their saucers. "It's time to talk strategy. With the Council gone, we've lost all coordination when it comes to dragons. Timeflash, I think your instincts about Heartsbane and the auras are correct. We'll have to come up with a plan to neutralize Tiamat from a distance, then free the Dragon Council. If we can nullify her powers, the Steel Guard should rejoin our fight and help us with her Followers. There are also the other Steel Guard outposts, although with Tiamat in charge of the Chrome Castle, we'll need a back door. Brian, do you still have access?"

"Uh…maybe," the young man said noncommittally. He stared at his phone.

"If the plan is to hit her from a distance, I could use more dragon bullets," Butters said and seemed unusually thoughtful. "I've never shot a goddess before."

"But the bullets were all destroyed," Sam pointed out.

"Not all of them," Drew said. "Although the largest cache is in Detroit. Brian, can you check on that?"

"Hmm?" Again, Brian didn't look up from his phone. His brow was furrowed.

"I'm concerned about the legitimacy of her claim," Timeflash said. "She did best the entire Dragon Council in combat."

"Oh, that's a bunch of horse crap. She must have tricked them," Amy said.

"That's happened before." The other woman shrugged. "Dragons respect power. The fact that we don't see any resistance means that at least some of the dragons out there are considering her claim."

"So, a dragon needs to beat her ass?" Hernandez nodded as if this were simply what must happen.

"But anyone who gets close enough will be overpowered."

"But Ky's amulet—" Sam tried to say again.

"I need bullets—" Butters cut in.

"Brian, can you get patched into the security cameras there or not?" Drew snapped at the Steel Dragon's brother.

"Sorry...I got distracted."

"Seriously, dude?" Keith snorted. "What could possibly distract you now?"

Brian grimaced and pulled a tablet out, went to what seemed to be a live newscast, and set up the device so everyone could see. "Tiamat is addressing the public, live and on TV. I was checking which channels are carrying it."

"Which ones?" Keith asked.

"All of them."

CHAPTER TWENTY

The cold water of the pond dragged Karl immediately from the lethargy induced by lack of air. He had been so sleepy and it had been so comforting to be warm and close to Jasmine. Now, however, the water all around him awakened him and forced him to face how little air was in his lungs.

Reflexively, he lashed out with shadow tendrils in all directions. Frantic, he scrabbled through the muck and probed for roots, stones, or anything to catch hold of. He needed to drag them to the surface. No, he decided quickly. He needed to get Jasmine to the surface. Karl knew that in the grand scheme of things, he and his powers were redundant. He had played his part and helped Kylara escape the plans of the Followers of Tiamat, the religion his insane father had always pushed on him. Now, he had to get Jasmine to safety. She was special and she was worth it.

Although that didn't mean he wouldn't try to get himself to the surface too.

He wrapped her bubble in a web of shadow tendrils like it was a precious egg as he used other dark filaments to pull himself ever higher through the pond but his progress was too slow. There were hardly any tree roots to grab onto this deep and there were no rocks to speak of. That seemed impossible. Surely pond muck couldn't go on forever. Then again, he would be a fool to think the rules of this realm were anything like those at home.

It was too bad that the rules weren't different with regard to how much air he needed to survive.

More tendrils surged from his fingers and drew him and Jasmine up another couple of feet. He could feel the bubble protecting her starting to go soft. She was running out of air. If she fell unconscious, there would be no way to save her, not at these depths.

Karl knew he had to do something fast and powerful.

To his surprise, he thought about what his father would say. *There is no power like the form of a dragon. Never forget that.* He had thought the existence of mages like Amy Williams handily disproved that and yet, his dragon form was stronger than his human body.

Determined to save Jasmine, he drew on the last trace of energy he had and took his dragon form. He had become discombobulated in the tight space and now faced down instead of up.

His enhanced gaze saw through the murk of the pond and the tiny square frame that had stopped their descent into some kind of a chamber below. He could never get through the opening now. It would be impossible at his size but maybe he could still affect whatever was down there.

Not sure where he had the strength to pull from, Karl breathed fire to the bottom of the pond. It didn't so much as darken the wood of the frame, nor did it make it through the opening, but not all was lost.

The fire super-heated the water below them and created a plume that pushed the two of them toward the surface. Jasmine launched out first, still conscious enough to grasp onto Karl's back when he emerged from the water too.

"Oh, thank goodness!" Tanya was beside herself. "Karl, your aura became so faint."

"Lack of air...does that...to a person..." He wheezed, sucked in huge breaths of air, and felt his strength and powers start to return.

He paddled to the shallows and used shadow tendrils to make a bridge for the mage to walk across to the shore. Once she was safely out of the pool, he changed into his human form and trudged out of the muck. He plopped down beside her and she promptly leaned against him.

They looked at the pond. As before, it was completely still like nothing had broken its placid surface.

"Did you get whatever was down there?" Tanya asked, which Karl thought was an exceedingly dumb question given that he could still see the flicker of light from the bottom of the pond. He didn't say anything, though. He was merely happy that he and Jasmine were both still alive.

"No. We couldn't make it," the mage said. "There's some kind of a frame down there but I couldn't see past that."

"There was some kind of chamber," Karl said. "At the bottom of the pond, there's a gate and past that, there's another room. In the light of my fire, I saw...something. I don't know what. It looked man-made though. Or dragon-made, I guess. Unnatural."

"Do you think it had anything to do with my powers?" Galen asked.

He snorted in derision. They had almost died while he had been chilling on the surface and he had the gall to ask about his lost abilities?

"No, I don't think so," Jasmine said.

"Sorry," Karl said caustically but the other boy didn't seem to notice his tone.

"Whatever's down there seems older than what happened to you, Galen—far older," Jasmine said. "I think... Well, this might sound grandiose, but I think it might have something to do with

Tiamat. She was imprisoned in this pond and it makes sense that there would need to be more than muck to keep her locked below. The room you saw, Karl…do you think it could have been a cell?"

"Who's to say?" he replied. He hadn't thought of the room's purpose, only that he'd wanted to get the hell out of the water. It was amazing that she was able to put all these clues together. His father was a fool for thinking mages were weak. Their shorter lifespans made them sharper and much cleverer than most dragons. She embodied both of these.

"I think we need to go down there," Jasmine said. "I know we came here for Galen, but I think this might be our true purpose. It might be the key to locking Tiamat away again."

"Then we try again," Karl said. "Although maybe the B-team should take a shift this time."

CHAPTER TWENTY-ONE

It took a moment for Kylara to process what Tiamat was saying on the small screen. Her attention was on the background, which was obviously what the usurper intended.

The self-proclaimed goddess stood at the foot of the tower. Behind her was the Dragon Council, all still frozen in stone that was black and as shiny as obsidian. They looked terribly fragile as if all she had to do was flick her diamond-encrusted tail and they would shatter to pieces. That was, no doubt, her intention.

The girl gasped when she recognized that it was not only the Dragon Council frozen in place behind their enemy. Amythist was there too. She looked proud and strong, even frozen in stone, at least at first glance. But as she tried to drag her eyes away from the frozen statues to the dragon in front of them, she couldn't help but wonder if other dragons would see strength in the old headmaster's eyes or foolishness.

Kylara could not feel the dragon goddess's aura but it was clear she was trying to calm her audience. Even in her dragon form, she seemed kind and motherly and her wide hips made her look like she was ready to bear a clutch of eggs.

"You have been too long without someone to care for you, my children," Tiamat said soothingly. "You have survived a world of chaos and I am proud of you all, but there is no longer any need to struggle. I also wish to welcome the mages and humans under the safety of my wings. You were wise to work together and because of that, I have not killed your former leader and instead, given her a place of honor."

The camera panned to the top of the skyscraper that was the Chrome Castle. There, on the drawbridge that served as a landing pad to the castle that topped the skyscraper, was the Steel Dragon. She was frozen in stone and looked both haughty and precarious. It would take little to snap the bridge she rested on and topple her hundreds of feet to break to smithereens. Kylara wondered if she was placed in such a way that she would destroy the rest of the Council as well.

"I approve of this Steel Guard," Tiamat said and still sounded so calm it hurt. "Those who have met me have accepted my rightful place as Mother and Goddess of this world."

"Only because of your aura, you monster," Hernandez all but growled at the tablet's screen.

"They have seen that I have the right to rule. I am sorry to say that the Dragon Council did not have the same vision the Steel Guard did. They tried to stand in my way and they had to be punished. I will forgive them, though, as long as no one tries to fight in their name.

"For now, I only wish for you to continue with your lives as you did before your mother returned. I like the industriousness of this age. You must continue to work and labor so you will be rewarded. I will see all of you very soon. When you see me, you will bow, and together, we will usher in a new age. I am your mother, my children, and you will all soon see that Mother knows best."

Applause and cheers followed. Tiamat inclined her head

slightly to indicate that she heard them before she left. The cameras continued to roll and highlight the petrified Dragon Council while the news reporters and anchors began to offer commentary on this "momentous" day. There was no partisan bias to the various news corps. Each and every reporter there was under the influence of the usurper's aura.

Finally, when the echo chamber that was the commentary on the various channels Brian opened tabs for became too much to bear, he turned it off.

"Well...that was a nightmare," Keith said, his smile tight.

"Everyone saw Amythist, right?" Drew muttered.

"Yeah, we saw her," Butters said.

"She was the only person who could stand against Tiamat's aura. She's the only reason Kylara was able to break free of it," Timeflash said and horror tinged her words. "Without her, what chance do we have?"

"We still have a chance," Hester said in a rather uncharacteristic show of optimism. "Kylara has her aunt's amulet now. Its twin kept her completely hidden from dragon kind for sixteen years. It can hold against Tiamat—it has to."

Drew turned to Ky, a blunt look on his face. "Do you think you can hold out against her aura now that you have the pendant?"

She tried to stay positive but it was difficult. "I'm not sure. Tiamat almost overcame me when I wore my mom's amulet," Kylara said. "And that was when she was imprisoned. Now that she's free and has a physical body, I don't think we can count on that being enough."

"But you're stronger too," Sam pointed out and took her hand in his. "You can beat her. You will."

"I agree that Lara's stubborn streak will come into play," Drew said and inadvertently used the name she had given when they'd first met to partially hide her true identity. "And it's certainly an advantage that we have a piece of tech we didn't have when we faced Tiamat."

"That pendant is not tech. It's magic," Amy quipped.

"Regardless, the greatest tactical advantage Kylara grants us is the ability to free the Dragon Council," he continued. "Our plan needs to focus on getting her in close enough to free them, then get them out of there again, possibly with her ability to take things to the...uh—Jesus, I can't believe I'm saying this—her ability to take us to the...uh, pixie realm."

"I agree. Kylara is powerful but Kristen is already a household hero," the mage responded. "We'll need her to rally the other dragons."

"And the Council too," Keith added. "They're all on the Dragon Council because they don't ever totally agree with Kristen. It means they'll be able to rally those who don't directly support the Steel Dragon."

"Idiots," Brian muttered. "My sister is so much more awesome than a fricking pond goddess ghost."

"Agreed!" Butters said and everyone laughed except the two students.

"How can you joke at a time like this?" Sam asked. Kylara was also appalled.

"Gallows humor is kind of our thing." Hernandez winked. "What better way to face your mortality than flipping the bird in the grim reaper's face and telling a joke about his dirty underwear?"

"No way the grim reaper wears underwear. He's only bones," Keith protested.

"Back to the matter at hand," Butters said. "I hate to sound like a broken record, but some bullets would help to level the playing field. I don't know her range but I know mine."

"Well, lucky for you, I happen to know a guy," Drew said and reached for his phone but grimaced when he recalled that it had been destroyed. Kylara knew the feeling. "Someone, give me their phone. Atramento, do you want us to bring you any fruit?"

"From that cretin? Absolutely not. It would rot before he even finished telling you what kind of fruit it was."

Drew winked at the dragon mage, took a phone from Beanpole, and placed a call.

CHAPTER TWENTY-TWO

"I don't understand. Who is this…cretin…you are speaking to?" Hester demanded of Drew. Kylara was not at all surprised that her mom had taken Atramento's assessment over the man's assurances that they could trust him. She was an ex-Dragon SWAT officer, as was Atramento, although he was truly a master of paperwork more than a combat specialist like Diamantine had been.

Drew had already hung up. "We need dragon bullets. I don't see any way around that. There is a good supply locked in the base at Detroit but that's not an option."

"We could sneak in," Keith pointed out. "We know the property better than she does."

"Than Tiamat? Definitely. Better than all the people she has under her control? Hardly," their leader countered. "We have to assume that stash is compromised. She has convinced all the Steel Guard positioned there to protect her. Surely one of them would have told her about that ammunition. It's likely either destroyed or under heavy guard. Even if we could find a way to get past Tiamat, it'd be a fool's mission."

"So…we're screwed then?" Sam asked.

"I just got off the phone with the guy in charge of the second stash," Drew said with a wink. "We'll need to move quickly as it's on the desert island in the Pacific where the technomages had commandeered that bunker."

"Oh, this will be fun." Amy smirked. "I had no idea he was still involved in that base."

"It's top-secret stuff," Drew said. "There is no reason for a mage—even one as powerful as yourself—to know all the details about how we train our best Steel Guards to be ready to fight against dragons. Assuming we make it through all this, it stays top-secret. Is that clear?"

"We've all already been there." Hernandez snorted.

"Not me!" Sam said.

"Your grandfather had, though," Butters said with a nod.

"I hope this trip can help us, Drew, but I can't open a portal to a random island in the middle of the ocean," Kylara said. "I have to be familiar with a location to go there. Finding an island would be like a needle in a haystack. Even if you know its general coordinates, it would take me hours."

"That's time we don't have," Sam said.

"I have all that all taken care of," Drew said. "Go ahead and step outside, Kylara. We'll wait for you to come back."

"If this is some nonsense about the adults being able to talk while the kids go out—"

"It's nothing like that, I promise," Drew said placatingly. "But go outside. Hurry."

She nodded although she didn't like his mischievous grin at all and complied. Surprised, she gaped at a portal flickering to life in the mountain meadow.

Its edges crackled with energy and the misty center cleared to reveal a tropical scene that could not have been more different than the austere beauty of the pine forests high in the mountains. Palm trees, vines, and flowers all battled for space. With such a profusion of green, she almost didn't see the volcano in the background nor the concrete bunker that was almost perfectly hidden by the climbing vines that covered it.

It took a moment before she noticed the man standing in front of the portal. He wore a floral print shirt and grinned like a fool. "Kylara Diamantine, we meet again although I doubt you'll remember me. Our first meeting was all too short, I'm afraid. I have to say your reputation precedes you. I never thought I'd meet another young dragon with a strange past and yet, here we are, ready to work together to save the other one. How about that?"

"Kylara, go! If you don't, he'll never stop talking!" Drew shouted from behind her.

"Now that's not true. I can stop talking any time I wish. You can ask any of the mages here with me. Ask them and you'll see."

"Go!" Butters shouted.

The dragon mage nodded—the SWAT team was grinning so it would be fine, she hoped—and stepped through the flickering portal.

No sooner did she leave the Rocky Mountains and step onto the tropical island than the portal flickered and faded to nothing behind her.

Kylara stood at the entrance to the bunker surrounded by a half-dozen mages who were breathing hard. Two of them had blood dripping from their noses, a sign of magical overexertion.

The one who had chatted so enthusiastically stepped forward, his hand extended in demand of a handshake. She took it and he pumped her arm until she wondered if he would have dislocated her shoulder if she had not had dragon strength.

"Kylara Diamantine," he said as if he tried her name for the second time and liked the feel of it. "I'm Larry Brockton. It's nice to meet you again."

CHAPTER TWENTY-THREE

"I'm telling you, I can do it," Galen told Karl. He had already explained that he could dive down there, that he was a vanilla dragon but had always been able to hold his breath far longer than most dragons could because he was a Stormwing. All Stormwings were familiar with water. Even those without weather control abilities learned at an early age how to hold their breath. He could do this.

Tanya seemed to believe him. It was the other boy who needed convincing—an odd event in that Midnight inadvertently showed that he cared about Galen's wellbeing. "If you can hold your breath for so damn long, why didn't you say anything sooner?"

"Because Jasmine fricking Patel said she could do it! Her family is more esteemed than mine and they're mages. Uh...no offense Jasmine." The disfigured boy nodded respectfully, something the rest of his family would have scoffed at him for doing.

"Whatever," the mage replied but she didn't seem too annoyed. He couldn't tell, though, as he couldn't read her aura.

"Fine. My girlfriend deserved that compliment, so fine. But if you could hold your breath for so long, why hide out in the desert? It seems like you should have headed to the California coast and spent your days fishing." Karl tapped the side of his head with one finger as if to bring attention to his genius brain.

"My family are storm dragons, Midnight. They like the ocean. I couldn't go there, not like this." It was an understatement but also something of a lie. He had gone to the ocean because—like Karl had said—the fishing was good, but he had seen one of his cousins flying overhead.

He was not certain that he had been seen but it seemed like his cousin had sensed something of his aura as he had spent hours circling above the cove where he had taken shelter and called lightning down to blast apart any seal or dolphin that showed itself. He had understood that those lightning bolts had been for him. "I swear I can do this," he said as he stopped himself from woolgathering.

Even without being able to read the other dragon's aura, Galen could tell Karl was not convinced.

"You know what? I say go for it. The worst-case scenario, well...it's been real, dude." Midnight shrugged.

"Karl!" Tanya snapped.

"He's right, though," Galen said. "If I have to sacrifice myself to help stop Tiamat...well, at least I'll die with honor."

"No one has to die," Tanya said, her voice pleading. There was no one whose aura he wanted to be able to understand more than hers. The way she looked at him—but no. It was pity he saw in her eyes. What else could it be? She was beautiful, and he was... Well, he was what he deserved to be—a monster.

"Indeed!" A raucous cry issued from the woods. Galen turned to see what appeared to be some kind of bird claws coming directly at his face. "No one has to die but ye, foul beast!"

The falcon slammed into his face. He screamed and fell back. While he tried to pull the bird and whatever yelled for his death from its back, he heard Tanya shouting at its rider to calm and Karl laughing maniacally.

"Ach, fine, fine. A friend, you say?" the being replied. In the next moment, the bird ceased its attack and Midnight wiped tears from his eyes and chuckled as he helped Galen to his feet.

"Are you all right, man?" he asked.

"Yeah. I guess there are some advantages to always having scales," he muttered.

"Oh, no! Galen, you're hurt. I wish Sam were here. He could heal you," Tanya said, moved closer, and pushed Karl out of the way.

"I'm fine," he said. In all honesty, he was. The falcon hadn't done anything worse than he had done to himself before he'd learned that he now always had claws on his human hands.

She nodded and took a step back. "Rider, this is Galen. He's a friend of ours who we're trying to help. Galen, this is Rider."

The newcomer was about twelve inches tall with oversized eyes and seemed to be wearing a beetle shell for a backpack. "You're a pixie," the boy said rather stupidly.

"Aye, and ye're an abomination to man and dragon, but ye don't see me pointing out how horrendous ye are." Rider spat to prove his point. The boy had never talked to a pixie before. They were tough little creatures, it seemed, and bold too.

"Rider," Tanya remonstrated. Galen was impressed that she had stood up to the twelve-inch-tall pixie with a single word.

"Oh, right. A pleasure." Rider bowed formally and spread the beetle shell on his back to reveal larger, translucent wings hidden within. He straightened and his back folded into itself so he looked like he wore a beetle backpack again.

"What are you doing here?" Jasmine asked him.

"Accomplishing my mission, that's what!" he said, so pleased with himself that his Scottish accent vanished for a moment. "I was sent to find you and bring you home! And I've done it! Well, almost." He opened a portal. "Eh?" He gestured for them to go through.

"We can't go, Rider, not yet," Jasmine said.

"Sure, you can. You kind of...well, step through." He motioned to the portal again.

"We have to do something first," Tanya explained. "This is the pond where Tiamat was imprisoned."

"Aye, I know that. All the pixies know that. It was us who kept her sleeping down there for so long."

"Then do you know what's at the bottom of the pond?" Galen asked.

The look of incredulity the pixie gave him was so pointed it put anything Karl had said to shame. "I have an idea...don't you?" he asked guardedly.

"I think it's a prison of some kind," the boy said. "And I think I can swim down there. If you could please give us a few more minutes."

"Fine." Rider snapped his fingers and the portal vanished. "Get on with it then."

"I'm still not sure you should go alone, Galen," Tanya said.

"I'm our best chance," he explained for what felt like the umpteenth time. "Maybe one of your dragon forms could dive that deep, but you couldn't get through the gate or whatever is at the bottom. I can. Plus, like I said, I can hold my breath. My scales will help with the pressure too. If I'm here for a purpose, this has to be it."

"I'd say so, yeah. It wouldn't make sense for anyone but you to go," Rider said.

"What's that supposed to mean?" Karl asked.

"Ask him." The pixie gestured with a thumb at Galen.

This was getting confusing, the disfigured boy decided.

"Still... Can't you drag me down there with you or something? Jasmine could make a bubble and I could..." Tanya's voice trailed off.

"I tried that. I don't have the range," Jasmine said.

"If ye needs a second down there, I can be him," Rider volunteered with a pronounced exaggeration of a Scottish brogue.

"If ye needs? Seriously?" Karl rolled his eyes.

"Yeah, that would be great. You'll be able to go down there too?" Galen said and relief replaced some of the anxiety he felt.

"Oh...uh, I...didn't expect you to say yes—dragon's honor and all," the pixie stammered.

"No worries if you're scared, pixie," Jasmine said.

"I have ridden grizzly bears and badgers, mountain lions, and mountain bluebirds. Rider fears nothing. Although I will need a mount if you expect me to go inside that...that...place." He shuddered.

Galen thought he understood. It wasn't the pond itself that frightened the creature but what had been there. He felt the opposite. Boneclaw had used the placid water to take his powers, not the dragon goddess who happened to be at the bottom at the time.

He stepped into the water and hoped that their conflicting fears would make them a strong team instead of a doomed one.

"All right!" Rider said and leapt into the pond—except he wasn't the one to jump. In the time it had taken for the boy to wade into the water, the pixie had removed the saddle from his falcon and fastened it around a massive bullfrog with four eyes and six legs.

"Thanks for coming with me," he said. He didn't know the proper etiquette with pixies but thought this one deserved at least that much.

"No problem, no problem at all. If the Big Pixie can be brave, little Rider can be brave too...right?"

To Galen, it sounded like he was trying to talk himself up.

"To be honest, I'm a little scared. You coming with me makes me feel way better."

Rider puffed up at that and spurred his four-eyed frog into the middle of the pool.

The boy swam after him and positioned himself above the glowing light at the bottom. He breathed all the air in his lungs out and sucked in a huge breath. Unhurried, he exhaled again and drew an ever-larger breath. He did this once more, then dove under the surface.

Galen pointed his nose down and kicked toward the bottom. His stumpy wings were not strong enough or big enough to help him fly but they helped him to swim. He focused on his stroke, tucked his wings in to cut through the water, then spread them out to push him deeper.

"Nice swimming there, kid."

He almost sucked in a breath of air in surprise when he heard Rider's voice. Thankfully, he managed to not accidentally drown but he did turn his head and slow for a minute.

"What? You've never seen a pixie riding a six-legged frog with a magical bubble of air wrapped around his head before?"

Amused, he shook his head in and continued his descent. The frog was a much stronger swimmer than he was and spiraled around him to keep pace.

"I have to say this is creepy," Rider said as the sunlight from the top of the pond began to fade with the depth. "I like the nighttime and all—it's a great time to catch raccoons or owls to ride—but weird, creepy ponds? That's entirely different."

Galen continued to swim. He was thirty feet down and more than halfway toward the hole in the bottom of the pond.

"How did you end up leaving that stuff there anyway?" Rider asked casually.

His mind raced with questions. What was the pixie talking about? He made it sound like he should already know what was down there waiting for him, which of course he did not. He had been there before. Boneclaw had used it to take the power this very pond had granted him, but he had never seen any lights coming from the bottom. For that matter, he had not known that Tiamat had been interred there. How strange to think one could overlook a goddess.

"Look at you, sluicing through the water," Rider said admiringly. His frog had slowed, reluctant to go as deep as Galen was. "It looks like I picked the wrong mount. Oh, sorry. I know how you dragons are."

The boy would have sighed if he could but instead, he pointed at the back of his neck and gestured for his tiny companion to approach. Rider must have waited for such an invitation and he did not tarry. He kicked off the four-eyed bullfrog and swam easily, his wings propelling him through the water as if it were air.

"Thanks, I appreciate you," he said as he settled onto his shoulders and dropped all pretense of a Scottish accent. "It's creepy down here. Good on you for coming, even if you had to."

Galen said nothing of course and merely continued his steady descent. They were almost at the wooden frame Jasmine had described. It honestly defied explanation. In the very center of this pond amidst the muck and grime was a square of empty space framed by heavy timbers. There was no mud on any of the wood at all. He could see through the aperture and it looked like there was another chamber below, almost as big as the pond he had already swum through had been.

"Well, that's weird, huh?" Rider asked. "It looks like someone's been dusting."

The boy was not sure if he had the lung capacity to go much farther. Already, his chest had begun to burn. He knew he had more than enough to get to the surface but he also knew that every foot of depth would bring more pressure and make the air he had seem all the more precious.

"What are we waiting for, Galen? Onward! To the depths we plunge! Yearrgh!" The last exclamation sounded decidedly more pirate than Scottish but Galen appreciated the sentiment all the same.

Besides, there was nothing to be done but continue toward the bottom of the pool. Jasmine had risked her life down here, as had Karl. In fact, all of them had risked their well-being to help him. Tanya had risked her life for him months before when she'd found him near the shore of this same pond battling the dragon skeletons he had somehow gained power over. He was not about to quit now.

Determined, he pumped his wings, kicked his legs, and pushed himself deeper.

"Mush!" Rider called and kicked his tiny heels into the sides of his neck.

He reached the frame, pushed both arms through to grasp the underside of the wood and pull himself through the hole, and tucked his wings close to his body so he could fit.

No sooner did he get his feet and the tip of his tail through than he became supremely disoriented.

It felt like the ground somehow raced toward him and dragged his feet past his head. He tried to hold onto the wooden frame to ground himself but could not. His stomach lurched as his sense of gravity shifted upside down, then right way up.

A moment later, he stood on the bottom of the chamber. Water poured from the hole in the ceiling above him but after the briefest of moments, it slowed and stopped as if someone had turned the water to a showerhead off.

"Well, that was something I never experienced before. Like a wee rollercoaster that was," Rider said and peered at the hole above them that was far more than an entrance. Somehow, it had let them through but kept the rest of the water out. Even the water that had spilled into the room with them was already vanishing as quickly as if it were a puddle in the heat of the desert, despite the room feeling cool and moist.

Galen looked up and tried to take in his surroundings. He stood in a fairly large, subterranean chamber. *More like subaquatic,* he thought. The walls were made of tightly packed earth, as were the edges of the floor. Beneath his feet—and taking up most of the room—was a stone floor. Most of it was made of unadorned cut stone—not squares or rectangles like humans would have done, he noted, but flowing shapes that fit together intricately. At the center of the stone circle, a smaller circle was marked out by a ring of black a few inches wide.

"I think maybe we need to head to the center," Rider whispered in his ear. For some reason, the pixie was still on his shoulder.

He nodded and moved toward the smaller circle inscribed inside the larger one. It was maybe ten feet in diameter and although its edge was black as if someone had used coals to mark it out, the interior glowed. He paused just outside its border and looked at its center.

A chest sat there, made of heavy wood that looked ancient yet still strong. The pieces of metal used to hold it together and for its hinges were all made of pure gold. The gold didn't glow, however, but whatever was inside the chest.

"It's kind of creepy that it's open," Galen said.

"Better than it being locked tight, don't you think?" Rider asked.

"I suppose so, yeah," he muttered and looked at the stone floor around the chest. There were shapes cut into the stone, radiating out from the chest. "Are those runes?" he asked the pixie but didn't exactly expect an answer.

"Not runes no… those markings are older than any written language or attempt at one," the creature said and sounded much older than he had thus far. "Those are some of the patterns of magic—the shapes and expressions that form magic in this realm and indeed, all realms. I think they're pretty."

"They are that," he agreed as the glowing light flitted around the Fibonacci spirals, perfect polygons, and fractals that all worked together to form a pattern he could almost grasp the grandeur of but not quite. He could recognize their beauty, though, and maybe that was at the root of all magic.

"Do you think it's safe to step in there?" he asked.

"For you? I'm sure of it," Rider said. His words didn't exactly comfort Galen as he didn't look at him but focused his gaze on one of the motes of light that raced around the geometric patterns carved in the center of the circle.

But he had come this far and was not about to stop now. He took a deep breath, stepped over the black border of the circle, and approached the open chest.

Cautiously, he leaned forward, looked inside, and realized that the glow came from some kind of strange incandescent...slime?

CHAPTER TWENTY-FOUR

Kylara hadn't felt chilly in the mountains but she now wished she were back in the cooler climate. The thickly jungled island they were on was hot and humid in a way a girl from the desert did not find exactly comforting. She was accustomed to being able to step into the shade and win respite from the heat but there, even inside the cavernous concrete tunnel that led into the chamber of a volcano, she could not escape.

It followed them inside, at home in the moist air as much as the sweet, cloying scents of the tropical flowers were. However, even though both her sense of smell and sense of temperature were both assaulted in ways she was not happy about, it was her sense of hearing that seemed most overwhelmed.

"Well, I never did think I would see the day that I would see Kylara Diamantine on my island! Then again, you can never tell who will become a Person of Consequence. I hadn't thought I would be one, for example. Murder investigators aren't famous very often. Well, not the real-life ones and their short-lived side-kicks—compared to dragons anyway—are even less famous. And yet I was one.

"I thought I still was until the Steel Dragon shipped me off to this island again. The first few months were fine, you understand, but after a while, you start to miss being able to go out to get a cappuccino or smoothie or whatever. Oh, that reminds me...where are my manners? Would you like something to drink? We do have the Pacific Ocean's best coconut milk."

"Uh, no thank you. We're in a crisis and I'm supposed to bring everyone here."

Larry nodded his graying head. "Drew did say you were all in something of a pickle."

"I'll bring them all here, then. Okay?"

"Oh, right. You can do that. Well, have at it. Here I was giving my mages a rest, although Lord knows I take it too easy on them. Why, in my day, we'd take on a dragon in the morning and bring a runaway mage in peacefully in the afternoon."

Kylara glanced at the five other mages. Each of them was still breathless from their exertion of opening a portal to the opposite side of the world and the subsequent march through the tunnels. Somehow, Larry was not winded despite him talking the entire time while they marched deeper into the shell of the dead volcano that made up the center of this island.

"I know we're in a hurry but we might as well get into the central chamber," he said and gestured to a doorway at the end of the concrete hallway.

"Sure." Kylara hurried ahead and stepped into the room, although room was an understatement for the space. It was the entire interior of a volcano. Some work had been done to level the bottom but other than that, it looked frighteningly natural. Veins of lava turned into black stone ran up and down the interior walls and the parts of the floor that had been leveled looked like lava flows from TV—the same lava flows that she had seen plucky British naturalists remind the watcher were often quite hot.

"This room ought to be big enough, eh?" Larry said. "If you

take the first shift, we should be ready to do the next—eh, mages?"

The mages grunted an affirmative toward their bossy supervisor.

"I don't know if that will be necessary," she said.

"I love the confidence. but it's a long way for mage gates." He winked.

Kylara did not bother to explain. She felt like this island already had far too much verbosity. Instead, she simply opened a gate to the pixie realm and opened a second gate from the pixie realm to the mountain meadow in Colorado. Although the distance between the two places was either thousands or tens of thousands of miles—depending whether one imagined portals taking their users around the surface of the earth or through it—for her pixie gates, all distances were essentially a few feet away from each other.

Drew had everyone ready. He gave the order and they hurried through.

Hester Diamantine came through first in her full dragon form and her diamond scales sparkled even in the low light inside the volcano. Keith and Hernandez came next, decked out with assault-style rifles and belts heavy with pistols and grenades. After them came Butters and Beanpole, each with cases that Kylara knew held sniper rifles. Butters had another case—another rifle?—while Beanpole had four pistols, no doubt to cover the more accomplished sniper. Amy Williams stepped through after them and rolled her eyes at the military-style movements of the others.

Brian, in turn, rolled his eyes at her riding a skateboard. The young man had a pistol, although the dragon mage was beginning to understand that the phone and tablet he carried were more effective weapons in his hands. Finally, the last two dragons —Sam and Timeflash—entered the portal.

"You can close it," Drew said to her with a nod.

"No Atramento or the pixies?" she asked and peered through the portal.

"Oda and Mari can get Atramento into the action if we need him. They want to stay behind in case Rider brings your friends to the mountains."

She nodded. It made sense so she closed the portal to Larry Brockton's slow clap.

"I gotta say, leaving the portal open while you talked with Drew was impressive. At this distance, I'm shocked you don't have blood dripping out both ears and dirty jeans from falling into the dirt. You want us to handle the rest, I assume?"

"This is it," Drew said flatly.

"Right. I know I've been out of the loop but you told me some nutjob calling herself Tiamat has the entire Steel Guard of Detroit under her aura. Unless you all stopped for an offensive on the way here, this won't be enough." The mage chuckled. Kylara didn't know him well enough to know if there was something hidden in that laughter and she couldn't sense his emotions while wearing her pendant.

"This will have to be enough," the other man said. "We work with what we have, not what we wish we had."

That—to her shock—left Larry speechless.

"Look on the bright side," Butters said and slapped the man on the back.

"What's that?"

"We added seven mages to our team."

Larry raised an eyebrow but a grin crept onto his face and a moment later, he was chattering away even faster than he had before. "You know, it's great to see you and all, but you do realize I live on a tropical island, right? Fresh fruit ripe for the picking, fish like you've never seen in the bay, warm days, and clear nights. You could have come and visited. I'm not saying I'm not happy to see you but just once, it would be nice to meet when it's not an emergency."

KEVIN MCLAUGHLIN & MICHAEL ANDERLE

Drew and his team laughed although their leader sobered quickly. "You know you chose the wrong friends for that, Larry."

"Yeah. I know, I know. Now. let me guess. You want old Larry to shut up so you can get down to bossing my mages around and looting all the gear I've saved for you to take and blow something up?"

"Oh, goodie, you do have explosives!" Hernandez beamed and held a hand out that Keith slapped a couple of large bills into. She shoved her winnings into her pocket.

"The long and short of it is we need to rescue Kristen and the Council. I think we'll have time to plan something that might work, but for us to have any chance at success, we'll need weapons, dragon ammunition, maybe a vehicle, and any other gear you have that you think might work. Do you think you can help with any of that?" Drew raised an eyebrow in question.

"Are you asking if I can rise to my purpose for being here?" Larry smirked. "Drew, you always were too much. I've been here training these mages and the recruits for months and you have the audacity to ask if I can help? Do you not remember who you're talking to? I am Larry Brockton. No! *The* Larry Brockton! You better believe—"

"All right, great. So yeah, Larry can help. Can we see the explosives now?" Hernandez interjected.

"Sure, right. Sorry. It's been a while with no one to keep me company."

"What about these mages?" Amy asked.

"Them and the recruits are no fun for a good time. Their eyes glaze over the second I get going, in fact—"

"I was merely being polite," the woman said and winked at the older mage.

"Oh, right, sorry. If you'll follow me." Larry led them from the central chamber into the concrete tube and through another door. They traversed another tunnel, this one narrower and tiled instead of floored with raw concrete. The door at the end of this hallway was incongruously technologically advanced for the island. Two cameras were mounted above it along with a keypad and some kind of recording device their guide whispered into.

The door was satisfied that all requirements were met and it slid open with the faint whine of an electric motor.

To Kylara, the room on the other side was like something out of a movie. Guns were stored there in many types, sizes, and models, although she couldn't name any of them beyond the most basic descriptions of what the Steel Guard had already told her. She had twice made the mistake of calling something an assault rifle that wasn't one and paid for it dearly in long-winded explanations about how no, this weapon was not technically an assault weapon.

Sam looked about as confused as she did. He nodded at all the chrome, scopes, and grips but didn't move to take any of it.

But to Drew and his team, it was like Christmas. They flowed into the room like rats into an undefended pantry. Everyone but Butters snatched what the dragon mage assumed was an upgraded version of their weapon. To these newer and shinier weapons, they affixed scopes, switched out components, and generally made a mess of the space that had been immaculately clean and meticulously organized only moments before.

They also exchanged their Kevlar vests for some that looked similar but she was certain were not. She did not know much about the technology that had been created by the technomages out of dragon body parts, but she had a feeling these vests would block the claw of a dragon better than regular Kevlar would. Although she didn't see what a vest would do against a dragon's fire breath, she decided that if it came to that, they would have already lost. There was no technology that would stop a dragon's aura. Well, none save the silver-and-turquoise pendant hanging around her neck.

Over these vests, the Steel Guard affixed ammunition belts that they stocked carefully with different kinds of bullets. Kylara felt so naïve. She had vaguely understood that there were different kinds of bullets but had thought the distinction ended at shotgun pellets and solid rounds. Instead, it seemed Hernandez and Keith's long-barreled automatic assault-style rifles needed different ammunition than Butter's sniper rifle, despite it being merely another rifle.

When she mentioned this to Butters he stared at her for so long that she thought his eyes might fall out.

"Merely another type of rifle? This is my baby. It's a modified .408 CheyTac..." He trailed off when he noticed her eyes glazing over. "This one goes bang-bang from far away. Theirs goes bang-bang very fast."

"Right. Sure," she said and let the marksman get back to further modifying his big, long gun.

They also loaded up on grenades and Hernandez took chunks of what looked like playdough wrapped in bags of gravel.

The recruits Larry had said couldn't handle his conversational prowess appeared. They were all either shirtless or wearing swimsuits and dripped sweat. He had sent them out to train and gather fruit. There were maybe thirty of them and together, they stank something fierce after their workout, but Larry still made them cycle through the armory and collect their weapons before they took to the showers. Fortunately, Amy didn't like the smell any more than Kylara did and created a breeze to suck some of the body odor away from them.

The young dragon mage wanted to feel relieved. She wanted to feel like they were now prepared to face Tiamat, her Followers, and the Steel Guard whose emotions she had swayed to her side, but she couldn't bring herself to feel anything but dread.

Everyone had taken a weapon. This was true. They had loaded their weapons and tucked a few extra bullets in magazines —she thought that was what they were called. But what were rounds? She was still uncertain but they had left the supply room completely decimated. Every crate of dragon bullets had been emptied. Every grenade had been clipped to a belt. They had seven more mages now, three dozen Steel Guard recruits who knew how to shoot and had ostensibly trained to fight dragons, plus four trainee dragons. It did not seem like much compared to what Tiamat had at her disposal.

"Remember, when we get to Detroit, we're aiming to wound, not kill. Once Tiamat is removed, her aura powers will be gone and the Steel Guard she had under her control will be our people again."

"Should we even use these then?" one of the recruits asked and looked at the weapon in his hands with an expression somewhere between terror and awe.

"We have no choice," their leader explained. "Regular bullets are like bee stings to dragons. Painful, certainly, possibly lethal in high enough numbers, but rarely more than annoying. Hitting a couple of them with dragon bullets will prove that we're a threat."

What he did not say was that if they had not secured this cache of bullets, the Steel Guard and Followers of Tiamat wouldn't even blink before they incinerated all of them. Even the mages wouldn't be able to stand against them. After all, Tiamat had far more mages than this under her sway.

"I don't want us to kill our allies, but if it's between you and them, take the shot," Drew said grimly.

The team Kylara had traveled with nodded. If they hadn't been in this same situation before, they understood the stakes of it. The recruits looked less certain.

"And Tiamat?" one of them asked.

"If you get a shot at Tiamat, take it. There's nothing I'd like more than a dragon goddess to fall to good old-fashioned American-made weapons."

"Yes, sir." The man saluted in the Steel Guard fashion.

"All right, you rookies go hit the showers. I want you in uniform and ready to deploy in ten minutes. Is that understood?"

KEVIN MCLAUGHLIN & MICHAEL ANDERLE

"Yes, Mr. Brockton the wise!" The troops marched away, carrying weapons in board trunks and bikinis.

"But I don't want to take a shower," Keith protested.

"Not you!" Drew snapped.

"Mr. Brockton the wise?" Butters enquired.

The old mage at least had the decency to blush. "Hey now, I told you I got bored out here. You never made your new trainees show you some respect?"

"There's nothing respectful about new trainees being forced to lie to their superior officer," Amy quipped.

Larry laughed drily. "Yeah, well, maybe if any of them were half the mage you are it'd be different."

"We're still here, sir," one of the mages said. They had not run off to shower with the recruits.

"Six months and none of you have a thing to say, and now we have company and you're all more than willing to throw old Larry off the back of the proverbial dragon? You know what? Never mind. Let's get down to planning this…what are we calling this? An infiltration? A rebellion?"

"An operation," Drew said firmly.

"Sure, right. There's no point in spicing it up or anything. If you would all follow me…"

They returned to the central caldera of the volcano, where he and the mages hurried to set up tables, chairs, screens, and a few projectors. They had barely finished and managed to run through their first version of the plan before a recruit ran into the room from a tunnel Kylara had not previously noticed.

"We're under attack!" he yelled breathlessly and pointed to the top of the volcano. He must have raced all the way down.

"What are you talking about?" Larry demanded.

"Dragons on the horizon, sir. A lot of them."

"How many is a lot?" Butters asked.

"Fifty, I'd say. Maybe more," the man replied.

"But that's impossible," Larry said. "Anyone who knew about this location is on our side now."

"Not necessarily, not anymore," Sam said. "Tiamat's aura could have turned any one of them against us and convinced them to reveal this location."

"But it would have taken them hours to get here," Drew said.

"Did you see any mages up there, son?" Larry asked.

"No, sir. I checked twice." He pulled a radio out and asked the same question of his partner who must have still been at the radio. "No mages."

"Go tell the guardsmen," Larry said.

"I already did, sir...over the radio."

Larry scoffed, pulled a radio off his belt, and turned it on. "Damn modern conveniences are more trouble than they're worth," he said, embarrassment in his voice at this tactical faux pas.

"If there are no mages, it means they had to get here the old-fashioned way," Timeflash said.

"But how could they find us?"

Brian looked up from his tablet. "Our phones. Damn it, I knew this was possible but didn't think it was likely. Why did I have to be such a good teacher?" he lamented to the world at large.

"Phones on the table—*now*," Drew barked. Everyone obeyed except him and Kylara of course, whose phones had already been destroyed. He moved quickly along the table and crushed each device with the butt of a pistol.

Brian grimaced when the man destroyed his tablet but he didn't move to stop him from doing it.

"Now we have a choice," Drew said. "We can run or we can fight. Without phones, we hopefully won't be tracked again."

"I say we fight," Hernandez said and stood quickly. "I want to make things go boom."

"Okay, can I get some opinions from someone besides the pyromaniac?" their leader asked.

"I'm with Hernandez," Beanpole said, and his soft-spoken words forced everyone to listen because his reaction was so unexpected. "If there are no mages, we can likely assume that these are the Followers of Tiamat, perhaps those who were positioned somewhere in the South Pacific. This is a force that could come to her aid after we begin our fight with her if they can establish a portal. If we can disable them now, we should try."

"Oh, we can disable them," Larry said. "And I'd rather give them a fight before they try to sniff out any intelligence we have stashed here. They might not be great at computers but we have maps of safehouses I'd need to destroy before I leave. I wouldn't want any of our other outposts exposed."

"What do you think, Ky-lara?" Drew asked. For some reason, him emphasizing the "Lara" in her name like he always did seemed to carry extra weight like he was still the nice guy at the diner helping a runaway.

She dragged in a deep breath and looked at everyone around her. Was this insanity? Were they out of their minds to think they could stand against a goddess? They were so few and she had so many under her sway—people who were better trained, or better armed, or in better control of their powers than she and this tiny band of allies were.

"Was Tiamat there?" she asked the recruit who had come down from the roof.

"Tiamate?" he asked and mispronounced the name slightly.

Kylara nodded and stepped back from the table before she transformed into her dragon form. Ever since Tiamat had inhabited her body, her scales had turned black although they sparkled with a hundred colors in the light.

Like the goddess, her scales were also encrusted with diamond, although that was a power she had received from her mother and Tiamat had stolen from her. Well, not quite, not if the legends could be believed and Tiamat's spilled blood truly had brought magic into this world. If that was all true—and she found it increasingly hard to doubt—the diamond scales had come from Tiamat via her mother.

"She would have looked like this—the same scales."

"But curvier," Amy said. "More feminine."

"No, ma'am," the recruit said. "I checked colors but there was nothing like that...uh, like you, ma'am," he said firmly.

"Then I say we fight," Kylara said. "No mages? I would bet this isn't a Steel Guard garrison, then. It has to be the Followers of Tiamat. Which means that when we eliminate them, there will be nothing left of her when we defeat her."

"When, not if. I love the confidence," Hernandez said.

Drew grinned. "Great. So despite having the ability to teleport out of here, we'll face these dragons and fight."

"I wouldn't have it any other way," the demolitions expert said.

"Someone help me to the top of the volcano," Butters said. "This poor young lady needs to see what this baby can do," he patted his sniper rifle.

Plans were laid quickly. In moments, the defense of a deserted island in the Pacific would begin. The pervasive hope was that when the time came to battle a goddess, they might stand a chance.

CHAPTER TWENTY-FIVE

Drew seemed to have far more compunction about using Kylara for the vanguard of the defense than she did herself.

"There has to be another way."

"There's no time for this, human." Hester Diamantine growled her impatience. "My daughter could have held her own even before she had the powers she does now."

He tried to protest further but she silenced him with a snort. "Amy, it has been a long time since I fought with a mage on my back but I'd be honored if you would join me in battle."

"You're asking if I want to ride a diamond-encrusted dragon into battle?" The mage grinned and sent her skateboard to rest against a wall. "Because there's only one way to answer a question like that." She vaulted up, caught herself with her telekinesis, and flipped to land on Hester's back.

"Fine," Drew said as if he had a choice. "Hester and Kylara engage them out there. Sam, you can heal the dragons so I want you to hang back and be ready to support them."

A man more concerned about his appearance than actual tactics might have balked at being put on second-string defense, but Sam only nodded. His powers were unique in that they could effectively extend what Kylara would be able to do. He understood his role well.

"Larry, do you want to join me for old times' sake?" Timeflash asked the aging mage.

"You're asking if I want to climb on your back, fly into a battle that will almost certainly result in my death, likely from being incinerated by dragon's fire?"

"This is the Cult of Tiamat we're talking about," Kylara interjected. "The chances are you'll be killed by ice or acid or by one of them controlling the ocean itself."

"Well, in that case, sign me up," Larry said and scrambled onto Timeflash's back. He turned to his mages and trainees. "Mages, your priority will be defense. We can't afford any casualties, not when we're already outnumbered and this isn't even the big battle. Drew will lead the recruits in firing at these dragons. Your job is to make sure they don't get incinerate—uh...frozen or melted by acid. Recruits, listen to Drew and don't get killed, all right? Let's put all that target practice to good work."

"Yes, sir!" the troops barked.

"Oh, and Jesse's in charge," Larry added before Timeflash took to the skies.

"What? Jesse? She's a big eh!" one of the other mages protested.

"That's why she's in charge!" the mage shouted as the dragon whisked him away to the approaching wall of dragons. They were still a mile offshore, at least, but Kylara knew that would be covered quickly by dragons flying at speed.

"We'll take as many as we can," Drew said.

"So will we," she replied and launched skyward with her mom to join Timeflash.

They rose quickly above the volcanic island. Despite her knowing exactly where the entrance to the base was, she was amazed at how quickly it vanished into the fecund growth of the jungle. Hopefully, that would buy the team there some safety but she wasn't about to bank on that.

"They're bringing a storm with them," Hester said and nodded at a wall of gray clouds behind the dragons that was veined with twisting bolts of lightning. It looked like the storm had a heart with a furious pulse.

"They were," the dragon mage said and drew on the first of the many powers she was sure she would use in this battle. She knew she could summon a storm of her own but she had a different idea. Instead of eclipsing the sky with clouds and rain, she called upon gale-force winds and sent them a little above the heads of the approaching dragons and the storm one of them must be bringing with them.

The wind sliced through the storm clouds and sheared them away into nothing, so when the battle was finally joined, it was the bright oranges, reds, and purples of a sunset they fought under rather than the heavy clouds of a conjured storm.

"For our mother!" one of the cultists cried and all hell broke loose.

Chunks of metal streaked across the span of air between them aimed at Kylara's two teammates. She used her powers to divert the metal into the sea and away from Timeflash. Hester caught the strike in her diamond chest, though, and laughed.

"You'll have to do better than that!" she shouted, raised her claws, and sliced the belly of a dragon she flew past. Although she didn't touch the dragon's wing, it snapped in half as if some giant had cracked it over its knee like it was kindling.

"You're welcome!" Amy shouted at the dragon she had maimed as he tumbled into the water.

Three dragons attacked Kylara—one with acid, one with a cloud of sand particles, and a third that could control horrible, bloody-eyed birds that struck at her eyes but didn't seem to be able to touch her.

She was able to neutralize the acid as soon as it touched her but she knew no one else had the ability to do so. Thinking quickly, she wound the acid dragon in tendrils of shadow and jerked her toward the one using the cloud of sand. The bound dragon exhaled a thousand droplets that melted through the sand dragon's cloud and struck him in the face. The wounded attacker fell from the sky.

The dragon mage breathed ice on the acid dragon's claws and the weight caused her to plunge into the water below.

Now, she had the horrible, bloody-eyed birds to contend with. She tried to dodge but they seemed to be able to anticipate her every movement, stayed with her, and harried her head. When she did a barrel roll, the creatures somehow rotated with her.

"Ky, what are you doing?" Sam shouted.

"Trying to lose these birds!" she yelled in response.

"What birds?"

Kylara looked past the teaming mass of birds at the dragon who was controlling them. She realized then that it wasn't birds her adversary was controlling but her perception of them. This dragon could create illusions in the minds of others—a powerful trick until it was revealed.

She sprayed acid at the illusion dragon. He screamed in pain and the bloody-eyed birds vanished as the attacker plummeted into the sea to attempt to wash the acid away.

With all immediate threats now dealt with, she pumped her wings and wheeled to regroup. She had made it past the wall of attackers so could now see them from behind as they approached the island.

Or tried to, she thought grimly.

A splash of crimson exploded from a dragon and he fell from the sky. A second later, the sound of the gunshot reached her ears. More dragons fell, and the sounds of more gunshots followed like staccato punctuation to the dramatic moments.

For a blessed moment, she thought the battle might have been over that easily, but whirling shields of metal ripped from a ship that had sunk near the island appeared in front of the rest of the assaulting dragons.

Kylara glanced below and saw that the metal-controlling dragon—although injured—was still alive and used his power to great effect.

She swooped down and froze the water around the metal dragon but it was too late for a quick victory.

The cultists had broken formation. They soared and spiraled as they approached the island. Shots still rang out from the defenses but far fewer. Drew had doubtlessly told his team and the recruits to conserve their ammunition and only take a shot if they thought it might strike and most of them seemed to be obeying the order.

A flash of light at the top of the volcano and another dragon splashing into the sea helped her understand how Butters and his sniper rifle were indeed different from the rest of them.

An attacker reached the volcano and exhaled a cloud of what seemed to be acrid smoke but it was blown away before it could reach the sniper. The mages had no doubt created that particular gust of wind. They would do their job as she would do hers.

Kylara turned her attention to the dragons in the air all around her.

Timeflash and Larry held their own against a dragon who attempted to knock the mage from her back with blasts of concentrated air.

Amy and Diamantine were far more effective. Hester was able to get in close and used her diamond scales to protect her body to great effect. This allowed the mage to use her formidable telekinetic strength to grasp dragons and either drive them into each other or hurl them into the sea.

Despite these victories, there were so many more dragons that it was impossible to stop them all from reaching the island. Already, a dozen soared around the volcano and seemed to flit about like swallows to avoid the staccato bursts of gunfire that attempted to eliminate them. They blasted the jungle below with what Kylara could only describe as the elements. Wind, water, fire, and ice all decimated the jungle and the people hiding within.

Another invader had landed on the beach and lifted pillars and ridges of stone from beneath the sand to create bulwarks the other dragons could land behind. She realized immediately that she had to stop him. A dragon's healing power meant that even a few minutes could turn a mortally wounded combatant into a fresh fighter.

She dove down and used her power over stone to sink the plinths into the sand.

Two dragons came in on either side of her as she approached the stone dragon. One blasted her with fire that he seemed to have almost telekinetic control over. It took the blurred form of a snake and tried to swallow her while the dragon on the other side launched bolts of electricity from her claws at her.

Rather than trying to determine the best powers to neutralize these abilities, Kylara called on the forms of magic she had the most practice with. Her eyes blazed with light and she looked the fire-breathing dragon in the eye to blind him. The snake of fire still poured from his throat to snap at her but missed. She looked at the lightning dragon as well, but her adversary turned her head before the light could blind her.

Unperturbed, the dragon mage lashed out with shadow tendrils, encircled her, and dragged her closer. A headbutt with diamond-encrusted horns rendered the lightning dragon unconscious and likely concussed.

But before she could fall, she froze in midair. She hung there, her eyes half-open but sightless from the concussion and her mouth agape with a tendril of electricity wrapped around and through her teeth—like a frame from a movie on pause.

Kylara's first thought was that the illusion dragon had struck again but this seemed to be a power far beyond the one she had faced. The entire battlefield was frozen in time. Confused, she observed the scene like it was a macabre three-dimensional painting.

A cultist clutched a bullet wound in his chest. Droplets of blood hung suspended in the air while the back of the dragon was still unhurt. The bullet had paused in mid-flight—after it had struck the dragon's chest but before it had exited their back.

Amy stood atop Hester's back, her face a twisted mask of rage like a psychotic Valkyrie, albeit one wearing a baggy hoodie emblazoned with a rhino tagging a dumpster with a spray paint can.

Her mom was stuck in mid-battle with a dragon with stone skin. Flecks of granite were suspended in the air all around them.

Bullets were frozen in mid-flight too, as were the clouds of flame, poison, and ice from the dragons.

Everything seemed frozen, in fact, except for the massive wingless dragon who surged from behind a stone pillar and bull-dozed into Kylara with such force that she catapulted back and cracked another pillar in half.

"Did you forget about me?" asked Bull.

"With a face like yours? How could I?" Kylara replied and planted her feet firmly in the surf-dampened sand. In reality, she had written the unstoppable dragon off. The last time she'd seen him—had it only been a few days?—she had opened a portal and sent him to the northern reaches of Canada. The only explanations were that Tiamat used her ability to gate or forced the mages to use theirs to extend her reach.

"Maybe you'd like an imprint of it in your skull?" Bull roared and charged again.

Kylara raised a barrier of shadow webbing but he tore through it like it was cotton candy.

She made a wall of ice and her attacker simply plowed through it.

When she put a stone pillar in his path, the massive dragon cracked it like a twig.

Out of time, she planted her feet—she had the same power too, after all—and lowered her diamond horns to meet his.

Their skulls met with a resounding thwack and the dragon mage hurtled away from the point of impact, past a dragon frozen in flight with fire bubbling out of the back of its throat, and into a stone pillar. It cracked and the top fell on her. She seemed to remember something about having to be in motion to make her power to be unstoppable work.

Bull understood this far better than she did and drove into her a second time before she could gain momentum. Again, she pounded into a pillar of stone. Oddly this one didn't fall on her but froze.

That made her realize what was going on. It was Temporus, the dragon she had first met when he had frozen time for Kylara and Kishar to discuss her position as the Sum of All Dragons. He had frozen time—or more accurately, put her, Bull, and himself in what could loosely be described as a speed bubble. Obviously, this was some ploy to remove Kylara from the battlefield. She had to find him so if Bull gained the upper hand in this fight, someone would be able to come to her aid.

The momentum dragon wasn't about to let that happen, though. He charged at her and she barely managed to dodge. He shattered the rock that had stopped her like it was nothing but a sandcastle in the path of a jock at the beach.

Kylara reached out with her shadow abilities and felt behind all the stones that had been raised on the beach, knowing that Temporus had to be close.

"You already tried that, sparkly little dragon." Bull trampled over her shadow tendrils and snapped the ends off those he stamped on.

When she couldn't find the time dragon, she raced forward

and activated her momentum power as she dismissed the probing tendrils of darkness.

This time, when their horns hammered into each other, the force flung them both back to topple and roll in the sand.

Bull found his feet quickly, though, and pawed the ground like his namesake. "Finally, a challenge. I like that diamond skin. Do you think Mother Tiamat will give me some if I split you in two?"

His grotesque threat gave Kylara an idea. Instead of meeting his charge, she jumped behind a boulder and changed to her human form. He didn't notice as he was too focused on adjusting his course to pursue the illusion of her dragon form that she had made leap out from behind the boulder at the exact second she had hidden behind it.

While the imaginary birds had been both annoying and even somewhat embarrassing, she had to admit that this illusion power was an enormous advantage.

"Coward!" Bull roared as he chased her illusory form into the surf. It was easy to outpace him, not because he was slow but because an illusion didn't have to worry about finding its footing. Fortunately, Temporus had frozen time so she didn't have to bother to make the water splash convincingly as the illusion went deeper and deeper.

"How do you think Bull got here, you moron? By flying?" He had no wings but it seemed he could swim about as well as he ran. He picked his legs up beneath him—and made her think of a hippo with a tail—and began to swim with powerful strokes.

That was exactly what Kylara had hoped he would do. She froze the water all around him, trapped him in place, and robbed him of his momentum.

"Coward!" Bull roared.

She ignored him and turned to the stone pillars that had been raised from the sand. "Your plan failed, Temporus, so you might as well put time back to normal and try to vanish in the chaos."

No answer came, which did not particularly surprise her. The time dragon had not seemed like a fighter.

"Have it your way," she replied and took her dragon form again. She thought she might be able to overwhelm his ability to make a bubble of time. But while she seemed to have more raw power due to being…well, a dragon, pixie, or mage, depending on who you asked, she lacked finesse compared to most dragons and had never tried to freeze time. Instead, she opted for a different tactic.

She made all the stones protruding from the sand sink slowly below the surface.

Their withdrawal was rewarded with a yelp of fear as Temporus was revealed. He was in human form—his arms covered in watches like they had been the last time she had seen him—so his scurrying seemed especially pathetic. Kylara wrapped him in shadow and thunked his head against the sand.

He fell unconscious and the chaos of the battle sprang to life again.

Amy and Hester were still a powerful duo with diamonds for defense and arms of invisible force to attack. Timeflash and Larry were harrying a storm dragon—likely a Stormwing related to Galen—and seemed to give far more than they took.

One of the pockets of recruits had fallen. A burned-out patch of jungle revealed a square, concrete entrance to the base hidden within. Their fallen bodies confirmed the bitter failure of their retreat.

Kylara was about to leap into battle when a stone erupted from beneath her feet, took her by surprise, and knocked her on the jaw. She had forgotten about the dragon who had raised the stones, an enemy who should not be overlooked.

Two more stone boulders surged from the sand on either side and crushed her between them. It might have been enough to crack her rib if she were not wrapped in diamond. Still, she didn't like her odds and became airborne in time for a dragon to bury its claws into her bruised ribs.

She was about to retaliate when she realized it wasn't an enemy, but Sam. His claws infused her with healing energy and energized by the infusion, she called on a wave from the sea to power onto the shore and drag the stone dragon out into the deep.

When she looked at the sky around her, more dragons plummeted to the jungle below. Timeflash and Larry had routed the storm dragon and Kylara sensed that the winds he was calling were those of retreat.

"Return to the mother!" a dragon with the ability to make amplified calls with an inflatable throat sack bellowed into the chaos of the battle.

The cultists who were still fighting did not need to be told twice. They flew back the way they had come and made no effort to save their dead or even check on their wounded. In a few minutes, the island was quiet again, save for the cries of the injured and dying.

"Well, that was fun," Larry said from Timeflash's back as he flew overhead. He carried a captive dragon in human form and dropped him to the ground in front of Kylara.

She wrapped the dragon with shadow tendrils as Sam flew away to call others to guard the prisoners.

The wounded didn't put up much of a fight, especially not once they saw that their captors had mages with magic-dampening cuffs.

"Please, let me heal first," one of them begged. The dragon mage made a show of securing one dragon who had resisted. As soon as he was cuffed, he sagged and his bruises now refused to heal.

When she told the one who had asked that he could heal as long as he waited on his knees, the other prisoners fell into line. Being denied their powers was bad but being forced to feel actual pain while their powers were denied? That was not something dragons often had to live with.

Larry and Timeflash returned eventually, and the mage's earlier good mood had been shattered. "We lost nine people," he said, his eyes already puffy as if he'd cried himself out. "Nine goddamn people. Eight of my dear recruits and Jesse." He shook his head. "You think it will get easier but it never does, goddammit. It never does."

Drew tried his best to comfort him but his words fell on deaf ears. None of Drew's team had been lost. Larry didn't point this out of course and surely he didn't hold it against the man, but Kylara could see it hurt that the men and women he'd been responsible for training had lost their lives.

They convened shortly after in the central chamber of the volcano.

"We need to move. Now that she knows where we are, we have to assume this location is completely compromised," Drew said. His team had already begun to gather what supplies remained. There was not much.

Larry returned with his people, although two of the mages were missing. "I completely agree. I left two mages to guard the prisoners in the cells below but they're both skilled with portals. If Tiamat returns, they'll get out of here. What's our plan?"

"Our plan?" Drew asked. "I assume you and your team have a safe house to go to."

"And miss this fight? I wouldn't miss it for the world. My feelings aside, those are the stakes, aren't they? We either help you now against wildly unfair odds or wait for Tiamat to round us all up one by one. For me, it's not much of a choice, you know what I'm saying?"

"Of course not—"

"Plus, this is Kristen we're talking about. Have you met her mom? Do you know what she would do to me if I sat back and did nothing while her daughter was frozen in rock? No way. We're coming with you. If there's a plan to save her, I'm in."

"Are you sure about that?" Butters asked.

"What's that supposed to mean? Do you doubt my loyalty? Seriously? After all we've been through together?"

"I'm only saying the next step will involve subterfuge, which means you'll have to stop talking at some point." The sniper chuckled when Larry reddened.

Kylara hoped that gallows humor would save them yet.

CHAPTER TWENTY-SIX

Galen did not know what to make of the sparkling slime. It seemed incongruous that something that unimpressive filled the ornate chest in the center of the circle of geometric designs in the room beneath the pond. The chest, though? He assumed it was what had held Tiamat's spirit. "This chest—it was her prison, wasn't it?"

Rider shrugged. "Ach, prison is a human term. We call this her resting place but yes, this is where she slumbered for so long."

"But what is this…goo?" he asked, reluctant to touch it unless he had no choice. It was thicker than water—more like jelly, although ribbons of light moved through it to a kind of rhythm, like heartbeats. He still hadn't fully regained his breath after he'd come close to drowning at the bottom of the pond and moving through the strange membrane into this room. As his heartbeat slowed, the pulsing lights of the slime seemed to slow as well. Could it sense him? Did that mean it was a part of Tiamat?

The pixie snorted. "You still can't tell?" The little creature seemed frustrated.

"I don't think it's part of Tiamat."

"Well, of course it's not part of Tiamat! She was set free. It's yours. I thought you dragons had aura senses or whatever, yet you can't sense your essence?"

"My essence?" This was beyond confusing to the boy— although, there was something about the slime that was inordinately inviting.

"Isn't that why you came here in the first place? Weren't you looking for magic?"

Galen blinked, although he was unable to move his eyes away from the glittering goo. "Yeah, but I couldn't find it in the pond."

"Maybe because it's down here, not in the pond."

"So you're saying this is the magic that Boneclaw took from me?"

"At least part of it, yes!" Rider transformed into a ribbon and whipped around the room, showering sparks in his wake. "Come on. Touch it already. Isn't there a dragon goddess you're supposed to help fight? Why are you so squeamish? You're lucky! The chances are your magic would have been reabsorbed into the pixie realm but it somehow reached this room and the chest kept what was left of it intact."

The disfigured boy didn't know what to say. This was why he was there and why he had contacted Tanya and asked for help. He had hoped he could regain his powers but part of him believed that he deserved to be the monster he had become.

After all, he had never fit in with the Stormwing family. His lack of storm powers had caused the family to treat him like a runt. While he might be worth sending to school in an age when vanilla dragons were allowed such privileges, he certainly was not worth holding any kind of position in the family. He had always known that he was essentially a powerless pariah to them but had he rejected them and forged his own path because of the way they treated him?

The answer was an unequivocal no.

Instead of showing true grit and becoming better than his family—like Karl Midnight had—Galen treated everyone else as terribly as his family treated him. He had been rude to mages as well as vanilla dragons. When he'd had the opportunity to seize power, he had—and had promptly been corrupted by it.

Even when he had the opportunity to stand against Boneclaw, he hadn't. He was a failure and part of him—a far larger part than he had ever admitted to himself—had expected to burn this final bridge to the only group of people who had ever shown him any real kindness and spend the rest of his life in exile.

Except that he now stood in front of a chest that contained what he had lost.

"I don't want to be the same person I was," Galen said to Rider, who had once more taken his mostly human form. "I don't want to take my dragon powers back and become a bully to those who need help and a lapdog to those that don't."

"Then don't do that, mate." The pixie slapped him on the back. "It's not the power that makes us who we are. It's what we do with it. Look at me. With my natural ability to ride any beast, I could be a king or a conqueror of the planet. Imagine, with war elephants and those super-fluffy kittens at my disposal, I could ride over the entire world but I don't. It's all about our choices."

"But how do you know what's right?" he asked, shocked that he was asking serious advice from a being who had threatened to rule the world by saddling fluffy kittens.

"You can't. But if you surround yourself with people who you think are good, they can help steer you in the right direction. Now, will you touch that slime or what? I'm booooooored!"

Galen took a deep breath, made a promise to himself to try to be the kind of person Tanya might come to respect, and stretched his hand toward the goo.

His claws poked effortlessly into the jiggling mass as if it wasn't there at all. He pushed in deeper until the flesh of his fingers touched the slime. It was cool and sticky like he was pushing into a chest filled with grape jelly.

In fact, it did not seem to be anything but a cheap prop until one of the ribbons of light inside the slime found his hand. It seemed to strike him by chance but as soon as it touched him, it flowed from the slime into his body. Interestingly, it continued to pulse as it did so and must have been connected to the rest of the light as all the glowing strands followed the first to flow into the boy through his hands.

In seconds, the light was all gone, absorbed into his skin. The slime in the chest—now devoid of this animating force—melted into nothing like snow on a warm day. But unlike snow, it left no liquid behind. The chest was empty and dry as if it waited to hold something else.

Galen took a step back when he felt the magic—his magic—flow through him. Rider had been right. He felt more like himself —stronger than he had before—and his aura sense was back. He could feel Karl's care for Jasmine and Tanya's concern for him from where they waited at the shore of the pond.

He looked at the claws on his hands and wondered how long it would take to make them go away or if he would forever be cursed in this form. Is that what he wanted? Did he truly believe he deserved to suffer?

No. That was not what he wanted.

Maybe it was what he deserved, but the boy did not want to live out his life as an abomination. He wanted to become what he had been because that was the form in which he could help others. If he remained trapped in this form, he would never be accepted by his people or humans. How could he make anyone's lives better if he was greeted by screams every time anyone saw him?

This thought triggered something in his magic. Galen's heart bloomed with joy as the claws retracted into his fingers. The scales followed. They folded one by one to reveal human skin. He touched his face with his hands and felt his extended jaw retract. His dragon teeth shifted until he had the handsome white smile he had missed every time he had seen his reflection in a pool of water since Boneclaw had stabbed him.

His legs mended next. They'd had an extra joint like dragon legs did, but no longer. His feet turned to normal human feet and made his lack of shoes a problem again. He tried to flick his tail and pump his stumpy wings but both were gone. The only thing that remained of the monster's body he had been trapped in was his wisps of lanky hair, but his scalp was skin again instead of patches of scales and hair.

Tears came to his eyes. He was healed. After all this time, he was healed! He was himself again. A boy who could become a dragon—or could he? He badly wanted to check to see if he could indeed take the form of a dragon but there was no room in this chamber. Well, that wasn't quite true. There was room to become a dragon but not to leave if he could not take his human form again. He wanted to get out of there and see the world again more than he wanted that form of power.

"Rider...thank you. I'm—"

"Not so freaking ugly anymore. Congratulations!" His tiny companion flitted about impatiently.

"Although I guess we have a new problem." Galen gestured at the exit to the room twenty feet above them. "I might be able to jump up there with my dragon strength but I don't see how I can jump and have enough air to swim to the surface."

"That sounds like a headache. Let's do it my way instead." Rider zipped around him, faster and faster, until a platform of sparkling energy formed beneath his feet. It gave a little lurch as it elevated.

Seconds before they reached the gateway to the pond, his ears popped. In the next moment, he was in the pond but instead of having to hold his breath, Rider had created a bubble of air around his head so he could breathe.

"Why didn't you do this on the way down?" Galen asked and chuckled at the absurdity of the question.

"You were all broody and acting like you had to be brave or whatever," the pixie replied from his bubble of air. "Plus, you didn't ask."

Galen decided he would have endured far worse to gain his human body and dragon powers than swimming through a creepy pond.

They breached the surface of the water and swam toward shore as Tanya cheered, Jasmine golf-clapped, and Karl grinned and shook his head. "You were supposed to find a way to stop Tiamat, not fix yourself!" the other boy joked.

His feet touched the slimy, silty bottom of the pond. Even that was a joy and he barely noticed Midnight's snark. His feet had been scaled, taloned dragon feet for so long that he had almost forgotten the simple pleasures of his feet sinking into cool mud. He strode to the shore and stepped from the water. Once on the bank, he looked cautiously over his shoulder to see if the pond was still as it had been.

It was and not a ripple marred the surface to show his passing.

"Galen, you did it!" Tanya said and embraced him in a warm hug. Even that would have been enough, but coupled with him being able to sense her aura was enough to move him to tears. She was proud of him, thankful, and overjoyed at what he had accomplished. He did not know if he had missed being able to hug people more or being able to feel what they were feeling. It was a blessing that he had gained both abilities.

"Not bad, man. Not bad," Karl said and shook his hand when Tanya finally let him go. "You said you would be happy if you could simply be in your human form. Is that what happened or can you still take your dragon form?"

"I don't know," Galen admitted. "There wasn't space down there to check."

"There's room here," Jasmine said.

He nodded. They were right and he had to know. It would be

fine—more than fine—if this was the body in which he lived for the rest of his life but... Well, if he still had the power to become a dragon, wouldn't he be able to help even more people than if he were only a human?

Half-afraid of failure, he reached inside himself and tried to transform. A well of energy roiled inside him that had been lacking while he had been in exile in the desert. He could feel it churning inside his chest but it was not what it once was.

With effort, Galen tried to stretch his core of magic from his chest into the rest of his body. It did as he asked although there was not much of it, so the process was far from effortless. Still, it worked. As he called on the magic to suffuse him, his body responded. A mist surrounded him as his legs extended, his arms grew claws again, and wings and a tail sprouted from his back. For a horrible, agonizing moment, he thought his transformation might stop there, but he pushed past the block and felt himself grow in size until he achieved his dragon form.

"Galen! You did it!" Tanya said. He felt like the old him might have made some petty, mean-spirited quip about stating the obvious, but the new him—the him he wanted to be—was thankful to have someone to share his excitement with.

"Not bad, dude," Karl said.

"Can you still feel them?" Jasmine asked.

Galen didn't have to ask who the "them" she was referring to was—the bodies of the dead, the remains he had desecrated.

"I cannot," he said and realized that the truth of this statement made him almost as happy as being able to change into his dragon form. "But I can feel your auras again and that's more than I had hoped for."

"We can feel you too, man. You seem tired," Karl said.

"Don't push yourself," Tanya added.

Galen nodded. It was true. "My dragon form...it is harder to stay like this." He released the magic he had called from the center of himself and his body reverted to human form.

Karl and Tanya shared a look and their auras flashed concern before they got them back under control.

They were right. This was odd. Before, both forms had felt like they were on completely even ground. It took energy to transform from his dragon form to his human form, or vice versa, but it didn't take any energy to maintain either form. There had been nothing to maintain. He had been a dragon, which meant both the human body and the dragon one were his.

Perhaps that feeling would return with time but he felt different at the moment. His human body felt like the natural fit —like he could stay in it effortlessly and forever. His dragon form required his concentration and a flow of magic to maintain.

"We can work all that out later. Kylara's probably waiting for us," Galen said. "I bet our hour is almost up."

"Oh, your hour is long past," Rider said. "We need to return to your world. The others will be looking for us."

"They'll need to know about this place," he said. "There's a chest down there—the one Tiamat was trapped in. We can use that."

"Not if we don't go home. Now let's move before I summon a battle kitten!" The pixie opened a portal.

Galen didn't bother to explain the pixie's delusions of grandeur to the others as they walked through the gate. Who was he to judge? After all, Rider had ridden him.

CHAPTER TWENTY-SEVEN

In the end, everyone agreed to go to Kylara's first idea for a safe-house—the castle of the Prairie King, a self-made monarch now dead for centuries.

Kylara, Drew, Sam, Amy, Brian, Larry, and Hernandez all stood in a circle in the courtyard of the castle. The oak trees Tanya had made grow when the keep had come under attack so long before were even bigger than they had been when the dragon mage had last seen them.

Most of the walls still stood but none of them were in any better shape than they had been on their previous visit. Still, they provided welcome elevation in the endless sea of rolling grass. Drew's team, plus Larry's mages and recruits, all manned the walls or were stationed in the grass on what counted for nearby hills. Even though they no longer had cell phones and therefore no simple way to track them—hopefully—they did not want the Cult of Tiamat to surprise them again.

They were about to commence planning when Kylara felt a strange tugging at her. She turned and felt as if someone was pulling her hair—or, more specifically, that someone was trying to pull her hair with telekinesis. No one was there and Amy was in conversation with Larry, so it wasn't either of them.

"Kylara? You're essential to all this. Are you all right?" Drew asked.

"Yeah, I'm fine. I only…I thought that I felt something."

He nodded, although he seemed as distracted by the plan as she was by whatever she had felt. "The biggest issue will be Tiamat's aura. There's a real risk that if we get too close, some of us might lose our ability to think for ourselves."

"Not think, but feel," Timeflash interjected. "Tiamat can't change your thoughts. No dragon can. But she can make you feel like you'll need to protect her. Larry, your recruits might be especially vulnerable."

"Still, we might have to use them to draw her out and get her away from the Council so Kylara can get in. It reminds me of this time with Windlock when we knew a dragon was holed up in a cave and we had to get him out. Now you won't believe this but I swear the payoff is worth it…"

Kylara's attention drifted from his words when she felt the tugging sensation again. It seemed like someone was trying to get her attention—like they had tapped on her shoulder but through a blanket or a thick jacket.

She turned and was shocked to see the outline of Jasmine Patel's face for the briefest of moments before she vanished.

"Jasmine!" she blurted, which quite effectively stopped the mage's story and any further conversation of tactics.

She opened a portal quickly to the pixie realm but didn't see her friends there. Of course she did not, she reasoned to quell her panic. If Jasmine had contacted her using a spell, it would not have worked from the pixie realm. Which meant they were back. She opened a second portal to the school where she had last seen them but the land outside the Lumos School ground was pleasantly quiet. Her senses alert, she glanced at the buildings and noted that no repairs had been done and also that they were deserted. That was probably for the best, given that Tiamat was still at large, but it did not answer the question of where her friends might be.

After a moment, she remembered that the pixies Oda and Mari had sent Rider after her friends. If he had found them, he would likely have brought them to his home in the Rocky Mountains. She opened a portal and was delighted to see Tanya and Jasmine staring at something behind her. That meant she was directly in their line of sight.

Tanya yelped with joy and Jasmine stopped mumbling and opened her eyes.

"Oh, my God, Jasmine, it worked! Kylara, you're here."

"Of course it worked. It's a communication spell. That's the point of them," the mage replied.

"Where's Karl? Is Galen all right?" Kylara asked as she stepped through the portal. Even with all her experience, it was still odd to step from what was essentially a two-dimensional hole and find things on the other side of it.

Despite the strangeness, she never expected to find what she saw.

A boy was seated in a chair in front of Karl, who held a long knife raised above his head.

"Karl, what are you doing?" She gasped.

"Oh, hey. Jasmine's spell worked? I'm finishing what I started," he said, lowered the knife to the boy's scalp, and dragged it across the last few wisps of hair. He had been shaving his head.

Then Kylara realized who he was. "Oh, my goodness—Galen?"

"In the flesh." Galen smiled.

She couldn't believe she had not recognized him sooner although it made sense in an embarrassing kind of way. In all honesty, she had never thought he'd be healed. She had accepted his half-human, half-dragon form as who he was and hadn't expected to see him as his old self again. And yet, there he was, freshly shaved and wearing a cable-knit sweater.

"Uh, Kylara? We can't plan how to undo Tiamat's petrification without your ability to…you know, undo petrification!" Amy shouted from the other side of the portal.

"Is everything all right?" Tanya asked.

The dragon mage could not help but snort a dark laugh. For a moment, she thought she understood the allure of gallows humor after all. "No. Nothing's all right. Come on through. You have so much catching up to do."

Tanya nodded and followed her. The others came as well except for Rider, who waved farewell and vowed to return when they needed him most, riding a battle kitten.

"I think everyone here knows Jasmine, Karl, and Tanya," Kylara said to the assembled group—a war council, she decided, as it was how she thought of them. "For those of you who don't know, this is Galen Stormwing."

There were dark nods at his introduction. What he had done with the bodies of dead dragons was public knowledge to this group of Steel Guards. It made sense. After all, they were tasked with protecting the world from threats exactly like what he had represented.

"Are you still a necromancer, kid?" Amy asked bluntly.

"No, ma'am. I'm merely a vanilla dragon now," Galen said and sounded relieved. "Although I can't even hold that form for long, honestly."

Drew nodded. "Then I'll have to ask you to give us some space. Vanilla dragons haven't proven to be effective against Tiamat. You're a liability. I'm sorry, but there it is."

"But I have intelligence on Tiamat!" Galen protested.

"He truly does, Ky," Tanya said.

"What is it?" Kylara asked and to her surprise, Drew, Larry, and Amy all demurred to her and looked at the boy to answer.

"Uh, right," he said, instantly and unmistakably nervous. "The pond where she was captured…there's a chest at the bottom of it where she can be imprisoned again. Rider thinks if you can get her down there, it should hold her for another couple of millennia as long as the pixies keep her asleep like they did before."

Everyone paused and looked at each other for a moment. Finally, Butters spoke. "Well, I'll be, kid. That's some rock-solid intelligence right there."

"But I'm afraid it doesn't change much," Drew said. "Unless someone disagrees, I still think our plan needs to be to get the Dragon Council unpetrified first and deal with Tiamat second."

There were nods at this. "I think I could handle her in a fight but not with everyone she has at her disposal," Amy said.

"What about Heartsbane?" Timeflash asked. "If we can free her of Tiamat's aura, she'd be a powerful ally."

"We can't assume that it's even possible," Drew said. "To be honest, her falling means we need to be even more careful about us getting too close because her aura is almost as powerful as Tiamat's. However, I don't see why the goddess would have petrified the Council if she could sway them with her aura. Them being able to speak for her would be more valuable than using them as statues. If we can get them free and together, their auras might win us some of our allies back. Ultimately, it means we'll be playing a game of cat and mouse."

"Please don't tell me we're the mice," Keith muttered.

"Kylara's the only person who can restore the Council so she'll have to go in," their leader continued over Keith's objection. "I hope that this pendant of hers will afford her some cover but we can't rely on that. Our job will be to distract the cult, the Steel Guard under her aura, and Tiamat herself."

"I'd like to go on the record that this sounds like a bad idea," Butters said. "Like, a very bad one."

"Lucky for you, Butters, you'll have a different position. You'll be stationed on the tallest skyscraper we can get you on. If you get a shot at Tiamat, you take three. Is that understood?"

The sniper nodded.

"The rest of us will try to lure everyone else away from the castle. If we can get the Steel Guard far enough away from Tiamat, they should break free of her aura and possibly join us."

"She won't simply let you take them," Kylara said.

"Right. Which is why I'm hoping that if we can engage them and get them to follow, she'll come too so they don't get too far away," Drew said.

"I'm sorry, maybe I missed something, but why can't Kylara simply teleport in there?" Karl asked.

"You know that security you have at your school?" Amy asked Karl.

"Yeah? What about it?"

"It's a joke compared to what Drew and I set up," the mage declared. "Kylara can't portal in, not if she wants to step back to earth in one piece."

Drew nodded. "Unfortunately, the security systems are... robust. That's another reason we'll try to draw them away from the Chrome Castle. We can't mount an assault on that base. Not with the numbers we have. Hell, not with five times this many people."

"It doesn't sound like great odds," Keith said.

"Three hundred says we'll make it," Hernandez said to Keith. "Two to one, your favor."

"Done." He smirked although his expression fell after he shook Hernandez's hand. Perhaps he realized that if he won the bet, he might not be alive to collect his winnings.

"How will I get in, then?" Kylara asked.

"That's where I come in." Brian stepped forward. He looked weirdly naked without a tablet or a smartphone in his hand. "I spent way too much time playing with Legos and Minecraft."

"Minecraft was out when you were a kid?" the Rookie asked.

"Uh...no, not exactly," Brian cleared his throat. "The point is, I have designed a ton of fantasy buildings, so when my sister wanted a skyscraper where magic police and dragons could work together, I jumped at the opportunity to play architect. I know every floor of that building, down to the bronze faucets in the bathrooms. I'll escort you in through a secret entrance while the rest mount their assault."

"Timing will be crucial," Drew said. "If Kylara and Brian enter the base too soon, Tiamat might be able to change his emotional state toward the mission."

"With all due respect, Drew, I don't think that will happen," Brian said through clenched teeth. "I know I've had my doubts on that score but that's my sister she has turned to stone. I understand that the rest of you respect her and I understand that y'all probably love her like a sister. But she's my sister. I have been kidnapped, chased through a damn Pacman maze, and had my home invaded, all so dragons could get to Kristen. Frankly, I don't see how Tiamat could make me stop caring about her."

Drew nodded at the angry outburst, not one to argue. "Beanpole will also tell you when the bulk of Steel Guard has left the area to make sure you two don't get caught by those without the same...bond Brian has."

"Right, of course," the young man said. He agreed to the plan but didn't apologize for his outburst. Kylara respected that, and she also hoped that his feelings would prove a useful asset. Amythist had said that some people couldn't be convinced of some things. Auras could be used to rally or suppress emotions, but it was difficult to make someone feel the total opposite of their natural state. Brian's love and loyalty to his sister ran deep.

"Well, I guess my only question is when do we start?" Larry asked.

Drew glanced at his watch. "Shall we say ten minutes?"

CHAPTER TWENTY-EIGHT

If Drew had known that one night, he would have to lead an assault on the defenses of the Chrome Castle, he might not have made them so damned good. As it was, he knew that once they were in visual range of the castle at the top of the skyscraper, they would be in danger.

But they had to get close enough to be perceived as a threat so he led his team down the boulevard that ended at the gates of the Chrome Castle. They didn't march toward the inevitable conflict. That was both too dangerous and too obvious. Instead, they flitted from alley to parking lot, hid in the lee side of buildings, and cut through coffee shops or clothing boutiques that had not even existed on this stretch of street before Kristen had commissioned the Chrome Castle to be built.

He was on point with Timeflash. She needed to be on the very front line so she could feel for Tiamat's aura. He had argued against her position at the front but she had insisted. She was not a dragon who excelled in combat. Her unique skills were best suited to rebuilding once the smoke of battle had cleared. Losing her to Tiamat's will would be bad but not as bad as losing Hester or even any of the younger dragons, as odd as it seemed to him.

But Hester, a former member of Dragon SWAT, had backed the kids up. They were powerful in a fight, especially when working together.

The rest of the Steel Guards who had once worked on the Detroit SWAT team with him were close, save Butters and Beanpole who were already in position on the top of a skyscraper. Larry, his mages, and the recruits followed Drew and his team. Behind them were the rest of the dragons—Sam Lumos, Karl Midnight, Tanya Fastwing, and Galen Stormwing—and the mage Jasmine Patel. He had insisted that Hester stay with them too and she hadn't argued.

Step by step and store by store, they proceeded up the wide boulevard until there was nothing between them and the grounds of the Chrome Castle but an empty street. This was as close as they could get. Hell, this was closer than Drew had wanted. If the Chrome Castle's defenses had been reprogrammed to recognize him and his people as enemies, they would probably be dead already.

But their position there meant it was time to launch their attack. He thrust his hand out from the shadows of the dumpster behind a vegan burger shop and set their assault in motion.

At the very end of the street, from the roof of a store that somehow only sold jeans, Amy launched herself into the middle of the street, landed on her skateboard, and propelled herself forward with her telekinesis. As she rolled down the boulevard, she busted a few ollies and did a few kick-tricks as if she owned the place.

The sound of the wheels rolling over the asphalt and the clack of the board as it left the ground and thunked down echoed between the empty storefronts. It was only an hour after dark, yet the shops were all empty. Brian had issued a false alert about a gas leak in the area which made everyone evacuate. It might not have worked in any other major metropolitan area but in Detroit, this close to the Chrome

Castle, people were quite accustomed to doing as the authorities asked.

Drew watched Amy roll up the street and hoped this wasn't as crazy as he thought it was.

She crossed the street between the Chrome Castle and the rest of the city, threw her arms out, and ripped the gates out of their mountings. Some level of the defenses was still intact as lights flashed in the skyscraper, the doors in the lowest level flung open, and well-dressed men and women poured out.

"I come for Kristen! Is one of you overgrown lizards going to do something to stop me or will you run to your mommy?"

Out of the entire plan Drew thought this was the most insane part. Why would anyone rise to such an obvious piece of bait? It seemed he still had much to learn about dragon arrogance.

The well-dressed men and women who stormed across the grounds changed to their dragon forms and took to the skies.

He made a quick appraisal of the dragons through a scope. While he hadn't been able to discern anything but their clothes when they'd first appeared, now that they were in their dragon bodies and flying toward them, it was easy enough to tell their identities. Or it would have been if he recognized any of them, which he didn't. These weren't Steel Guard dragons under the sway of Tiamat's aura then but cultists, willing Followers of their goddess.

Satisfied that these weren't any of their dragons enslaved by Tiamat's aura, he gave his team the signal that approved lethal force.

Amy also clearly recognized that these were not her coworkers. She hurled one of them to the earth as if the massive, scaled, fire-breathing beast of legend were nothing but a mosquito. That action effectively drew the dragons' attention even more.

The mage skated past Drew and his team, who were still hidden in the shadows. The dragons followed and exposed their sides to those who waited in ambush. The trap was sprung. Their different groups waited until they would no longer be firing at each other before they unleashed a barrage of dragon bullets into Amy's pursuers.

Dragons screamed in pain and plummeted onto the asphalt. Some were dead already, killed by skilled shots. Others shrieked from the agony inflicted by the bullets that could tear through them as easily as regular bullets ripped through everything else but dragons.

Those who were wounded were not given a chance to take to the air. Sam Lumos, his team of friends, and Hester Diamantine lunged into the battle, dispatched those whose healing abilities would put them back into combat, and ensured that those who might be incapacitated were sufficiently wounded that fighting was not an option.

Drew turned away from the sounds of bones breaking and flesh tearing and looked at the Chrome Castle.

"Anything yet?" Drew asked Timeflash.

"I don't sense her. She must still be inside with the Steel Guard."

"Then we make it clear that her Followers won't survive without reinforcements." He signaled to Larry and his mages. They attacked with invisible ropes made of mental powers to drag the dragons who had made it past the barrage of bullets into range again. The recruits were better shots than he had hoped and more dragons fell.

"That did it," Timeflash said darkly. "I feel her now."

"Tiamat might enter the battle soon," Drew yelled to his team. He still didn't want to use radio as the Steel Guard was likely monitoring their communications, but the sounds of battle were so loud now that he wasn't worried about being overheard. "Make sure someone on each team keeps a bullet in the chamber for her!"

But she had made no effort to come out yet, Drew was chagrined to see. Instead, the dragons of the Steel Guard poured out of the Chrome Castle with mages on their backs and human soldiers raced across the grounds.

"These are our people, Larry," Drew shouted, knowing that his team didn't need reminders to spare the lives of their comrades.

As the dragons approached, he set his jaw. Those who had joined the Steel Guard did not deserve to die. They were brave—braver than the mages or humans. When Kristen Hall had led her revolution to make the world a more just place for humans, mages, and dragons, it was humans and mages who benefited most. They gained rights that had been denied them for centuries.

Dragons were the losers of the deal. It made sense—from the perspective of self-preservation, anyway—that they would resist Kristen's "new world order." Yet these dragons had joined her, almost always sacrificed wealth and prestige to do so, and sometimes sacrificed their relationships with their family.

They didn't deserve to be mowed down because Tiamat had bulldozed their sense of what was important.

Reluctantly, he took careful aim and shot a dragon by the name of Whipstrike through the wing. The dragon landed heavily and the mage tumbled from his back. He might have felt relief that the mage didn't get up from the bloody smear they had left on the asphalt of the street but he felt nothing but the knot in his stomach grow tighter.

Keith had switched to regular bullets and methodically shot the legs of the human members of the Steel Guard who ran toward them. He wiped tears from his cheeks to make sure they didn't interfere with his aim. Drew clenched his teeth. Sometimes, he hated magic. These were their brothers and sisters, not their enemies. They wouldn't be in this situation if not for magic.

Sam and his team abandoned their battle with the remaining members of the Followers of Tiamat—those were better targets for Larry's recruits, anyway—and engaged with the Steel Guard.

It was a strange feeling to see a dragon Drew had helped train have its wings ripped off by Diamantine and feel good about it. But there it was. He already knew he would have nightmares about this day.

"Drew," Butters' voice said from his radio. He looked reflexively at the sky. They had agreed that the marksman would break radio silence with this simplest of all codes if and only if one condition had been met. He squinted into the night sky and saw her.

Tiamat.

Her scales were dark but even in the light of the moon, they glittered with a hundred different colors. He couldn't hear the distant echo of the sniper rifle over the din of the battle, but he knew that Butters was doing his best to bring a goddess down.

Tiamat roared and filled the air with flames. They animated and each tongue of fire became a serpent or a hawk that sought one of Drew's allies.

In the next moment, Butters hit her.

She screamed in pain. Her wings flapped in a futile attempt to keep her aloft before she pounded into the earth.

A normal dragon would have felt and been injured by the impact. Instead, dirt cracked the asphalt of the street and rose to catch her. She touched down gracefully on this landing pad and walked—no, she strolled, Drew had to admit—into the battle.

His heart filled with terror, but it was still his heart. Tiamat wanting to kill them instead of converting them was their best-case scenario. He laid down covering fire, which she blocked with a whirling shield of metal. Still, he held her attention and that mattered most.

While dragons battled above, mages wielded the elements, and humans exchanged gunshots with each other, Drew tried to hold the attention of a goddess so Hernandez could get close enough to blow her to smithereens.

CHAPTER TWENTY-NINE

Leaving her friends, allies, and mentors to fight a battle while she snuck off felt wrong to Kylara, but she understood that she had no other choice. She hated it but she understood.

What she did not understand was where Brian was taking her. Instead of leading her toward the Chrome Castle or even around it so they could enter from the back, he seemed to be taking her away from the battle completely.

"Are you sure we're going in the right direction?" she had to ask eventually. The sounds of gunshots could be heard echoing across the city. She needed to be in that battle, helping her friends.

"Yeah, I'm sure. You don't exactly build a secret tunnel into a base and forget where it is. What, are you getting tired or something?" Brian was already breathing heavily as they had been running at a good pace for a few blocks.

She was not winded, of course, as she had dragon strength to fuel her muscles. It would take far more than a brisk pace to tire her out.

"I'm simply making sure you're not lost."

They had entered a part of the city that had yet to be redeveloped. Old warehouses constructed of crumbling brick, rotting wood, or rusting metal made up the landscape and were a testimony to the industrial past of the city.

"Kristen bought all these blocks," Brian said. "We didn't want our hidden entrance to be the only place that looked like crap."

"Leaving all these buildings to rot so you can have a back door seems a little much."

"We've already revitalized blocks of the city. We plan to do this area next year if...that is if you can... We have to save my sister." He came to a stop at one of the buildings. It was a smaller warehouse, made of wood and paint that had long since faded to a nondescript brownish-gray.

Avoiding her gaze, he fiddled with the combination lock on the chain that kept the door shut for a moment before he found the numbers he was looking for and they entered the crumbling building.

"A padlock? Couldn't someone simply cut through that?" Kylara asked.

"They could," he said and hurried to a smaller room inside the warehouse—a bathroom with no door that looked like actual hell. "And if they broke in, they'd go to the workshop and find it held nothing of value. No one comes to the stained bathroom, though."

He entered the space, felt the stained tiles—which honestly made her skin crawl—and pulled one loose to reveal the electric eye of a camera. When he stared into it, a click came from somewhere else in the building.

Brian put the tile in place again. "We only have thirty seconds. Come on."

Quickly, he led her out of the bathroom toward one of the two heavy doors at the back of the building. He picked up a five-foot piece of rebar that leaned against a wall. Kylara thought he might use it to force something, but he simply held it like a walking stick as he opened one of the doors. She had expected it to reveal nothing but the outdoor space behind the warehouse. Instead, she saw a narrow staircase.

"The other door heads outside, of course. It's something of an optical illusion." He winked.

The wall was a few feet thick, she realized. Hollowing out part of it for the stairs was an easy enough feat to accomplish when your building material was rotten wood. She followed him down the tight, spiral staircase and noticed with some relief that it had been reinforced. It was much stronger than the building above it.

They descended for what seemed like forever and the staircase widened only slightly. It was far newer than the warehouse above, although dusty with disuse.

"Are you sure we'll be able to get in?" Kylara asked.

"Well…as certain as I can be. I never thought we'd face a dragon who could turn my sister to stone and our people against us, but besides Kristen and I, there are only two other people who know about this entrance. I don't think Drew will betray us to Tiamat."

She made a mental note that he did not tell her who the other person who knew about the entrance was and hoped that wouldn't be a problem. They reached the bottom of the stairs and were stopped by an even heavier door than the one at the top.

While the one above had been made to match its surroundings, this one made no concessions to camouflage. It was shiny chrome and so thick that she doubted she would be able to get through it—certainly not without alerting whatever systems her companion was currently attempting to bypass.

"Come on…" Brian muttered under his breath. "Don't be as smart as me…don't be as smart as me…" His hand was pressed to a touchscreen and his eyes were open wide to another camera. The system appeared to be satisfied with his biometrics as the door hissed and swung inward for them to enter.

"Thanks, I'll take it from here," Kylara said and was about to put on a burst of dragon speed to race down the long, barren tunnel lit by flickering fluorescent fixtures every thirty or so feet.

"No, no, no, hold up. Have you never played RPGs?"

"What?"

"Final Fantasy? Zelda? Dungeons and Dragons?"

"What are you talking about?"

"You don't make a door and then not boobytrap the tunnel that comes after it," Brian said as if such paranoia should be obvious. "Stay behind me, all right? There are a few more…uh, inconveniences ahead."

Kylara nodded, still confused until, after about a hundred feet, he slowed and extended his piece of rebar carefully in front of them. He whacked the floor and six barbs launched from either wall. They crackled with electricity for a moment, then fell still.

"Darts tipped with claws connected to wires connected to enough electricity to bring a dragon down." He winked.

"Impressive," she murmured and wondered if such a combination could have brought her down. Probably not, as it took more than dragon claws to pierce her skin.

But it seemed he had planned for even a being such as her to try to traverse this tunnel. The next boobytrap released a cloud of gas laced with neurotoxins that would render anything with a nervous system immobile for hours, he explained while they waited for it to clear. It left a sticky film on the concrete floor and walls that she did not dare to touch.

None of the entrapments were magical in nature except the last one. To her shock, Brian walked past the laser sensor that triggered it. A silver net dropped from above and snapped around him with magnets. Kylara knew the silver that had been used—it was the same enchanted material that robbed a dragon or mage of their magical abilities—but to him, a decidedly non-magical individual, it was nothing but an inconvenience. He untangled himself and led them to another staircase that ended at a heavy door that responded to his biometrics.

They stepped out of the security tunnel and into the basement of the base itself in what appeared to be a storage closet of some kind.

"All right," Brian whispered. "From here, we need to move up through the three basement levels and we're in. Should we try to free the Council and Lady Amythist out in front on the ground level or go straight to the top to my sister?"

"I will continue to the Council. Once they are free, I hope they can distract Tiamat long enough for me to reach Kristen. You need to get back to Drew and tell him that I made it in."

"Wait, what?" Brian's whisper grew into a louder yelp. "You think I'm going back?"

"I couldn't have made it this far without you, Brian, but I have to go the rest of the way alone. I have my pendant to protect me and the powers to free the Council. You have neither. You have to get to safety."

"No thanks. Tell me, do you have the access codes and expertise to reprogram the defenses of this building against Tiamat?"

"Well, no I—"

"And do you know how the alarm system works and how to disable it if someone manages to activate it before you crack their head?"

"Not exactly but—"

"Do you have what it takes to kill the dragon who was in your head?" Brian pulled out a pistol that was doubtlessly filled with dragon rounds.

"I will stop Tiamat," Kylara said.

"Not without my help, you won't. I know I'm squishier than you. So do Drew and the rest of them, for that matter. But we're in this to win. Kristen is my sister. I'm not going anywhere until she's free. I understand that I can't tango with a dragon. Hell, the only reason I haven't pissed myself at the idea of doing this is because I hope Hernandez has enough C4 to make Tiamat into nothing but a stubborn stain. But none of that means I'll simply walk away."

"Okay, okay. I'm sorry I said anything but stay behind me, all right?" Her skin made a shift from its regular coppery texture to diamond armor.

"Yeah, I planned to do exactly that, thanks. The controls for the alarms are near all the doors. They look like a power receptacle. If someone presses one of those, we're toast."

"That's good to know. Are you ready?"

Brian checked his gun. "Ready."

Kylara sent a tendril of darkness under the door into the hallway. With luck, no one would see it.

"What the hell is that?" a man demanded from the other side.

The dragon mage did not hesitate. She kicked the door in front of them hard enough to knock it off its hinges and hurl it into the man who had noticed her shadow powers.

Two more guards at the end of the hallway reached for pistols at their waists.

"Don't let them fire. The sound will trigger the alarm!" Brian shouted.

"It would have been nice to know that sooner," she said and launched shadow tendrils across the floor and up the men's legs to hold their guns firmly in their holsters.

"And you wanted to send me away," he said as he sprinted to keep up with her. She reached the guards first, clunked their heads together, and left them in a pile while he worked the door.

It clicked open at his touch and they hurried up a flight of stairs to the next level.

Kylara peeked out and yanked her head back as a guard turned to face her.

"Did you hear that?" the guard said to her partner.

"Yeah, it sounds like all hell is breaking loose out there."

"Nah, it sounds like something is happening below."

"Maybe we should check it out—"

"Nice work, showing initiative," the dragon mage said, swept the legs from under one, and tackled the other to the floor. They moaned in pain and she wasn't sure what to do as they made too much noise and would surely alert someone. She had the power to make them be quiet—she could freeze them in stone exactly like Tiamat had the others, but no. She wouldn't— couldn't—do that to these people.

"Closet!" Brian said and opened one.

Kylara sighed in relief, threw them in, and tossed in a potted Ficus plant that had struggled to survive under the harsh light of the fluorescents. With a little light to make it grow, the two guards were soon restrained when the roots exploded from the plant and bound them.

"At least they won't suffocate in there," her companion said and closed the door on them. He opened the door to the next basement level.

They raced up the steps to find many more guards on this level.

"Goddammit," Brian cursed. "I hope Drew and the others are doing better than we are."

She said nothing. One of the enemy had seen the door open and she launched herself into battle.

CHAPTER THIRTY

Drew broke cover, ran out in front of Tiamat, and sprayed her with rounds. She blocked them all. A piece of floating metal took one, a plinth of soil another, a web of shadow the next, followed by any number of other shields. She could switch between powers as fast as he could fire bullets. He might have given up the fight if he were doing something besides trying to distract her.

But Hernandez was in position. She'd dropped a duffel behind the dragon and was now getting clear. He didn't know how much C4 and dragon shrapnel she'd loaded into it but knowing his demolitions expert, it was far more likely to be too much than too little.

With the package in place, he raced into cover as Keith and the recruits laid down covering fire. By some miracle, he made it alive and still able to feel for himself.

Hernandez yanked her remote control out. "Are you ready to see the insides of a goddess?" she asked.

"Blow her to h—"

"No, don't! It's a trick! I just shot in the head and it went straight thr—" Butters voice was cut off by the sound of enough C4 to level the city block detonating directly beneath Tiamat.

The explosion blew a hole in the street, destroyed the jean store and the café across the street, and blew back the wall on the entire front side of the grounds of the Chrome Castle.

Unfortunately, it didn't so much as leave a mark on the target. It took him a moment to realize that it wasn't because she was so powerful but because it wasn't her at all. It was an illusion of her.

Drew knew there was a dragon who could make illusions but Kylara had said she'd seen her body floating offshore at the island where Larry had trained his recruits. She'd been killed during the battle there. But Tiamat seemed to have all dragon powers. She wasn't limited to ones she'd absorbed like Kylara and their Hail Mary pass at eliminating her had been thoroughly foiled.

But what could they do? The dragon mage was already inside with Brian, trying to free Kristen and the Council. Tiamat must still be in there too, watching this whole thing play out from a place of safety. She had seen the explosion—the whole damn state of Michigan must have seen that explosion. This must have been why she sent the illusionary dragon out—to draw whatever attacks it could—and it had worked. Hernandez couldn't have any more explosives and judging by the Steel Guards flying up toward a conveniently nearby skyscraper—Butters' position was compromised.

"What do we do now, sir?" Hernandez yelled, but he could hardly hear her over the ringing in his ears. Still, he knew the answer to the question all the same.

"We show Tiamat that we're still coming for her," Drew said, stepped out of cover, and bellowed, "Charge!"

He raced directly at the dragon and ran straight through her to prove definitively that she was an illusion. That was good. It meant he and his team had been outmaneuvered but not that she was invulnerable. Still, this would be close.

His team and Larry's recruits rushed forward toward the now nonexistent gates of the compound. The illusion of Tiamat vanished, having served its purpose.

More Steel Guards streamed from the interior of the Chrome Castle. "Keep 'em busy!" Drew shouted, still reluctant to kill allies.

His team knew what they were doing, however. They shot them in the legs or arms and aimed for the chest if and only if the Steel Guard wore a bulletproof vest.

But the effort to not kill their friends cost them time and maneuverability.

The members of the Steel Guard they had already been battling reformed and joined forces with the Cult of Tiamat to surge into the invading forces' flank. Drew didn't particularly want to push much closer, so this was good. They would fight there, draw Tiamat's eye, and give Kylara enough time to turn the tide of battle.

"Larry, I need you and your mages over there *now!*" he yelled and directed the old mage to their exposed side. The mages managed to get shields up but the cult members—despite lacking the formal training of the Steel Guard—had powers that made standard tactics less than effective.

A dragon who could burrow through the soil like it was water burst out of the earth behind the line of mages and might have slaughtered all of them had Amy not chosen that moment to drop from above on her skateboard. She slammed the dragon into his hole like the world's most epic game of whack-a-mole.

Undeterred the dragon simply erupted in another place, flung recruits like shrapnel, and dragged one poor soul into the earth with him.

"We need to create a perimeter!" Drew yelled at Larry, Hernandez, and everyone who could hear him. In the noise and mayhem of battle, it seemed like no one at all.

"You got it!" Tanya shouted and landed in her dragon form. The next time the dragon tried to thrust through the dirt, it became tangled in the roots of trees and grasses at her command.

Diamantine was able to basically become a wall. Her diamond scales made almost all of the attacking dragons' abilities moot.

"Sir, we have an opening!" Keith shouted from the front of their little unit.

"Then we take it!" Drew replied and ordered the team to advance.

With Amy and Diamantine guarding their flanks, Larry and his mages at their rear, and Keith and Hernandez showing the recruits how to storm a base, they made better progress than he had ever hoped for.

Before long, they could see the obsidian-black statues that had once been the living members of the Council. They stood at the base of the Chrome Castle, frozen in time and blind witnesses to the battle that unfolded for their benefit and because they had not been able to do what Drew now had to accomplish.

He glanced up. It was hard to see in the night but he could still see the Steel Dragon at the top of the Chrome Castle. Hopefully, Kylara was already halfway to her. He didn't think they could win this without Kristen.

"Forward! We hold the statuary until Kylara gets here!" he shouted to his team. He had never expected to use the word 'statuary' in combat before but he had given up pretending like his life was anything like he had imagined it would be.

He narrowed his eyes when one of the statues unfurled its wings. When it had been motionless, its wings had looked black like all the other statues but now, they glittered with a hundred colors—a thousand—in the light of the full moon. Tiamat raised her head and stood before them, regal and powerful, a goddess.

"That is your plan, then?" she all but purred before her aura rolled over Drew.

It was unlike anything he could have imagined.

He fell to his knees as he felt dozens of emotions all at once and then in quick succession, all of them more powerful than he had ever experienced.

An overwhelming sensation of love swamped rational thought. First, it was the love he had felt for his mom as a kid—love that had only intensified as he'd aged and realized how hard her life had been given that she was single and worked more jobs than she had ever let her young son know. Tiamat worked even harder, though. She cared for the entire world and was willing to make it a better place. But...she wasn't...his mom.

He pushed back and felt fear take hold in his chest. She was more powerful than any dragon he had ever seen. With no effort, she could destroy society, decimate the human population, rain fire on the earth, and make the seas rise to bring Armageddon itself. But...only if...he let her.

Awe transfixed him—at her power, her age, and at the fact that the Mother of All Dragons stood before him and willed him to join her. It was a generous offer, truly. The kind of offer he'd be a fool to resist. But...if she was so powerful, why force him to feel this way?

Love took him again—the love of a father for his daughter. He was not a dad and never had been. There'd been one girlfriend who had gotten pregnant, but the baby hadn't lived past three months. He hadn't thought about that in a long time but he thought about it now—about how much he had wanted to protect that baby from a dangerous world.

Then, his thoughts shifted. It was Kylara he truly thought of as a daughter. She was young, arrogant, and had a problem with authority, exactly like he had as a kid. He had joined the Detroit SWAT team to try to make it better—first, for people like Kristen and later, once he became a Steel Guard, for people like Kylara.

Thoughts of her filled Drew's heart and gave him the strength to raise his head and look at Tiamat. The dragon's eyes sparkled with flames of a thousand colors. She tried to crush his emotions but could not. He felt love for his fellow teammates, not this self-proclaimed goddess. He feared a world where she became its ruler, not a world without her. He was in awe of her, certainly, but in the same way that he was in awe of a hurricane that could flatten buildings. His love for those who needed to be protected would not be turned against those same people.

It took effort and he knew full well that it might result in him being incinerated, but he took a deep breath and stood. Deliberately, he raised his chin even further and looked Tiamat directly in the eyes.

"You have no power over me."

He knew the gesture was nothing more than symbolic and that it might damn well cost him his life, but when she opened her mouth, he did not flinch or run. It was a pleasant surprise when nothing came out except her laughter.

"Such power," she said sardonically. "Too bad your team does not have the strength you possess."

Drew looked to his left and saw Keith and Larry on their knees, groveling to their new master. Larry's mages had fared no better and neither had the recruits. All of them supplicated themselves before this being of unimaginable power.

Oddly, however, Hernandez was still on her feet and cursed a storm under her breath while she stared at Tiamat like she had stolen the demolitions expert's bag of toys. It was true, in a way, and the thought almost made him smile.

He turned his head and saw that on the other side, Kylara's friends had succumbed. Sam, Jasmine, Tanya, and Galen all bowed before the goddess. Timeflash had fared no better. Even Hester Diamantine sat in her diamond-scaled dragon form, her front legs crossed and head lowered to rest on them.

"Diamantine, you have to resist! For Kylara!" Drew shouted at her.

"Don't you see?" she responded. "Our surrender is the only way she lives. Nothing is more important to me than Kylara. If we resist, Tiamat will kill her, but if we join, The Mother of All Dragons will give her a place of honor. Can you not feel it to be so?"

"She's tricking you!" he yelled.

The dragon said nothing and lowered her head again.

"Sam, Tanya?" Drew shouted.

"Kylara cannot resist this," Tanya said. "She was always the worst with auras. We have to convince her to join us."

Sam looked at Drew and shook his head.

Beyond them, Amy Williams still seemed to be herself, but barely. She remained standing and swung her arms around in her great loops that created a swirling vortex of wind, psychic energy, and only a mage could say what else. It seemed to be working, though, as she did not drop to her knees and instead, glared at Tiamat. Unfortunately, it seemed to take all her energy simply to keep their enemy's magic at bay. She was effectively stalemated.

"Impressive," the goddess dragon said, "The three of you resisting. Perhaps you need more of a push."

Drew did not think there was a dragon who could have made his blood run colder than her but he hadn't anticipated that Heartsbane would join the battle.

She flew in from the Chrome Castle and over the heads of the Dragon Council members still petrified in black stone.

In the shocked silence, she landed and transformed into her human form. As usual, her pretty face was framed by blonde French braids that were so light, they looked like white gold. Her true power had never come from her dragon form but her ability to rally people's emotions.

When she approached them with a demure smile, her barbed tongue was held in check for a moment, either by her will or Tiamat's. Drew could not guess but it worried him more than anything else about her.

She approached Amy first, and his heart began to hammer in his chest. If Amy was converted, all was surely lost.

But it was not Heartsbane who broke the silence. It was

Hernandez. Her mumbled cursing grew in volume until he could make out words between the expletives.

"Melissa! Melissa, what in the hell are you doing?" she shouted.

Melissa Heartsbane paused and appraised her, then glanced at Tiamat.

"You may do as you wish as long as you serve me," the goddess said.

She nodded and walked toward Hernandez.

"That's right! Get your pretty little ass over here," the demotions expert yelled. "This is what you are, huh? When push comes to shove, you get shoved, huh? You spend your whole life manipulating people—manipulating me—and the first time someone who can stand against you shows up, you simply roll over? You're pathetic! You're pathetic for how you lied to me and for how you refuse to resist her."

Something like regret flickered over Heartsbane's face. "I never manipulated you," she said to the woman.

"That's bull and you know it! You're nothing without your powers and now, you're not even that. You could never have got in my pants without doing exactly what Tiamat is doing to you now."

"Why do you speak to me this way?" the dragon said, her voice more placatory than Drew had ever heard it. "After what we shared?"

Hernandez spat on the ground in front of her. "If I mean anything to you, prove it. Kiss me without your aura. Let me at least see what that's like."

"I never used my aura on you like that."

"Bull!" the woman roared.

"It is fine, my daughter. If you can convince her to our side with a kiss, then let it be," Tiamat said.

Heartsbane nodded. She was so calm it was uncanny as she approached Hernandez.

The demolitions expert stopped her cursing and looked Melissa in the eyes and for a moment, Drew saw something he rarely saw on her face—vulnerability. Then, the two women embraced and the world seemed to hold still.

A second later—or a minute, he had no idea—they pulled apart. Hernandez was no longer cursing and his heart sank.

But Heartsbane turned on Tiamat. She smiled. "The Mother of All Dragons is weaker than one trash-talking cop who likes playing with explosives?" She snorted. "You're pathetic."

"That's my girl!" Hernandez crowed to the moon above.

"Cute," the dragon goddess growled, "but ultimately irrelevant."

Tendrils of shadow radiated from her claws and bound Hernandez, Heartsbane, and Drew. His arms were tethered to his sides as the ropes of darkness tightened around him. The two women fared no better.

Next, Tiamat turned her attention to Amy. She exhaled and ice began to form around the swirling vortex of power that the mage worked so hard to maintain. Surprisingly, she did not push into this defensive zone but instead, made a massive block of ice that completely encapsulated Amy and her magic shields.

Drew struggled against his bonds and was punished for his efforts. The earth rose to encapsulate him and replaced his shadow restraints with those of rock. They were defeated. Even though he had retained control of his mind, he had lost the battle.

CHAPTER THIRTY-ONE

Kylara stood on the far side of twenty guards. All but one had been knocked unconscious. The last one still standing had unfortunately had his wrist broken thanks to her enthusiasm. He clutched it and scowled at her.

"Has Tiamat ordered all the troops out into the battle?" she demanded of the whimpering guard.

"Yes, ma'am. Everyone but us humans. The mages and dragons she has will wipe your resistance out. You can't stand against her. No one can."

She wanted to take her pendant off and use her aura to make him see that he had been tricked by a dragon, nothing more, but she did not dare. Already, the silver-and-turquoise pendant felt warm against her chest. Tiamat was using her aura and her aunt's pendant was protecting her from it.

"The human guards are still inside?" Brian demanded, having stumbled past all those she had knocked out.

"Most of them, yes, sir," the man said and nodded hurriedly. "Tiamat doesn't understand the building—bless her ancient soul —so she's relying on us to help her."

"That's good to know," Brian said. "Kylara, can you, uh..."

She nodded and karate-chopped the guard to render him unconscious.

They snuck quietly up the steps to the ground floor of the Chrome Castle building. It was a large room, an entrance designed to impress those who came to visit the Dragon Council. Thin pillars decorated with simple chrome patterns supported a ceiling that was high above and gave little cover to the dozens of Steel Guards who watched the battle through the windows all around the ground level.

There was no way she would be able to move past all of them without being seen. Even if she used her shadow powers, there was simply too much open space and too many glaring lights shining against the night sky outside.

"I can feel her," Brian said. "She's using her aura against our friends."

Kylara's hand brushed her pendant. She couldn't feel exactly what was happening but she could feel the warmth.

"You have to get the Council free," Brian said and pointed at the statues outside the front of the building. In the light, they were little more than silhouettes.

"What about your sister?"

"I have to get to the building's defenses before you go up there. That drawbridge she's on...well, have you ever seen a cartoon where the king can make the floor drop out from people who displease him?"

"You didn't." She clenched her jaw.

"Kristen never used it but I couldn't help myself. If someone realizes what we're up to before I have control of the Chrome Castle's defenses, Kristen takes the plunge. It might not be a problem for a normal dragon, but given that she's frozen in stone..."

"How do we get there?" Kylara asked.

"It's ten floors up. I know a way in but that guard said there's nothing but regular people here. I can take them—well, as long as there aren't too many. If Tiamat's out there fighting our friends…"

Brian didn't have to finish as they both knew how that battle would go. She needed to free the Council. Hopefully, they could stand against Tiamat's aura and could turn the tide of battle.

"I don't see how I can get past them without being noticed," she said.

Brian shrugged. "Not to put this all on you, but it kind of is so go do your dragon thing," He waved her off.

Kylara couldn't help but chuckle. It was insane to think they were trying to subvert the will of a goddess and he believed that her "dragon thing" would somehow solve their problems.

Although it did give her an idea. It was insane, undeniably dangerous, and a bigger risk than she knew anyone would want her to take but if it worked, she'd be happy to ask forgiveness. Besides, there wasn't anyone around so she couldn't exactly ask permission.

"As soon as I take my dragon shape, head to the stairs," Kylara ordered and pointed across the room to where another stairwell waited.

"Your dragon form? I thought you could use your shadow powers or—"

"You said do my dragon thing. I'm doing it. Got it?"

"Sure, yeah." He nodded.

"And don't run. Wait—go downstairs and put on one of those guards' uniforms."

"Good plan!" he said exuberantly, ran downstairs, and reappeared a minute later in a black-and-silver jumpsuit. "All right. Let's do this."

"And Brian," Kylara said before she took her dragon form, "If you feel fear, where should you run?"

"Upstairs?"

"Exactly. Upstairs is the safest place for you to be and the only way to make the battle outside safe for our friends. Got it?"

"Yeah, but why?"

The sound of battle intensified from outside. "No time." Kylara removed her pendant—as dangerous as it seemed, she saw no alternative—and transformed into her dragon body.

Radiating confidence was at the very center of her plan, so she stamped out into the first floor of the Chrome Castle building. She tried not to think about how her hips were not quite as wide as Tiamat's, her waist was not as pinched, or how her chest didn't swell in its dragon form as the Mother of All Dragons' did. Instead, she focused on the fact that she knew her scales were identical to Tiamat's and sparkled in the same hundreds of colors, and that the people in this room were there because of the terror she had put in their hearts.

The dragon mage rallied her aura to reveal how she felt about herself. She was a powerful, unstoppable dragon. The people in this room should both fear and respect her.

It worked. The Steel Guards in her path scurried aside and those who saw her coming saluted. She didn't allow herself to feel nervous or anxious and simply continued to walk until she was outside. A single glance over her shoulder gave her a glimpse of a terrified Brian when he broke his stride and raced up the stairs. Fortunately, no one else seemed to notice him.

Kylara turned to the entrance of the building and walked through the gaping hole where the front door had been. Kristen had specifically made the entrance to the first floor human-sized. That way, dragons couldn't barge in and bully all the smaller, non-fire-breathing people in the lobby.

Tiamat had not liked this attempt to use architecture to create equality, so she'd broken a hole and used her ability to control metal to make a twisted frame around the opening. Kylara strode through and resisted the urge to put it back as it should be.

She left the lobby and stepped out onto the top of the stairs. Below, at the foot of the stairs, were the petrified bodies of the Dragon Council and Lady Amythist. Beyond them were her friends and she could see at a glance that their battle was lost. All either kneeled or were bound by magic of one type or another.

Between her friends and the petrified Dragon Council was Tiamat.

The black dragon had not turned—a lucky break for Kylara, who transformed into her human body and put the turquoise-and-silver pendant around her neck. As soon as she did so, the pressure of dread she had felt pushing at her consciousness was gone. She was protected again.

The dragon mage wrapped herself in shadow and stole down the steps.

CHAPTER THIRTY-TWO

Brian hurried up the stairs. At first, he avoided the temptation to run and walked as fast as he damn well could. As he climbed higher, he increased his speed to a run, despite the fact that it made his legs burn from the exertion. The place appeared to have been cleaned out. What members of the Steel Guard were left seemed to be deployed entirely to the first floor. With luck, they had left his operations room locked but not melted shut. He thought his odds were good though. The dragons and mages who could do such a thing had tended to overlook his technological skillset.

Cautiously, he left the stairwell and saw that the entrance to his operations room was, in fact, not completely destroyed.

"Oh, hell yes," he whispered and jogged down the hallway to the door.

This was his opportunity to help his sister. After everything she had done for him, he had always wanted an opportunity to save her. He had been able to admit to himself that it was a foolish dream. Surely life would be better if Kristen was not kidnapped or captured or had people trying to kill her. He had long ago resigned himself to being a supporting character in her life. After all, she was the Steel Dragon, the most powerful dragon in the world—at least she used to be. He was merely tech support.

And yet today looked like it would be tech support's day. He had not been able to see out into the darkness outside the Chrome Castle, but the fact that there had been a battle at all seemed to indicate that the full defenses of the building had not been activated. If they had, the mages might have stood a chance but the dragons shouldn't have been able to survive. His assumption was that Tiamat had convinced someone to make the Chrome Castle treat her like a friend but had not possessed the foresight to reprogram the system to make it treat Brian, Drew, and the rest of them as enemies. The fact that his biometrics still worked confirmed this.

Still, Brian felt palpable relief when he used the palm reader and retinal scanner outside the operations room and the system granted him access. The latch on the door clicked. Before it could slide open, he drew his pistol. Not activating the full potential of the system was a mistake he expected a dragon to make. Leaving a guard behind seemed like something a dragon might consider.

While he knew that it might be a friend, he clenched his teeth and braced himself to do what would be necessary to save his sister and everyone else he knew. He kicked the door open and leveled his gun at the interior of the operations room.

Thankfully, no one was there.

He let himself breathe again and slipped inside.

As he sat at the console, he realized he was an idiot who had left the door open. He stood hastily and closed the door but before it could click shut, someone's foot slipped into the gap.

Panicked, he slammed the door on the foot, but the owner of it did not withdraw. Instead, they kicked the barrier inward and thrust Brian back.

He tried to raise his gun but before he could, the man

slammed into him. He knocked him off his feet and the pistol clattered from his hand.

Brian tried to stand but his assailant already had a gun pointed at his forehead.

"Joe?"

For a moment, he could not believe it. He did not only know the man holding a gun to him, but he had trained him to be his lieutenant of operations. He wouldn't call Joe a friend—despite an interest in tech and its security implications, the two did not see eye to eye on much—but an acquaintance, certainly.

"I wondered when you'd show up, Brian," Joe said.

"They left you in charge?" he asked and tried to not look at the gun while he got Joe talking.

"Tiamat wants me downstairs with everyone else but she doesn't understand this system. This can protect her."

"That's why I'm here," he said and took a tiny step toward the man. "The system is being underutilized. The Steel Guard should never have made it this far."

"Not another goddamn step, Brian. If you were with us, I would have seen you before Drew and those morons outside attacked. The system is being underutilized because you left a firewall you never gave me access to get past."

"Here, let me show you," he said and gestured at the computer as slowly as he could. He put his hands on the back of the chair and when Joe's gaze flicked from him to the keyboard—he wanted to see whatever password he would input—he threw the chair back.

It slammed into Joe's gut, who doubled over.

Brian drove a shoulder into him and knocked him to the floor.

His former teammate was not disabled by the fall, however. He hadn't even dropped his freaking gun and he brought it up and fired twice.

Reflexively, the young man fell prone and his elbows

hammered painfully on the tile. That was good. He did not think he would have noticed his elbows if a bullet had ripped through him. In front of him was the gun he'd dropped.

He snatched it, aimed, and squeezed the trigger before Joe could fire a third shot.

The man uttered a wet, throaty yell and clutched his neck. Blood seeped between his fingers and he fell back to sprawl in an awkward heap.

Brian knew he would hate himself for this later, but before he checked the fallen Steel Guard, he shut the door. It clicked shut and the locks automatically engaged.

Now, he was alone with the man he'd shot.

Pushing his instinctive reluctance aside, he went to Joe, who was a mess of blood. His hands had already fallen away from his neck and both lay limp at his sides. He tried to feel for a pulse but there was nothing there.

"Oh, Jesus," he said and his shoes stepped in the man's blood as he stumbled back, leaving a trail that pointed to the murderer. "Oh, goddammit," he said and fought the tears that stung to his eyes but was unable to keep them from falling.

There was nothing to be done. He could grieve—would have to grieve—later. He had known this might happen. Joe was the only other person who had known the back way into the Chrome Castle and he had expected to encounter him sooner. When he hadn't, he'd allowed himself to hope he might be in the clear. He had not thought he would have to…that he'd…he never wanted to kill anyone, even if he knew he had to.

But those feelings could come later.

Right now, he was the only human alive who could turn the tide of battle against a dragon goddess and her cult.

Even though he hadn't seen anyone, he wasn't about to assume that the gunshots would go unheard. The Chrome Castle had systems to detect such things and many would know how to follow the system to the source of the gunshots.

Brian didn't have much time but his fingers hopefully wouldn't need much.

They sprang into action and almost moved of their own accord to activate systems that had gone untouched, designate erstwhile allies as targets, and engage safe zones and redundancies that had been in place and simply waited to be activated.

He could do this, he told himself when a hand pounded on the door.

All he needed was another minute.

CHAPTER THIRTY-THREE

Step by step, Kylara slunk toward the Dragon Council. She was wrapped in shadow with a hand clasped around her pendant. To enable her to move more quietly, she had turned her skin to normal and tried to not breathe as she took each step as silently as she could.

Tiamat's back was still to her. She merely needed to be a little closer so she could send out the swirling mist that would return the petrified dragons of the Council to their normal forms. Her pendant seemed to conceal her from the Mother of All Dragons, who had not turned.

Her attention was on the small group of allies in front of her. Based on who was restrained and who knelt freely, it looked like Drew, Hernandez, Heartsbane, and presumably Amy had remained free of her control. The girl did not know who else would have been contained inside a miniature glacier and besides, the mage was nowhere to be seen.

"I value strength, even the stubborn strength of humans," Tiamat said to Drew and ran a claw along his cheek. Bound in the earth itself, he could do nothing to escape her touch. Still, he jerked his head and her claw cut into his cheek. "But you must understand that you are dispensable."

He looked away from her and by chance, his gaze fell on Kylara. She knew he couldn't see her, wrapped in shadow as she was, but he saw a smudge of darkness and recognized her plan and how tenuous her situation was. He winked.

"If I'm dispensable, why am I still alive?"

"The world has changed. I can see that in the way your cities glow and in the languages you speak. People like you—stubborn people—could be of use to me."

"You're a filthy liar!" Hernandez shouted.

"Quiet!" Tiamat said and shadow extended from the woman's body to cover her mouth. "You are only alive because your attempt on my life was brazen enough for me to make an example of you when this is all over."

Judging by the look in the demolitions expert's eyes, she was cursing something fierce, but the web of shadow across her mouth muffled her words.

"You expect me to join you when you threaten my friends?" Drew demanded roughly.

The goddess' attention snapped back to him. Kylara continued her approach. She had to get closer. The fact was that she had never used the un-petrifying smoke in her human form and was not sure if she could. But she knew that to rescue the entire Council, she needed to be as close as possible.

"You fascinate me," Tiamat said. "She does not. On the contrary, she is a violent ape who has learned how to use but another iteration of fire. However, if you submit to me, I will spare her. Resistance is futile. Either you submit and serve me willingly, or you will die in ways you had never imagined. But why do this? Why take your own life when the alternative is to join me and have your life taken care of? I am the Mother of All Dragons. They will always be my firstborn but humans have a place in this world too. Even if you do not share my blood, I will take joy in watching you grow and in the things you will build for me."

Kylara felt her pendant, still clutched in her hand, heat crazily. She would have dropped it if she didn't know exactly what that meant. Tiamat was using her aura to its full effect. Even without targeting her directly, it was incredibly powerful. Fortunately, the pendant was able to protect her, but would it if the dragon attacked her directly?

It was probably wiser to not test it. She was almost in a position to free the Dragon Council. Together, their auras would be able to combat Tiamat. They had to.

"Do you swear you'll free her?" Drew asked.

"There is no oath I can make to a human." Tiamat chuckled as if he were a child demanding extra dessert before he had eaten his vegetables. "But I give you my word that I will spare her if you kneel and swear your loyal intention to me."

He drew a deep breath, looked at the night sky, and glanced at Kylara. After another wink, he blinked twice, perhaps to cover the signal.

"I did not know you would be so merciful. I'll kneel and swear my intention," he said from within his prison of earth.

The black dragon gestured to him with a claw and the earth packed tightly all around his body sloughed away. Free, he breathed deeply and looked at her.

"Now, kneel," Tiamat ordered.

Drew made a show of kneeling. Slowly, he bent his knee and dragged it out as much as he could without raising suspicion. Kylara used the precious seconds he was giving her to get into position.

His knee touched the ground.

"Now, your intention," Tiamat said.

"Right. I intend to put a bullet through your damn skull!" His gun was already drawn and he fired a string of shots at her.

Not a single one of them got through.

The same dirt that had been used to constrain him lurched into place to rob each bullet of its momentum. They fell one after the other at her feet.

"Foolish human. You have neither the power to stand against me nor the wisdom to see the futility of such a gesture." Tiamat growled.

"I don't know about wisdom, but I'll show you power!" The top half of the block of ice imprisoning Amy Williams blew to pieces and the mage launched into the sky. Her skateboard came to her and glued itself to her feet.

Kylara did not know if Amy had somehow sensed her or if she had simply heard Drew's gunshots and saw that the time to fight was now. Her motivations were irrelevant, however. Either way, this was the opportunity to free the Dragon Council.

She dropped the shadow she was hiding in and called on her inner magic to summon the mist to reverse the petrification.

Tiamat roared as Amy launched a spike of telekinetic energy at her. She absorbed the blow with a wall of ice but she did not appear to like the outcome. The mage had completely obliterated the frozen shield so instead of making the black dragon look strong, it made her look weak.

The goddess launched into the air and released a multitude of energy blasts at her magic-wielding foe. Fire, ice, lightning, and wind pummeled the slight figure in quick succession, but Amy was powerful. She flitted constantly on her skateboard, avoided the full brunt of any of the blows, and used shields to stop anything from hurting her.

Kylara reached deeper for the power to free the Dragon Council, but she could not find it. Kishar had been able to do it from her human form, hadn't she? Surely she could too. She knew that if she transformed into her dragon shape, Tiamat would see her so she dug deep.

Amy continued the fight. She didn't have power over as many elements as the dragon goddess did. Although the girl had seen the world's most powerful mage control elements before, she did not bother with any of them now. Instead, she tried to hurl her enemy back with thrusts from shimmering blue shields. She lifted boulders that had been artfully placed about the grounds of the Chrome Castle and threw them. Between the rocks, she ripped trees from the ground that were far larger than they should have been—they had been dug up with massive equipment during Kylara's internship and transplanted there—and used them to try to spear the Mother of All Dragons.

None of it worked. While she could use her telekinesis to lift boulders, Tiamat could control the stones themselves. The dragon goddess let her hurl the boulders but before any of them struck her, they veered away from the will of Tiamat.

She did not seem to have any direct power over the trees, however. Instead of making them swerve away, she took turns striking them with lightning, melting them to a pulp with acid, or simply incinerating them. In one particularly frightening display, she used the exact power that Kylara tried and failed to summon to transform a tree into black stone, which she then shattered into shards with her diamond-encrusted tail.

It was obvious to the dragon mage that Tiamat could crush Amy, but why didn't she? Why even let the mage lift the boulders at all? She still had Hernandez and Heartsbane wrapped in shadow, despite being in the middle of a fight. If she willed it, she could have left the boulders stuck in the ground, resisting Amy's power. Instead, she let the woman rage against her like a toddler working through a tantrum.

One of Amy's nostrils started to bleed and Kylara thought she understood. Tiamat was not all-powerful. She had not been able to crush Amy's will—an aspect of the mage that was not magically augmented at all—so why would she be able to defeat the mage if she used her magic? Rather than trying to destroy her, she was playing it smart and letting Amy tire herself out so she could simply kill her.

Kylara could not let the dragon goddess get her chance.

Risks be damned, she changed into her dragon form. She reached inside to her font of inner magic and felt there was more to it now than there had been in her human form. At last, she found the petrifying power and inhaled a great breath of air in preparation to free the Dragon Council.

She exhaled and tendrils of mist came from her nostrils and seeped through the Council.

Up above, the battle had taken a turn for the worse. Tiamat had yet to go on the offensive, and the exertion of needing to constantly attack was costing Amy. Both nostrils and an ear were bleeding and her movements were sloppy. No longer did she flit about on her skateboard, doing kick tricks to avoid or deflect attacks. Instead, she clung to it with both feet and one hand while her other hand tried to keep her attack active against the goddess.

Kylara sent the healing mist farther and farther from her. There were so many members of the Council and it took longer than she had thought it would. She had only ever used this power to bring one dragon back before—Lady Amythist–and even that had taken time. Thawing this many at once was not working.

Above her, Amy screamed when her skateboard was split in half by a beam of light.

She managed to dodge a few more strikes from Tiamat and yanked herself out of the way by pulling on her hoodie, but she had never been able to fly. She had always used her telekinesis to make her skateboard levitate, then stuck her shoes to it. Now that she had been denied that board, she didn't have the same agility.

When Tiamat called a blast of lightning down from the clear sky above them, the mage was unable to dodge. There was a blinding flash, a crack of thunder, and Amy fell through the night sky. One of her sleeves was on fire and trailed smoke as she plummeted.

The goddess dragon did not allow her to fall as far as the earth, however. Instead, she spun and timed her strike perfectly so her diamond tail caught the mage in the gut and flung her into a window of one of the lower floors of the Chrome Castle.

No movement came from within the dark hole her body had created. Kylara knew that the smartest thing would be to assume that Amy had given her life.

She had to make it worth it, she decided, and tried to push out more of the creeping mist. Her only hope was to free the Council, and she had to do it *now.*

Already, the mist had risen and almost surrounded Lady Amythist. She didn't know if there was a certain amount of time required or if a level of coverage had to be achieved before they would be restored. With her friends' lives and the fate of the world hanging in the balance, she only knew that nothing else mattered. She had to push out more of the mist at any cost.

Kylara knew she was close. She thought she could see Amythist's eyes start to twinkle. She *would* free her!

In the next moment, a beam of light streaked into her back and slammed her face into the ground.

She knew it was Tiamat. Who else could it be? But she didn't fight, not yet. Instead, she tried to exhale more of the mist.

The beam of light expanded and in its flow, the mist coming from the young dragon mage evaporated to nothing. All her effort had been for naught.

"This was your grand plan?" The black dragon laughed from above.

The ground beneath her shot up like a giant piston and threw her high. By some stroke of luck or mercy, she had not made the entire area around Kylara shift. If she had, the statues of the Council would already be broken.

She caught the air in her wings in time for a powered gust of wind to throw her back toward the Chrome Castle.

"I knew you were there the entire time." The Mother of All

Dragons laughed. "I had expected you to challenge me in front of your little cadre of mortals but instead, you tried to free these politicians?"

Boulders lifted from the earth and hurtled toward her. She tried to use her ability to control stone to stop them and managed to block the first three, but not the fourth or the fifth or the sixth.

They pounded into her and glass shattered behind her as she bulldozed into the lobby of the Chrome Castle. She only stopped moving when her head struck one of the pillars supporting the skyscraper above it.

"Foolish girl. I had hoped to use you to spectacular effect but instead, I'll gut you and watch you bleed out like the mammal you are."

CHAPTER THIRTY-FOUR

"How did you know...I was there?" Kylara choked the words past broken teeth. Being a diamond-scaled dragon meant that her teeth—made of bone—were one of the more vulnerable parts of her. Driving through plate glass and into a pillar hadn't hurt her all that much, but having boulders batter her face had left a mark. Although—like a supercharged shark—she was already pushing out more teeth.

"I could feel you when snuck beneath the earth like a spineless worm," Tiamat said, flew into the hole she had created with the girl's body, and landed in the lobby of the ground floor of the Chrome Castle building. Her talons clacked on the tile as she approached. "I could feel when you tried to use your aura to control the pathetic monkey guards in this building. I could feel when you tried to hide from me and when you tried to approach those simpering fools trapped in stone. I could feel your fear and I could taste it. You cannot hide from me. I. Am. A. Goddess!"

The dragon mage rolled out of the way as her enemy pounced and struck the floor with such force that she broke a hole into the lower level. The black dragon did not tumble through, though. She caught herself with a web of shadows and reformed the concrete and steel of the building into steps that allowed her to approach effortlessly.

"What hope do mortals like you have fighting against me? I existed before dragons and before magic. My spirit was enough to overwhelm your pathetic mind. You stand no chance."

Kylara forced herself to stand. Despite having been slammed through a glass window, she felt fine. Great, even. She was ready for this. "The point is to not weigh my odds. The point is to do the right thing."

"Oh?" Tiamat laughed. "And what, may I ask, is the right thing?"

"Kicking your teeth in seems like a good start." She used the steel beneath her to shove herself forward. At the same time, she lunged toward her adversary and made acid drip from her claws and teeth.

The goddess roared as she drove into her. Her claws found her enemy's chest but they couldn't rip into the diamond scales. Even the acid did nothing, neutralized by the same power she had used to create it.

Kylara tried to snap her jaws onto Tiamat's neck but was met with a blast of light in the face. She catapulted away, temporarily blinded, which allowed the other dragon to pound into her. Another plate glass window exploded at her back. She landed in the dirt, her vision still gone, and the dragon goddess attacked.

But she had senses beyond sight. Her ability to control the weather let her discern the flow of air currents when her enemy moved. Together with that, she was able to control stone and the earth beneath her feet responded to create a wall of earth and rock in front of the dragon goddess. The impact and crunch of broken bones sounded wonderful.

When her vision returned, she saw her enemy's healing power was also being used to full effect. Whatever bones had shattered in the dragon's body were already healed.

"Do you see how you cannot defeat me?" Tiamat asked.

"I see how you have the same powers I do."

The goddess growled and blasted her with another beam of light. She was not about to fall for the same trick twice, however, and created a shield of interwoven tendrils of darkness that absorbed it.

Tiamat increased the strength of her beam and it began to burn through the shadow, but she was not the only one with a well of strength to draw on. The young dragon mage tightened the weave of her shadow web. While the light continued to chew through, it met with increasing resistance. The Mother of All Dragons roared and strengthened the beam even more. The girl felt certain that she wanted to overpower her and show her that in a test of wills, the goddess would win.

And for all she knew, she might well. Kylara had not won her victories by simply overpowering her enemies. She had learned to rely on her allies and that together—but fighting smarter—they could rise to any challenge. Her friends couldn't be a part of this fight, but that didn't mean she couldn't use what she had learned from them.

In the sky above them, the stars winked out as clouds condensed into existence. They grew from white puffs to thick gray thunderheads. Then lightning sizzled from above at her command, while the shadow web between her and adversary continued to defend her.

But Tiamat was ready. Spears of stone rocketed from the earth. There were three of them, each thinner than a tree trunk, and they arched into the sky above the black dragon.

Kylara's first blast of lightning struck one of these stone lightning rods and was wicked into the earth at her opponent's feet. Her second lightning strike caused one of the thin, stone lightning rods to explode. Unfortunately, the dragon goddess caught her third, fourth, fifth, sixth, and tenth strikes with the stone fingers.

Her laughter was lost in the cracks and booms of thunder.

Lightning illuminated her and made her usually dark scales seem as bright as day as they twinkled in all their colors.

The young dragon mage blasted ice next, which Tiamat melted with fire. She tried fire and wind but these were blocked with stone.

Next, she made her throat inflate with air so she could create a sonic boom to rupture the goddess's eardrums, but the wily dragon punctured the throat pouch with a spear made of metal ripped from the Chrome Castle.

Suddenly, she seemed to vanish and Kylara felt pain in her shoulder. Her enemy had stabbed her but was gone.

She froze time as Temporus had and revealed Tiamat moving at superhuman speeds. With time slowed, she healed easily from the wound.

The Mother of All Dragons scowled and released the flow of time. "You are clever—far cleverer than being in your mind led me to believe."

Kylara winked at her and lunged forward. Her adversary dodged her first strike and her second, then lashed out but missed. She dismissed the illusion of herself she had created and barreled into her. The goddess soared over the landscape and she grinned. She had summoned her ability to augment her momentum and had used it to great effect against her foe.

But Tiamat spread her wings before she made impact with the earth and caught a wind she had summoned. "This is such fun!"

She flew over the girl and rained acid, fire, pieces of metal, and stones but her quarry blocked it all with shadow, walls of earth, and her diamond scales.

Kylara sent a single ribbon of shadow into the darkness of the night. At its tip, she created a noose. The goddess flew into it and she tightened her trap, hauled on the shadow rope, and used the black dragon's momentum to pound her into the ground.

Tiamat made every one of her scales glow with radiant energy, which made the shadow evaporate, but the girl had anticipated this. She called on the plants all around her enemy to grow. They responded, both to her magic and to the light that poured off the black dragon like she had hoped.

Vines wound around the goddess and held her in place long enough for acorns hidden beneath the surface to burst into life and grow into trees that wrapped her in a cage of oak.

As the plant prison grew all around her, Tiamat began to laugh. "You truly are clever," she said and the vines closest to her were set alight. The oaks touching her began to smoke, then smolder, and finally ignited into a fire that burned hotter until all the captive had to do was shake and the trees fell away, reduced to nothing but charcoal. She had used one of the first powers Kylara had absorbed—the ability to heat or cool her skin—to escape her greatest hope to contain her.

"This won't be resolved by powers, will it?" The goddess growled in irritation.

"If you're surrendering, that's fine with me," the dragon mage replied.

"We could play this game all night and nothing would be clear," Tiamat said and ignored her attempt to call her a coward. "It is time to settle this the old way. After all these millennia, the old ways are sometimes still best."

Without further warning, the Mother of All Dragons rushed out of the bonfire she had created with nothing but the touch of her skin. She bulldozed into her and launched her away thanks to her use of the momentum power.

Kylara twisted in midair, used her wings to slow her fall, and managed to land on her feet, although her momentum was such that she slid back and her claws ripped long gashes in the grass.

That was when Tiamat gave up on her powers and attacked with tooth and claw.

The young dragon mage blocked the first two strikes but left herself open and felt teeth sink into her neck.

She got her back legs between herself and her foe and managed to shove the dragon off her.

"You fight like a cat when you are a dragon," the goddess sneered.

There truly was no time to say anything in reply as her enemy launched another assault. Kylara thought she knew something about duel training. Hester had taught her well and she knew how to use her diamond scales to great defense, but against the black dragon's diamond-tipped claws, those defenses were rendered obsolete.

Her greatest, most familiar strength turned into a weakness as Tiamat demonstrated repeatedly that she could pierce her flesh if she wished to. The black dragon fought like a viper and moved too quickly, and the younger dragon hesitated for too long in her reactions to each attack. Every time she tried to fight back, the goddess moved out of the way and struck.

She tried to summon a shadow web to defend herself, to call down a bolt of lightning, and to spray acid in her foe's face, but the strikes were too fast and too vicious. She targeted her armpits and the joints of her arms and seemed to understand dragon anatomy to a supernatural degree. Her teeth found nerve endings that caused so much pain they made any attempts to summon magic fail.

Kylara was stunned. There was so much to dragon combat she simply did not understand. Her mom had done her best to train her but she had taught her ways to defend herself with her diamond scales that would not serve against Tiamat. The black dragon was slowly eviscerating her and there was nothing she could do to stop her.

Grimly, she made her mind up to not give up. She twisted beneath her assailant and used shadow powers to help her spin free. The goddess let her spin and held a claw to her throat that ripped into her flesh.

The dragon mage gasped in pain, the sound wet and ragged as blood gushed from the wound in her throat.

Tiamat stabbed the tip of her tail through the palm of one of her claws and pinned her to the earth as she screamed in pain.

With a free claw, she grasped Kylara by her jaw and forced her to look into her eyes.

"This is such a tragedy—such a waste," the dragon stated coldly. "You could have been someone in my new regime. You could have been a dragon of consequence in the world and history itself. Instead, you will merely be a cautionary tale."

CHAPTER THIRTY-FIVE

Tiamat pulled the tip of her tail out of Kylara's palm and raised it over her head. The young dragon mage tried to lift her limb to knock her adversary aside, but the black dragon had already thrust the spike on one of her knees through her bicep. She found it darkly hilarious that she had not even noticed. The rest of her body was in too much pain and she had lost too much blood for something like a gaping hole in her arm to draw her attention.

Her enemy brandished her tail in readiness. At some point, Tiamat must have used her storm powers to blow the storm clouds away because Kylara was able to see the tip of her tail silhouetted against the moon. It flicked between shapes—first, a diamond-tipped barb, then a pitchfork of bone, a spherical club of bone, a spiked end, and a dozen others before it settled into the shape of her choice—a silver ax-blade. It was the same as Kristen's and it seemed bizarrely appropriate that the Mother of All Dragons would use the Steel Dragon's—her hero's—tail to sever her head from her body.

The massive appendage straightened and rose to its full

height, but scant seconds before she arced it toward her neck in a fatal strike, she was hurled aside.

With a roar of rage, the goddess staggered back as she was struck repeatedly. Kylara tried to overcome her confusion. She had thought she was the last dragon to stand against the usurper's aura and was certainly the last one with the ability to control stones or metal in the way that whoever now controlled them used them against her foe.

"Now's your chance, Kylara!" Brian shouted over loudspeakers.

Of course! He had activated the gun emplacements of the Chrome Castle. They could not be loaded with dragon bullets as Tiamat was still alive, but the volleys hit hard and he did not seem to make an attempt to conserve ammunition. Merely the force of the barrage of rounds was enough to push Tiamat away.

Unfortunately, the dragon mage was bleeding in a dozen places, bruised in a hundred, and her neck was still a gaping wound. She tried to right herself but could see her opportunity slipping away. The goddess had created a wall of stone between her and the emplacements on top of the Chrome Castle to buy herself enough time to regain control. It was unlikely that Brian would have the opportunity to hit her as hard again. Still, she was too injured to use the chance he had given her.

Or so she thought until Sam landed beside her in his dragon form. He lowered his muzzle and touched her neck gently a little below her jaw. Healing light flowed from his body to hers and she began to heal.

"I thought she had you under her control," Kylara said.

"She had convinced me that it was the way to protect you. When she attacked, it was harder to believe."

"Thank you, Sam."

"Yes, thank you, Sam," Tiamat sneered from a tunnel of stone she had wrapped up and over her. A shot rang out from up above and blasted flecks of stone off the tunnel, but it was too thick. Brian had seemed more than willing to throw ammunition into her but was less enthusiastic to pummel her stone defenses. "I see your headmaster was correct. My aura skills need practice. If you would please leave us. I look forward to using the next millennia to turn you against this pathetic excuse for a dragon."

She lunged out of her stone tunnel and brought a shadow cape with her to protect her from the guns far above.

Kylara transformed into her human form and the black shape careened overhead.

Tiamat whirled, still on the offensive. "A neat trick but it won't work again," she snapped and lunged forward.

This time, the dragon mage transformed into her pixie body. The massive beast would have plowed through her and left nothing but a bloody puddle on the ground, but catching a pixie was a different thing entirely. She transformed to sparks and slipped between the dragon goddess's claws despite her enemy's dragon-like reflexes.

"This is pathetic!" the goddess screamed and strengthened her shadow cloak to protect herself. "This is not how dragons fight."

"But I'm not only a dragon...or a human...or a mage, or even a pixie. I'm all of them. I'm more than all of them."

"And to think you were supposed to be the Sum of All Dragons," Tiamat sneered. She inhaled and blasted an inferno of flame that engulfed Kylara's pixie form.

Thankfully, she wasn't only a pixie. She took her human form and used a web of shadow to protect herself. More rounds pounded into the black dragon and thrust her back. The dragon mage ran forward, jumped, and transformed into her dragon form to use her momentum ability to augment her force and catapult her adversary well out of attack range.

Still, the Mother of All Dragons wasn't hurt and simply roared, spun on massive wings, and streaked into a new attack. Her concentration had been shaken, however. She had forgotten to protect herself from the threat above and another barrage of bullets toppled her before she could regain her balance.

Kylara—still in her dragon form—pounced on her and savaged her chest with claws dripping in acid.

Tiamat didn't take this easily, of course, and slashed wildly but she simply shed her bulky dragon form and became a pixie again.

The black dragon lurched toward her and sprayed ice.

Seconds before the attack reached her, she turned into her human form and heated her skin to melt the ice. She then took control of the water, shaped it into a massive fist, and drove it into her assailant's face.

The dragon was knocked back but she seemed uninjured until more bullets rained on her exposed belly.

She roared in pain and lunged at Kylara, who took her diamond dragon form at the last moment and anchored herself to the ground using earth and shadow. Tiamat bulldozed into her but had not expected such resistance from the body she had attacked—a human body.

Leaving her enemy no time to recover, the dragon mage struck with her claws and tail and ripped diamond scales out that were slow to heal. She then became a pixie and flitted away in a ribbon of sparks so Brian could unleash another storm of lead.

At least a dozen shots battered the Mother of All Dragons before she managed to create a barrier between her and the Chrome Castle.

"Enough of this!" she screeched. The bullets had finally cracked some of her scales. One side was bleeding from the shots and she still had wounds inflicted by Kylara. Even though the scales were diamond, they were artifacts of magic. It meant if Tiamat became overwhelmed while using her other powers—like the barrage she'd tried to kill her young adversary with combined with healing—the diamond scales were not as strong, nor would they replace themselves as quickly.

Unfortunately, Tiamat understood this as well as she did, if not better.

"Destroy those weapons!" the goddess ordered and Kylara's friends hastened to obey. Timeflash and Karl sprang into action. Jasmine climbed on Karl and Larry climbed on Timeflash and they took to the air and headed toward the Chrome Castle, impervious to its defenses simply because Brian was a good guy who was not about to shoot his friends or a couple of kids.

Tiamat threw boulders at Kylara, who dodged them in her pixie form but did not retreat. Already, Karl had grasped one of the massive guns with his shadow tendrils and yanked it from its moorings.

The young dragon mage knew she did not have much time to finish this. She streaked toward her enemy and changed from a shower of sparks to a glowing dragon. If she could only overwhelm the goddess, she could end this. She would overpower her, knock her unconscious, and take her to the pixie realm and lock her away. As she flew, she used her powers to hurl stones, metal, and lighting. She summoned ice, fire, acid, and raw lighting and struck like Armageddon itself.

CHAPTER THIRTY-SIX

Unfortunately, it seemed even Armageddon was not enough.

With one of the guns already ripped free and hurled off the Chrome Castle and another effectively neutralized by Timeflash and Larry, who were between it and Tiamat, the dragon goddess had begun to recover.

Kylara attacked with everything she had but Tiamat was able to counteract or neutralize her powers. Her defense wasn't quite as powerful as before but better than she had hoped. She dodged a strike from the dragon mage's claws and it was evident that the scales she had ripped free were almost regrown. Too easily, she redirected a blast of lightning and used the moment to heal the bruises from the bullets.

In the next moment, the goddess surged forward, drove into her, and hurled her back.

Without hesitation, she transformed to her pixie form but her enemy remained close like a cat chasing a butterfly. She couldn't quite catch her but she stayed so close that she could not risk taking her dragon form without being pummeled.

More gunshots rang out, but Tiamat blocked them. Kylara used the moment to take her dragon form and attack but the black dragon caught her with shadow and flipped her into the line of fire. She felt pain and was pushed into the larger dragon, who ripped at her underside with savage strikes of her claws.

"It's over. You cannot overpower me, not without your *friends*." Tiamat sneered the last word as if nothing was more laughable than the idea of having people you cared about in your life. The worst thing was that she was right.

Without a doubt, she could not win this alone.

She had never been able to succeed at anything alone and had always relied on others, be it her mom, her friends, her mentors, or a gaggle of pixies. While she knew she was not strong enough to defeat Tiamat alone, she also realized that she did not want to be. She was not the Sum of All Dragons, she knew that and could not rival her enemy in the skills that she controlled because Tiamat was a dragon while she was something more.

When the Mother of All Dragons launched herself into yet another devastating series of attacks, Kylara stopped pretending she could win this fight alone.

She opened a portal directly in front of her adversary and sent her into the lowest level of the basement. The briefest moment of silence followed, in which she wondered if her aim had been as good as she had hoped. There was little time to worry, however, as the entire Chrome Castle shook as if a bomb had detonated in its basement and she knew that Tiamat had not been bound by the magic-dampening trap she had hoped to use against her.

Still, whether it worked or not wasn't her primary purpose. She honestly did not think she could beat the enemy by teleporting her away. If it hadn't worked on Bull, it was even more unlikely to work on Tiamat. All she'd wanted was time.

Kylara vaulted skyward, pumped her wings twice, and changed into her pixie form. Wings in the subtly beautiful patterns of a desert moth propelled her upward past the shining windows and chrome framing of the skyscraper the Steel Dragon had built and was now trapped at the top of.

She landed on the drawbridge that jutted out from the stylized castle atop the skyscraper and gave it its namesake. Kristen stared out across Detroit, her eyes unseeing and frozen in black stone. Below, the small group of friends knelt no longer. It seemed Tiamat traveling through the pixie realm—even for a second—had been enough to disrupt her aura power. They shook themselves from their stupor and tried to formulate some semblance of a plan to resist the dragon who had turned their emotions against them. She hoped fervently that she was about to give them a symbol that might help them to do exactly that.

The young dragon mage changed to her dragon form and exhaled a cloud of mist on the Steel Dragon. Despite the wind, the vapor did not blow away. Instead, it rose to enshroud Kristen, sank into the stone that trapped her, and began the slow work to liberate her.

The drawbridge shook and Kylara knew Tiamat had emerged from the basement. She could hear her screaming threats as she rose to crush her enemy. Worse, she could feel her coming and sense her power. She did not prepare for battle, though, because she could not win this by herself. Instead, she tried to completely surround the leader of dragons with the mist that would free her.

The process took far too long.

The goddess rose above her. Her wings were larger than they had been, now augmented with shadow, and her claws each glistened with a different dragon power.

"A very clever trick, girl," she growled. "One I should have thought of. I never had the ability to go into that realm, you know. It is not the power of a dragon and I hate that place!

"However, as seems to be your standard, you completely failed to use it to its fullest potential. Like the Lumos boy you have feelings for, I will show you your mistakes over the next thousand years. There are realms worse than the one in which I was trapped. There are realms where you will pray for your death or will dream of something as comforting as eternal darkness. You will come to wish that I had simply trapped you in stone forever."

"I doubt that." Another dragon rose behind Tiamat. He was rotund with drooping mustaches, even in his dragon form. It was Lord Orenclaw, one of the Dragon Council. "Your use of the aura powers goes against Dragon Council by-laws."

"I'm afraid I must agree with Lord Orenclaw for once," a serpentine green dragon said. Lady Jade! The attempt to free the Dragon Council had worked. "You're completely out of order."

The two dragons attacked Tiamat. She roared and deflected their strikes easily enough, although the task became more difficult when the other members of the Council joined the attack.

"You are a usurper!" Orenclaw roared as he battered and slashed with heavy strikes.

"An anachronism of the past with no place in the present!" Lady Jade's attacks were not as strong as Orenclaw's but for every one he landed, she landed five.

"Followers, to me!" Tiamat roared, the sound augmented by magic and supernaturally loud.

Her Followers obeyed, although they didn't decimate the Council as their mistress wished them to do. Kylara's friends were free to act now. Amy—although injured—was back in the fight, as were Karl, Jasmine, Larry, Timeflash, Tanya, and Galen. What had looked like a defeated force now rallied to fight the dragons with reckless abandon, although not all of them.

The Steel Guard still fought for Tiamat, perhaps because they had been under her control for so long.

Nevertheless, hope surged again until lightning sizzled from above and struck the base of the platform that kept Kristen Hall —still frozen in stone—elevated above Detroit.

The wood splintered and the platform fell.

Gravity clutched the Steel Dragon and she dropped.

Kylara had come so far and had been so close. She didn't know what to do but fall with her.

They plummeted together as the battle raged above. She could not believe she had failed, that she had been so close and it had been for nothing. Kristen would shatter to rock shards in moments.

She frowned when she saw a fleck of stone flake away from the Steel Dragon to reveal a steel scale beneath. Another followed, and another. Soon, they fell through a rain of black flecks of stone until the trapped dragon was free and soared aloft through the detritus of her stony prison.

Effortlessly, she spread her wings and caught the air and together, Kylara and Kristen landed on the grounds of the Chrome Castle.

"Are you all right?" the dragon mage asked tentatively.

"What I am is completely done with this bitch."

Her face set in a cold rage, Kristen Hall joined the battle.

CHAPTER THIRTY-SEVEN

Tiamat was the Mother of All Dragons. She always had been and always would be. It seemed that in the ages during which she was kept from this world, many dragons—even some of her most devoted Followers—forgot what that meant and what kind of power she commanded. Some of them had expressed astonishment that Kristen Hall had the ability to turn her skin to steel.

This came as no surprise to her, of course. Steel had not existed in the quantity in which it existed today, but there had always been dragons who could mimic the materials around them. Being able to turn to steel was no different than having granite skin or diamond scales.

So, when Kristen fell from the roof and was released from the stone prison she had trapped her in, she felt it. Not only that, but she felt the girl's rage at being put in timeout and felt when it escalated into wrath.

She also knew that all children rebelled against their parents.

So, while the Steel Dragon tried to rise through the air to attack, Tiamat used the opportunity to make it clear that she was not special.

"End her," the goddess ordered and her Followers and the Steel Guards still at her beck and call obeyed.

A Stormwing summoned a storm and struck Kristen with electricity to hurl her from the sky as a twitching mess of misfiring nerves. The black dragon had augmented both the storm and the lightning blast, of course, but neither her quarry nor anyone else on the battlefield needed to know this. Her power could overwhelm any one of them. What they all needed to see was that those who followed her would be victorious.

To this end, she deliberately did not directly engage these usurpers to her power and the Dragon Council that had been warden to her throne while she had been exiled. Her attacks were not visible, hidden instead in those of her minions.

When one of her Followers attacked Heartsbane, she augmented their auras so the dragon could not overwhelm their emotions.

When the boy with shadow powers bound one of her dragons, she used a beam of light to break the bindings.

If plants bound one of her Followers, she used her powers to control the fire of another dragon and burn the plants away.

When one of the mages tried to crush a dragon with a boulder, she simply made the boulder slip free of their telekinetic touches.

She achieved all this effortlessly while she surveyed the battle from above and let herself heal. While she could join the fray, she found it unseemly to have missing scales and especially so when she could help from the sidelines and let her children teach the others a lesson in power—disobey Mother and suffer.

Controlled by the Steel Dragon's foolish brother, the Chrome Castle still attempted to aid the invaders and fired rounds unceasingly into the battle, though Tiamat had wrapped herself in cloud and shadow. The electric eyes of the human building would not find her. Still, she would like to see that building crumble. She had yet to find the proper use for humans in the family whose foundation she would build this day. Perhaps this was their purpose. Their sacrifice would end this battle and show the world in the days to come where humans would fit.

The Mother of All Dragons laughed into the clouds and watched the chaos unfold below while she bided her time. She would strike, oh yes, but only when she knew she could finally rip away what vestiges of hope these usurpers still possessed.

"Forward, dammit! Forward!" Drew shouted in an attempt to get Larry's recruits to fall in and keep up. It was hard to stick together given that the sky itself no longer made sense.

Lightning cracked from dragon to dragon. Fire erupted in balls, lances of flame, and sometimes far more fearsome shapes. In places, the ground was frozen, or ripped away, or blackened, or had become an impassable jungle.

Through it all, he pushed forward. If they could reach the Chrome Castle, they could use it far better than Tiamat's troops could. The stash of dragon bullets was there. If they could reach them, this battle would be over.

"We make for the basement!" Drew shouted to his team.

They were close to the building now, so close that they could make out the faces of the Steel Guards who still served Tiamat. Even with victory dependent on their actions, he did not want to kill these people. They didn't deserve it and if history had taught him anything, it was that they would need their allies more than ever when this was over.

"Recruits, do you know anything about hand-to-hand combat?" he bellowed.

"Yessir!" the closest one shouted.

"All right, then. Let's give 'em hell!"

He drove into the line of soldiers and used the butt of his gun rather than its barrel. The guard had fired at him but some of

Larry's mages were at the rear of the team and provided magical shielding. He knew from experience that fighting against people who were impervious to bullets was terrifying, no matter how many times you'd been trained to do it.

In shock and fear at the inefficacy of his attack, the Steel Guardsman cried out and crumbled when Drew swung the butt of his weapon into the side of his head.

A glance down the line told him that not all the confrontations had gone as well. Two recruits had fallen, bleeding out from bullets that got through the magical barriers. Hernandez had felled her target but Keith was still in combat with his.

They did not have time for this and needed the dragon bullets to turn the tide. The friendly dragons were outnumbered by Tiamat's forces. His only recourse was to eliminate them but to do so, he had to get through these human soldiers. The dragons with him could do it with a single breath of fire, something he did not want to allow.

Instead, he clenched his teeth and thwacked another head with the butt of his gun.

"It's always nice to have an intern come back!" Kristen shouted as she tangled with a dragon in iron skin who looked very much like her.

If this were a formal setting, Kylara would have let the Steel Dragon defeat this mind-controlled ally fairly but there was nothing formal about what was happening. She summoned a bolt of lightning—she had noticed that it had hurt one metal-clad dragon and hoped it would hurt this one—and struck their adversary with it.

Thankfully, her hope was rewarded. The iron dragon screamed and fell, twitching like Kristen had moments before when she had been struck in a similarly dishonorable way.

"Kristen, we need to talk!"

"If you want to get hired, now is not exactly the time to talk benefits."

"I think I know how to defeat Tiamat!"

The Steel Dragon pulled back from the dragon she had been about to engage. "Tell me everything you know."

"There's a pond in the pixie realm. At the bottom is a room that contains a chest that sits inside a circle inscribed with magic. That's where she was trapped and where we think we can trap her again."

"That's a damn good plan," Kristen replied and spun to deflect some kind of mucous from another dragon. Kylara launched fire at the sticky liquid and burned it away.

"The only problem is—"

"Let me guess. Only you can go there?"

"Or a pixie."

"We're a little short of pixies right now. I love the little guys but they're not great in a fight. Are you sure you can get her there?"

"I've used the portals on her before but she's grown wise to them. I don't think she'd fall for it unless she didn't have a choice."

"Got it," Kristen said. "Kylara, you won't like this, but I need you to hold back."

"What?"

"We'll attack Tiamat and hit her hard. I can't have you in that fight."

"But—"

"Your role is yet to come. I need you ready so you can open a portal and put her in this box. Do you think you can do that?"

"I can fight."

"You will! But right now, I need you to be ready."

"Fine," she said, although she couldn't help but give Kristen a little healing light energy.

"I can't say what the right moment will look like. You need to be ready, all right? Can you hide?"

She took her pixie form and was now merely a speck in this combat of giants.

"Be ready," the Steel Dragon said. "Now, it's time to show this wannabe mother what my real mom taught me."

"What's that?"

"That bullies never win."

Galen only had eyes for Tiamat. She was at the core of all these troubles. This fight would not be over until she was defeated.

Yet she hid in the clouds right now and let both sides decimate each other while she gathered her strength.

He had no intention to allow her to keep doing that.

While he could not control the clouds like almost everyone else in his family, it did not mean that Galen Stormwing was afraid of a little rain.

Before he could consider the foolishness of his decision, he drew a deep breath, tried to fill himself with energy, and changed to his dragon form. He vaulted skyward and ascended quickly. His powers would run out and he did not have long to accomplish his plan. He could feel them slipping away already but he did not need much time. All he needed to do was show Kylara where Tiamat was and she would defeat the goddess. He was certain of this.

Moments later, he flew into the clouds. He could no longer see Tiamat but he knew where she was as he could sense her in the currents of air. She was there, watching from her perch above it all. Such a maneuver would have made his father proud but it only disgusted the young dragon.

He flew through the clouds and felt his powers leech out of

him, but before he could find his quarry, he found something even worse.

His cousin was in the storm, controlling it.

"So, the rumors are true!" Eustace shouted. "The prodigal son returns." Lightning cracked, and Galen barely had the where-withal to dodge. It was a good thing his father had forced himself to defend himself against his family's power so many times. That was a thought he never thought he would have.

"You're not my family. You never treated me like one of you." He brought his talons out and barreled into his cousin's chest. Storm dragons couldn't fight very well when controlling a storm. It was something he had learned to take advantage of and something even his father had hated to admit was true.

Eustace roared and thunder echoed his pain as Galen forced him from his place in the clouds.

A great gust of wind struck them. His cousin seemed to have expected it and caught it with his wings, but he had not. It thrust him off and he tumbled like a kite caught in a tornado.

Lightning struck and he dodged. It wasn't easy to dodge it, but no one knew how to do it better than he did.

"I had heard you were a monster, Galen, but it appears you are nothing more than the same pathetic whelp you always were."

"At least I learned a thing or two when I was a monster." He righted himself and soared toward his cousin.

Eustace used wind and rain to blind him. No longer able to see, he was not able to dodge the lightning that struck him.

He screamed in pain but didn't slow. For his opponent to control multiple aspects of the storm, he had to be stationary. This was knowledge he'd learned the hard way and used to good effect more than once.

Although still blinded, he made impact with sufficient force to roll the other dragon and began to claw and bite him as they fell together.

His cousin tried to escape but he ripped his wings to prevent his flight.

As they plummeted, the clouds fell with them as if they did not want to abandon their master.

Above them, Tiamat was now exposed.

Galen grinned, his mission completed, and slammed into the ground with Eustace. His last thought before he lost consciousness was how relieved he was to have shifted into his human form.

Even though his body was broken, he had tried his best to use what little power he had to help this fight.

"There she is!" Amy shouted. In normal circumstances, she would have simply launched herself at the self-proclaimed dragon goddess. Nothing about this situation was even remotely normal, however. She needed to protect her friends and—much as she hated to admit it—Tiamat had already proven that she could overpower her. It was a lesson she wasn't likely to forget as her head still hurt from the overexertion of her power and from being hurled into a wall.

When Kristen Hall swooped in, her steel scales glittering, the mage did not mind the idea of teamwork quite so much.

"Get into the building!" Kristen ordered Drew and his team. "Amy and I will take care of the mother."

"You mean your mama," Drew shouted as he saluted.

Amy lifted herself off the ground—even this made her head twinge with pain—and deposited herself on the Steel Dragon's back as her friend and boss flew past.

"Where's Kylara?" she shouted over the rush of the wind.

"Waiting for the right moment."

"That makes sense, but do you honestly think we can take Tiamat on?"

"Not like that you can't!" Sam said and swooped in beside them. As he gained altitude with the two of them, he stretched the tip of his tail to touch Amy and she felt her pain fade as his magic flowed into her. Much of her pain had stemmed from her depleted energy but she was now recharged.

"Oh, this will be fun!" she said, but before they could drive into their enemy, her legion of cultists intercepted them.

"We need to get her to the ground!" Kristen shouted.

"I'll put that on my to-do list!" Amy replied as she reached out with her magic, caught hold of a dragon covered in thorns, and threw him into one of his allies who was covered in some kind of slime.

The two unusual combatants collided and, unable to extricate themselves from each other, fell out of the battle.

The mage watched them fall and saw Drew, the other members of SWAT, and Larry's recruits gain entrance to Chrome Castle.

"Drew's almost reached the depot," she told Kristen, who had launched a stream of steel spikes at a dragon who tried to block them with ice.

"When he gets out, we need to be above these dragons so they can eliminate them."

Suddenly, the prospect of them getting out seemed much less likely.

A massive ball of flame bloomed about a third of the way up the building and shattered the glass in the floors above and below it. Worse, though, was the groan of metal as the building began to lean to one side.

Brian barely had an opportunity to blast Tiamat with his gun emplacements before she had ordered her minions to break his toys. Still, there were other ways to fight besides the big guns.

The Chrome Castle had any number of different weapons that he had installed. The trick would be to reconfigure the defenses. He did not dare to activate these until he knew they would not accidentally mow his team down.

Before he could make any progress on this particular nugget of code, someone pounded on the door.

"Yeah, give me a minute!" Brian replied—there was no point in pretending that the room was empty. "I had a burrito for lunch and black beans go straight through me."

"The mother will forgive you if you open this door."

"Yeah, I kind of doubt that."

No reply came, only the sound of a tool working. At first, he thought they were trying to cut through the door but then realized that whatever they were doing, it was outside.

The silence stretched until he couldn't take it any longer. He went to the entrance, tried to look past Joe's dead body—he still felt shame and disgust at himself for having killed the man—and opened the door.

There was no one there.

His gaze settled on the biggest bomb he had ever seen and he realized it was about to explode.

Brian didn't even have time to scream. Instead, he ran into his control room, kicked open a panel he had built but had hoped to never use, and jumped.

He slid down his escape hatch lined with spring-loaded blades that would let someone slide down but would cut the fingers of anyone who wished to climb up. Seconds later, the bomb above him exploded and the building began to lean.

The Chrome Castle was falling.

Drew and his team had reached the lobby of the massive structure when it became quite clear that their plan to get the dragon bullets was doomed.

It wasn't the explosion above that signaled this, nor was it the rain of glass and shrapnel that fell outside. It was the way one of the steel girders in the lobby seemed to crimp as the ceiling started to lean.

One beam might not have been enough to doom the entire tower, but the Chrome Castle was not exactly in its virgin condition. Other beams were already bent or destroyed—likely from when Tiamat had raced out of the building in such a rage. They had barely supported the structure above them. The explosion had shifted the stresses on the floors below even further and the steel beams all around them carried the brunt of it.

Another crimped, and another until finally, one broke.

"Out! Everyone out!" Drew hollered.

"But the bullets!" Hernandez shouted in response.

"Are worthless without people to fire them. Now get the hell out—that's an order!"

They left the lobby through the hole they had entered through, and not a moment too soon. The entire skyscraper tipped away from them. Gravity kicked in and it fell increasingly faster until the castle at its top struck the ground with such force that it made the explosion that had started its descent seem paltry by comparison.

He and his team had escaped but they had still failed.

Above them, Kristen and Amy tried to get through the cultists to reach their mistress.

Kylara's friends—kids—did their best to grant the two passage, but they wouldn't last long.

The Steel Dragon had never thought that watching the Chrome Castle tumble from the sky would come as an afterthought to her, but that was all the brain space she was currently able to afford.

She was far more concerned about the people below, but there was little she could do for them. Dragons attacked her from all sides in an attempt to stop her from reaching their mistress.

"You're a horde of mama's boys!" Amy shouted as she threw back those she could.

Kristen struck at others and attacked with claws and teeth made of strong steel. Dragon scale was tough but she was tougher. Those who came too close to her were forced to back away and lick their wounds. Unfortunately, for dragons, that did not take more than a moment.

The Dragon Council fought bravely, united as they had never been in debate, but there were too many cultists and too many members of the Steel Guard under Tiamat's control. She had to break through so she could give Kylara the opportunity she had promised, but how could she? They were outnumbered.

The thought almost brought despair but she fought it back.

Suddenly, a portal blazed to life in the middle of the battle. One of the enemy combatants flew through it but somehow, it didn't take them anywhere. Instead, dragons streamed from the gate.

They attacked as soon as they came through, sprayed fire at the cultists, and lashed out with everything they had. The Followers reacted to dodge these new arrivals' strikes and blasts of flame.

Something about the way these dragons fought wasn't quite right, Kristen thought. Their strikes didn't seem to do any damage. And while it was typical for dragon flame to bounce off dragon scale, their blasts of fire seemed particularly ineffective.

If the enemy had noticed the ineptitude of this new force, they didn't show it. They retaliated and cursed when their claws missed or their powers failed to kill their enemy and only served to drive them back.

Kristen forgot about all of it as she pounded into her foe.

She had longed to feel her claws bite through the goddess' flesh but she was not given the taste of this victory. The diamond scales of the Mother of All Dragons rebuffed her steel claws.

"Foolish child! Even if steel could hurt my diamond, I would simply take your form." Tiamat sprayed acid she was all but certain would melt steel, but it thankfully never had the chance to.

Amy deflected it and returned it to its source.

The black dragon roared and dove into a powerful assault. This was something Kristen could do. She answered the attack with a vicious strike. The two battled in the night sky and flames and lightning gave those below flashes of action.

Tiamat captured her opponent's neck in her jaws.

The Steel Dragon sliced at the nape of the black dragon's neck with her ax-blade tail.

Scales and blood fell.

The mage on Kristen's back fought with unbridled ferocity, more insane than either of the dragons simply because she battled with what could be called immortals while she was most decidedly not one.

But Tiamat quickly tired of these unrewarding contests between their claws. She exhaled a cloud of mist and the Steel Dragon felt herself begin to turn to stone.

"Fat chance!" Amy shouted and summoned a wind that was more than wind to blow the petrifying mist away.

Tiamat roared in frustration and looked as if she was about to do something even more devastating when a beam of light blinded her.

She screamed as a bullet hole bloomed in her chest.

Butters had been afraid many times. It came with being a member of SWAT and seemed to come doubly with being part of the Steel Guard. He felt no shame at this. Fear was something to be overcome, not avoided.

Of course, this philosophy was sorely tested when his place atop a skyscraper adjacent to the battle was exposed and a dragon came to incinerate him and Beanpole.

"Can't we take the elevator?" Butters pleaded to his partner and best friend.

"Not a chance."

"But my ankle—"

"Was healed."

It still hurt but Butters clenched his teeth and followed his friend down flight after flight of stairs. They felt a blast of heat as the dragon who had targeted them incinerated the top floors of the building. He was glad that the entire structure had already been evacuated.

They reached the ground floor before the elevator did and stepped out of the stairs while the elevator shattered as it finished its descent.

"Do you still want to take the elevator?" Beanpole asked.

"I owe you a beer for that one."

They left the skyscraper and joined the chaos of the battle. Beanpole had already chosen another location for them if the first one was compromised. It was on the other side of the battle, not in a building but at the top of a hill on the grounds of the Chrome Castle. A grove of trees there had been planted at the sniper's insistence at no small expense. The others had thought he had simply developed a fondness for pine, but he had other motives. He had seen the opportunity to make the perfect sniper's nest.

They reached it after what felt like forever. He did not know how many people died while he and Beanpole snuck across the ground, avoiding combat like mice avoided catfights. He knew he would learn the number and the names of those who had died later and that it would haunt him. The knowledge urged him to move faster, despite the lingering pain in his ankle.

They reached the foot of the hill and hurried to its crest, where Butters stretched on a bed of pine needles and tried to slow his breathing so he could take a shot.

He checked his ammunition.

"How many left?" Beanpole asked.

The marksman swallowed hard. "One."

His teammate nodded as if this was not terribly surprising. "You'd better make it count, then."

"I haven't shot a goddess yet."

Perversely, it seemed like that opportunity might still be denied them when the entire damn Chrome Castle tumbled.

Beanpole had chosen this position because of its distance from where they expected the combat to be. He had not expected the Chrome Castle to almost crush them.

Butters managed to both stay still and keep his bowels from letting loose. He would be proud of that later, although he wouldn't tell anyone but Beanpole of this tiny, personal victory.

The enormous building collapsed not fifty feet from where they stood. He felt the shockwave of the blast on his belly and the wind on his face. The pine trees were battered with broken glass and shrapnel but they protected the sniper hidden within.

During it all, he did not let his eyes drift from the battle taking place in the sky above.

He watched as Kristen struggled to break through the cultists and was amazed when a force of unknown dragons appeared to join the battle. From his vantage point, however, it soon became obvious that they weren't real dragons but illusions of them.

"Kylara found a way to fight without fighting," He chuckled and his partner grinned.

The illusion wouldn't last long, he was sure of that, but dragons were fickle creatures despite all their power. They

KEVIN MCLAUGHLIN & MICHAEL ANDERLE

stopped attacking the Steel Dragon to try to protect themselves from this new group of foes, oblivious to the fact that none of the illusory dragons could hurt them.

Butters kept his eyes on the battle between Kristen and Tiamat. It seemed like this was his chance. He slowed his breathing and waited for the right moment.

His frustration grew when it did not come.

The goddess was too good a fighter. She kept her adversary engaged until she seemed to tire of it.

When he saw a dark cloud stream from her, his heartbeat seemed to stop. He knew what it meant and had seen Kylara use it to free the members of the Dragon Council. Kristen would be turned to stone. She would plummet to the earth and shatter unless Amy could somehow save her, which seemed unlikely given that Tiamat had already overpowered her.

In the next moment, the Lumos boy broke out of the faux battle below. A light as bright as the sun glowed in his throat and he opened his mouth and blasted it at Tiamat.

It was now or never.

Butters took his shot.

The dragon mage had known that the illusions would do little more than buy everyone time. She had hoped to give the Steel Dragon a chance to defeat Tiamat, but it was already clear that would not happen.

The Mother of All Dragons was too strong and her powers too varied. Kristen could not defeat her. Only Kylara could.

So, when Tiamat was blinded and then shot, she did not hesitate.

She had been above the two combatants, waiting for her moment to strike in pixie form. She saw it now and took her chance.

In an instant, she transformed into her dragon form as she tucked her wings and streaked toward the black dragon.

Moments before impact, she activated her momentum power. That kept her enemy's attention on her rather than the portal she had opened behind her.

Kylara slammed into Tiamat and her momentum forced them through the portal into the pixie realm and the pool where the goddess had been trapped before.

They plunged in and fought tooth and claw even as the surface of the pool calmed and became as placid as it ever had.

CHAPTER THIRTY-EIGHT

Their momentum thrust them deep into the water.

Sunlight streamed through the calm surface of the pond and highlighted the invisible battle beneath the surface in streams of gold.

Despite her adversary being injured, she still wielded her powers with a level of precision and control that Kylara simply lacked.

Tiamat super-heated the water to scald her, so she used ice breath to cool it. When she opened her mouth to breathe the ice, her foe forced water down her throat. In search of some advantage, she tried to make her neck turn to gills as she had seen water dragons do but something blocked her. She reached inward and found the appropriate type of magic but when she summoned it and it reached her neck, it would not manifest in the pond.

Fortunately, the goddess' power to control the water also seemed to have been nullified.

"Clever," Tiamat said. She had gills—she was a water dragon, after all—and her voice carried through the water.

When she struck again, she charged her body with electricity that crackled across her skin and coalesced at the tips of her claws. It lanced across the pond but before it could reach its target it dissipated into nothing but the jolt of a static shock.

"What is this?" Tiamat raged. She called on muck from the side of the pond to hurl it into the dragon mage but it dissipated into nothing but silt. "How are you blocking me? This is not one of my powers you wield!" she roared.

Kylara did not understand what was happening, only that she had to breathe. She swam toward the top of the pond but before she could reach it, the black dragon grasped the tip of her tail and hauled her deeper beneath the glassy surface of the water.

"There is no escape. Not from the Mother of All Dragons."

She thrashed and fought to break free of the vice-like hold. Next, she made her claws drip with acid but it was washed away by the pond, then made them heat. By the time they touched her adversary they were cool. She had to fight but more importantly, she had to breathe. If she could only…get…free!

On instinct, she changed to her human form. No longer having a tail, she slipped through Tiamat's grasp. She kicked to the surface and tried to use her dragon strength to power her legs, although even that ability did not seem to work. Her dragon strength remained in the core of her body but by the time the energy reached her legs, it was gone, pulled out of her by the water.

Her lungs burned and her pace slowed, and she could fight no longer. She had to draw a breath.

The goddess caught her in a claw and pulled her even deeper beneath the surface. "Cunning. Something about this place blocks dragon magic. That won't save you, though. I don't know what you think to accomplish, child, but even without my powers, I can still end you." She brought the girl to her open jaws.

Kylara tried to break free. She tried to batter the huge claws with her fists. Nothing worked. Every time she struggled, her enemy merely squeezed tighter.

The pressure grew until the dragon mage thought her ribs would crush and pierce her lungs. She feared her heart would stop. Even though she knew it wouldn't work, she reached for her magic. She had to get free and one of her powers had to help her.

In her last moment of desperation, she found her pixie power and shrank. But Tiamat was ready for this change. She tightened her hand to snuff her life out and suffocate her under the surface.

The girl had not suffocated, however. When she became a pixie, she had created a bubble of air around her head like an astronaut from an old science fiction movie.

She breathed deeply and regained her strength. When the black dragon tried to squash her, she simply turned to a ribbon of sparks and escaped her clutches.

Her dragon powers were not working but her pixie ones certainly were.

Encouraged, she darted around her foe to leave bubbles and sparks behind her that the Mother of All Dragons swiped at but missed every time.

"What is this? How do you still have your dragon powers?"

"These aren't my dragon powers!" She giggled—the behavior of the pixies was infectious in this form—and launched sparks into the dragon's eyes.

The goddess roared and thrashed and the movements drew her deeper into the water.

While the pond had drained Kylara's dragon powers, they did nothing to her pixie ones. She found she could use the water to drag the dragon deeper, that she could call on the plants' roots on the walls of the pond to grasp her, that she could keep her disoriented with sparks and flashes of power.

"I am the Mother of All Dragons! You cannot defeat me!" Tiamat roared and her breath came out as a maelstrom of different elements. Fire, ice, electricity, acid, illusions of monsters, and a hundred other abilities all washed over her diminutive opponent.

Kylara created a shield of magic—exactly like her aunt could, and Jasmine—to protect herself. Human magic worked there as well, it seemed.

"You may be the Mother of All Dragons," she said from inside her cozy little bubble. "And when it comes to dragon powers, you have more than me. But I'm not only a dragon. I'm a mage and a pixie too. I'm the Sum of All Magic."

"You are nothing!" Tiamat's breath having failed, she struck out with vicious swipes of her claws.

The dragon mage retreated and buzzed back with wings that let her move through the water as easily as they did through the air. She overcompensated and burst from the surface of the pond.

Through the glassy surface, she saw Tiamat swimming toward her with anger in her eyes.

No longer trapped in the pond's draining energy, Kylara felt her full slew of powers return. She truly was the Sum of All Magic now. Her pixie powers, her mage powers, and her dragon powers all returned to full strength.

She grinned and plunged into the pond.

Before the goddess could attack, she struck with everything she had. She used telekinesis to push her foe deeper, pixie sparks to disorient her, and her dragon powers to weaken her.

The pond no longer seemed intent on taking her abilities. It appeared to understand that she was a pixie—one of the curators of this realm—and not its prisoner. She was able to use fire to burn Tiamat's scales, acid to corrode them, and ice to freeze and crack them.

They plunged deeper into the pool and left shards of scales floating all around them, a rainbow of colors that were no longer hidden by the darkness that must have been Tiamat's.

"You have proven yourself! Join me as equals. We shall both rule."

"Nah," Kylara replied and plunged the tip of her diamond-tipped tail into her enemy's chest.

The tip found the dragon's heart. The dragon mage felt her pain even through the protection of the amulet. Blood clouded the water and in a moment, Tiamat's scaleless body began to shrink. Where there had once been a dragon, Kishar's body now drifted toward the bottom of the pond.

But the Mother of All Dragons was not defeated.

The form of a dragon bubbled from the woman's mouth. It was almost invisible, more of a distortion in the water than anything else. If the dragon goddess had decided to run, she might have been able to, but her pride would not allow her to withdraw.

"You are more formidable than I thought," Tiamat said as she neared the bottom of the pool where the square of timbers framed the entrance to the chamber. "But you still lack control to use the most important of all dragon powers."

Kylara felt her amulet grow hot as her adversary tried to bend her to her will.

"You are a fool, Kylara Diamantine, she who could have been the Sum of All Dragons. I took your body once and I can do it again."

The ancient dragon's spirit swam toward her. Kylara had taken her human form and held her arms up to protect herself in what might have been a futile gesture if she were anyone else.

Her foe was rebuffed. She could not break through her diamond skin, nor could she puncture the sphere of telekinetic shielding around her. The crackle of pixie sparks distorted her vision and she could not break through the protective aura of the pendant the girl's grandfather had made for her mother so long before.

Tiamat screamed in frustration but the timbre shifted to terror when her spirit was wrapped in a cage of light and dark. She snapped at her bars, broke some, and bent others.

Kylara reinforced her cage, not with more dragon powers but with bars of pure magic. The prisoner crashed and thrashed against them, but—for the moment—the cage held.

The girl took hold of it and swam toward the bottom of the pool.

She reached the square frame and was not surprised to discover that the cage she had made fit the hole perfectly.

Once it was locked into place, she opened the bottom. Desperate to escape, the goddess fled into the chamber.

Kylara dropped in after her, relieved to discover there was air down here.

"You won't put me back!" the ancient dragon screamed from all around her. Her spirit had taken the form of a hurricane that spun around the edges of the space. Now and then, snatches of her features could be seen—the line of her jaw, the curve of her hip, or a flick of her tail.

"No, I won't," the dragon mage agreed. "You'll go willingly."

Sure that this was the only way, she summoned her aura. She had never tried to use it while she wore the turquoise-and-silver pendant. For her whole life, she had always been content to hide behind the powers imbued in the amulet, but was that what her grandfather would have wanted? To make something for his family to hide in?

That had not been what Hester Diamantine wanted for her.

Nor, for that matter, had it been what Amythist Skyjewel wanted for her.

Her friends did not want it for her either, and it wasn't what Kristen or Amy desired.

All of them had wanted her to see that she was strong enough —no matter what she was. They had all wanted her to fight for herself and others.

In that moment, she made the choice to do so.

Her aura was powered not only by dragon magic, but by pixie magic, mage magic, by the pendant itself, and by the memories of everyone she loved. With calm determination, she used it to not make Tiamat fear her but for the ancient dragon to see what she was.

She was Kylara Diamantine. Like everyone else in the world, she was her own person. While she could not win fights by herself any more than anyone else could, she could ask for help. She could use what people had taught her and could stand up to those who would turn her against those she loved.

Tiamat's spirit screamed as if she had slapped her. In her desperation to flee, part of her form passed over the circle in the middle of the room. In an instant, the geometric shapes inscribed on the floor began to pulse and shift.

They grew more and more complex like the infinite tessellations of fractals. This churn of geometric shapes seemed to draw the goddess into the center of the room in the same way that knitting needles might draw a thread.

The patterns shifted increasingly faster and more complex as more of the dragon was forced into the center of the room. The patterns extended onto the chest and a moment later, the Mother of All Dragons began to be sucked into it. Her airy form seemed to grow denser and coalesced into some kind of slime that filled her prison.

Kylara raced forward, entered the circle of geometric shapes, and stepped across the swirling patterns until she stood in front of the chest.

Tiamat tried to strike her with insubstantial claws as she grasped the lid. She pulled it closed while her captive struggled against her.

But she fought for everything while the black dragon fought for only herself.

In the end, it was not a contest at all.

With a grunt of satisfaction, she slammed the lid shut.

Tiamat, goddess and Mother of All Dragons, had been put to rest again.

CHAPTER THIRTY-NINE

Kylara half-swam, half-floated to the surface.

She crawled through the mud and flopped onto the mossy shore. After a moment, she pushed up to look at the pond, expecting to see Tiamat's shape rise from it again, but there was nothing. The surface was as calm as it had ever been. A leaf floated down and landed on the water and no ripple spread out from it. For once, the odd nature of this pool calmed her.

Satisfied, she drew a deep breath. She was tired, bruised, and pushed far beyond her capabilities. Her brain reminded her that she needed rest, food, and a shower, but before she could even think about getting any of those things, a portal snapped open.

In that moment, she wanted to cry. She was tired and simply could no longer fight.

But she had to, her mind insisted.

The dragon mage managed to stand and wondered which one of Tiamat's cultists had discovered how to enter the pixie realm.

Thankfully, it was not an enemy who emerged but Rider.

"Big Pixie? Is that you?" he asked.

"It's me," she said, never having been so relieved to see a twelve-inch-tall human riding an opossum.

"You guys, it's her! She did it!" he shouted and the portal expanded behind him.

Kylara started to cry when Tanya stepped through. She wanted to stand tall when her mom and Kristen Hall appeared but it was Sam who made her want to smile.

"You guys are a little late," she said and sagged into the muddy moss that ringed the pool. "The fight's over. The bitch Kishar is dead and Tiamat's spirit is back in the box. Did Galen—"

"I'm right here," he said. He was his handsome human self again.

"That was a good call, thinking of the chest. It worked like a charm and sucked her spirit back in like she belonged there."

"With luck, she won't get out anytime soon," Lady Amythist said and the wrinkles around her eyes crinkled when she smiled. "And this time, perhaps dragon kind can remember the threat she represents."

"Although we might need someone to check on her now and then," the Steel Dragon said as she stepped forward and shook her hand. "Congratulations on your success. I know words always fall short in moments like these, but congratulations all the same. You know, we would like to have you at the Chrome Castle next summer if you want."

The girl grimaced. "But it fell—"

Kristen waved her complaints away. "There's a reason we keep Timeflash on staff. It might take her a few days but she'll fix it. Copy machine and everything."

"I don't know, Kristen—I mean, Lady Steel. Being an intern again after this sounds—"

The woman laughed and cut her complaint off. "I felt the same way in the early days. There was nothing I liked less than the Paper Dungeon. Atramento had to practically twist my arm to make me file scrolls. But no, Kylara, I'm not offering you a position as an intern. I would love to have you as a fully-fledged member of the Steel Guard. Clearly, your exceptional talents shouldn't be wasted."

"Check the contract first," Hester said as she stepped out from the crowd and wrapped her daughter in a hug. "You might want to make sure there are bonuses for defeating a goddess and all."

Kylara smiled and melted into her mom's hug.

Somehow, being surrounded by all these people she loved who had helped her and who she, in turn, had helped made her cracked ribs not hurt quite so much.

CHAPTER FORTY

A few days later and back on the campus of the Lumos School, Kylara could almost convince herself that everything was normal again.

One would think that mages would be able to rebuild the brick buildings of the school with relative ease compared to conventional human constructive crews, but this was not the case. Most of their time in Professor Sharra's class was either spent arguing the various merits of different protection spells or watching the professor use those very same arguments—albeit more refined—against the other mages to get her way about the school's defenses.

The dragon mage had made the mistake of asking the professor why Timeflash simply could not restore the school buildings and was still paying the price of such a "foolish, dragon-minded attitude." She was currently writing an essay on how mage and dragon magic could and could not interact.

From what she understood, if Timeflash rebuilt it, the magic protections that had been baked into the brick wouldn't be rebuilt and the defenses would suffer. Normally, she might have phoned in an essay like this—that is, a punitive one—but there were relatively few students at the school. They had the campus basically to themselves, which meant Professor Sharra would read every word she wrote and expect mistakes to be corrected.

Worst of all, she couldn't even ask Jasmine for help. The mage had dared to ask Lady Amythist why they had classes at all. She was still helping with "extracurricular materials magic practice" —in other words, stacking bricks.

Although classes had resumed—Lady Amythist said doing otherwise would let Tiamat win—the school had a distinctly different feel to Kylara. The lack of students was part of it, of course, but there was more. It felt smaller, weirdly, despite all her classes being held outdoors during the construction. Perhaps it wasn't that it felt smaller, not exactly, but that it no longer felt so big and intimidating.

She still remembered her arrival—frightened, tired, and alone. Now, the Lumos School made her feel none of those things. This was her home, not least of all because the people she cared about were there.

Professor Sharra accepted her essay and in a rare show of kindness, didn't read it immediately. Instead, she dismissed her for dinner.

Kylara missed the dining hall. It was one of her favorite places but no longer. The roof had been cracked at some point by the cultists and the kitchen flooded.

Still, the staff had been evacuated and had already returned, although they now grilled in the green U of the school.

She waved at Karl and Sam, who were stacking plates high with smoked meats.

"Ribs—seriously, dude? Brisket is way better." Karl sneered.

"Brisket is greasy and over-salted. Ribs are better. Spicy and sweet from the sauce. Only a moron would think brisket is better than ribs." The golden dragon cast a scornful glance at the other boy's plate.

"It's all about the balance, you guys," Kylara said as she piled her plate with a little of everything.

"Says the pixie-mage-dragon," Jasmine called across the U and waved at Karl. She strolled over and went to hug Karl but paused when she saw the plate stacked high with meat, sauce, and beans.

"I was telling Sam how dumb he is for liking ribs more than brisket," Midnight said. "What do you think?"

"I'm a vegetarian," the mage said and caught a floating plate to serve herself a variety of side dishes. "So I think you're both morons."

"How did we ever beat Tiamat?" Kylara asked. "We can't even agree about barbecue."

"Well, yeah, but barbecue's not that important," Sam said.

"Speak for yourself, rib-licker," Karl quipped.

"No, Sam's right. We were able to battle Tiamat because of each other. But we only trust each other because we can be open. That's what I value most about being friends with all of you." Jasmine smiled.

"Wow, Jasmine, that was...a lot from you," Sam said.

"Yeah. I love you, babe, but you're kind of moody," Karl pointed out.

"Yeah, well, it's only because stuck-up Tanya isn't here. If anyone tells her I value her friendship, I will end you."

"There's my girl!" Midnight put an arm around her shoulder. She, in turn, lifted his plate with her magic and kept it from spilling on her.

"Speaking of Tanya, has anyone seen her?" Kylara asked.

"I think so," Sam said slowly. "Out in the woods. With...uh, Galen."

"Oh. Right. They've spent hours there, huh?" Kylara asked. "I guess we should give them their privacy?"

Karl laughed loud and long as he used his shadow tendrils to fill two more plates. "And miss a chance to see Galen try to bust a move? Come on. What could be funnier?"

Everyone laughed and began to stroll in that direction with their meals. It wasn't that Kylara wanted to interrupt but soon, the semester—such as it was—would be over and they would all scatter to their different paths in life. She still didn't know if she would go to Detroit to work with the Steel Guard, but she was certainly considering it. It would have been an easier thing to say yes to had Kristen offered Sam a job there too.

The future—both immediate and distant—seemed to weigh heavily on all their minds as they walked through the woods toward the training grounds.

"You won't believe this, Jasmine, but my dad asked if you would come and visit," Karl said and broke the silence.

"He wants round two?" Jasmine asked.

"His exact words were, 'would it be possible to see the Patel girl in action,' believe it or not."

"Creepy!" she said.

Karl chuckled. "For Sir Midnight, that's good."

"Like father, like son, huh?" Sam asked.

The other boy laughed. "Heh. I guess so. Good one, Lumos."

"Always a pleasure, Midnight."

Kylara enjoyed the feeling in the air—the feel of their auras— while it lasted.

"Do you want to go or what?" Karl asked Jasmine.

"Let's blow this place," the mage said. They had been eating while they walked. Now, everyone exchanged barbecue-slathered hugs and said goodbye. "And tell Tanya she's a snob with no fashion sense but that I love her."

"My pleasure," Kylara responded, knowing that if she told the girl that Jasmine had said something so kind, her roommate would never believe it.

They saw Galen and Tanya lounging against the base of a tree that was blooming despite it being the completely wrong season. What was funny was that she knew her friend thought she was being subtle. It was a laughable notion but made her endearing nonetheless.

"We got you two dinner!" she shouted to them.

"Oh, hey," Galen said and straightened way too quickly. "Thanks...for that."

"Is it dinner already?" Tanya asked and checked her phone. "Oh wow. The time flies—"

"When you're having fun?" Sam asked.

She reddened and Kylara felt a trace of shame in her aura.

"Hey, Tanya. No worries."

"I assure you, I have no idea what you're talking about," the girl said. "But also, we have so much to talk about. Dorm room? Eight this evening?"

"Eight thirty." Galen pretended to cough in his hand to cover the requested change in time.

"Eight thirty is fine," Kylara said.

"Right. Well. See you then. I'm going to go...on a walk," Tanya said, accepted the plate of food, and moved into the woods.

Galen, grinning like a fool, took his plate. "I too...am going on a walk...in the woods."

"Were we ever that awkward?" Sam asked.

"I don't know. I think we're still awkward," Kylara joked.

Sam laughed. "It's weird, I know. I have absolutely no issue with backing you up in a fight. You've saved my life—"

"You saved mine too."

"I know, that's what I'm saying. I've seen you bleed. I've seen you with broken bones, and yet it feels like when we're not in combat, there's a distance between us that isn't there when we're in a fight."

"There doesn't have to be," she said and took his hand.

He grinned that perfect smile of his. "You don't mind your boyfriend being a glorified medic when it comes to battle?"

"You don't mind your girlfriend being a false dragon, a mage, a pixie, and maybe the key to an ancient religion?"

"I think it makes you look cute."

She giggled. "What about all the weirdness that follows me around? My aunt who attacked us with elementals, the necromancer dragon, the world's frumpiest mage, and a goddess? Oh, plus my mom's handshake will break the bones in your hand."

He laughed. "I wouldn't have it any other way."

"What did I do to deserve a boy like you, Sam?" Kylara asked and removed her pendant so she could better feel his emotions pour over her and he could feel hers.

"Keep saving the world, and we'll call it even," Sam said.

They leaned closer and the late afternoon sun painted them with the colors of a spectacular sunset that she might have tweaked to heighten the colors. She felt his feelings for her—love, yes, but also compassion, tenderness, and how she made him feel vulnerable because he didn't want to lose her. It was almost overwhelming to be able to feel so much of someone else's emotions, but she decided she could take it as long as he was around.

The sun set and they kissed while the world faded to black all around them. Not that Kylara minded the dark. Sam was glowing from the kiss, after all.

The End

KEVIN'S AUTHOR NOTES
APRIL 21, 2021

Phew.

As I write this, the world is slowly coming back to some semblance of the old normal. I don't know if any of us will ever be precisely the same as we were before all this crazy stuff started happening in early 2020, but at least it's beginning to fall behind us at long last. We've got a ways to go, of course. But things feel like they're moving in the right direction at long last.

I hope you and yours are all safe and sound during these erratic times. I also hope we can learn to live differently, even better, as a result of this experience. My wife and I just finished watching an Apple TV show featuring David Attenborough as narrator called "The Year Earth Changed". It was a good program if you're into nature shows, and it spoke about how humans drawing back this year impacted the other species on our planet. Unsurprisingly, it was more helpful than not.

But it wasn't just other species that did surprisingly well. In the US, we've just found out that suicide rates in 2020 dropped to historically low levels. Seems like our jobs might be an even bigger source of stress for us than the pandemic was.

Don't worry, I'm not calling for some wild, radical change! But perhaps if we take a little more time to step back and observe the world, enjoy the sunshine and fresh air, and spend more time with the people who matter most to us, we'll find our lives better for it.

Just a thought.

One of the things I've started doing differently is a more regular workout routine. I'm running daily and using my Oculus Quest for extra workouts on top of that. That's a Virtual Reality headset; it's a remarkably great tool for getting in fun but challenging exercise! My current faves are Beat Saber, The Climb 2, and a Tai Chi program that I've used for cool downs. It's good stuff. Hey, I used to be in *amazing* shape back when I was in the infantry, but at forty-eight I'm seriously into 'use it or lose it' territory, so I figured a little investment in exercise was a good way to go!

This book is the end of Kylara's journey — for the moment, anyway. She'll show up in future books as a side character, though, so don't worry!

We're moving on from this book to another sextet called "The DragonClaw Sword". It's going to feature Galen heavily, because we think he's become a fairly interesting character over the past few books, and Michael and I decided it was time to give him his own story.

He'll be joined by Vala, the first ever dwarf mage. Not everyone is thrilled by the idea of a dwarf mage. In fact, some dwarfs will stop at *nothing* to make sure she's also the *last* of her kind.

Galen has plenty of enemies all his own, of course.

Two outcasts who find each other, each trailing their own line of foes. But together, they might just have what it takes to carve out a place for themselves in the world.

You'll be able to read all about it next month in "Clawing For

Survival" — and I think you're going to like these books. The first one is already done, and it's pretty darned good.

That's all from me for today. Thanks so much for reading all of these books! I hope you've enjoyed the voyage.

MICHAEL'S AUTHOR NOTES
APRIL 22, 2021

Thank you for not only reading this story but these author notes as well.

Normally, I riff off my collaborators' author notes, but Kevin got all "get in shape at forty-eight" on me, and I don't have much to admit in that arena.

The only positive news is I was 215.0 this morning when a month and a half ago, it would probably have been 216.2 (those tenths of a pound matter to me now.)

So, on to something I found interesting last night.

Picture this—I'm firing up the TV and choosing Netflix, trying to find something I want to watch. I'm not a big TV watcher, so this is not a common occurrence. I start with a Gabriel "Fluffy" Iglesias special, only to figure out I've seen this already.

So, I look around and find a really long story about He-Man and the Masters of the Universe. Not so much the storyline, but the success and how it became a billion- (that's with a B. Color me surprised) dollar business in just about five years, then plummeted.

I personally love business stories. Don't get me started talking about The Toys that Made Us (awesome) or The Food that Built America. Those food barons were vicious and sadistically creative about bumping off their competition.

Seriously, watch it sometime.

I was never into the He-Man phase. It started when I was a teenager, and frankly, I also hated the name.

"He-Man?" Could you possibly get *less* creative? By watching the show, I found out that not only was it possible, but they accomplished it dozens of times.

They also accomplished earning over a billion dollars, so that tells me how much I need to learn and not to judge names given to young kids' products since I don't know @#%@#.

Some of the art shown was amazing (at least to me), and I wonder if any of those guys are still working? It's something I should track down. For whatever reason, I was drawn to one of the original creators working on the He-Man project, Ted Mayer. He designed some of the vehicles not only for He-Man, but went he on to work on *Teenage Mutant Ninja Turtles* as well.

(Here is his website if you are curious: http://www.ted-mayer.com/index.html)

While we work on the larger opportunity for LMBPN Entertainment, the mother company of LMBPN Publishing, I hope to get a chance to learn from people such as Ted Mayer.

I'm fifty-three years young at the moment, and I believe I have a lot of opportunities to do fun things if I learn from others.

Who knows? Maybe I'll get a chance to talk with Ted someday.

I doubt it will be a chance meeting while jogging. Just saying.

Ad Aeternitatem,

Michael Anderle

Steel Dragon Series

(with Michael Anderle)

Steel Dragon 1

Steel Dragon 2

Steel Dragon 3

Steel Dragon 4

Steel Dragon 5

Dragon's Daughter

(with Michael Anderle)

Never A Dragon (Book 1)

Dead Dragon New tricks (Book 2)

Thicker Than Blood (Book 3)

Dragon Fire and Pixie Dust (Book 4)

The Cult of Tiamat (Book 5)

The Sum of All Magic (Book 6)

Adventures of the Starship Satori (Space Opera blended with military SF)

Finding Satori - prequel short story, available only to email list fans!

Book 1 - Ad Astra: Book 2 - Stellar Legacy

Book 3 - Deep Waters

Book 4 - No Plan Survives Contact

Book 5 - Liberty

Book 6 - Satori's Destiny

Book 7 - Ashes of War

Book 8 - Embers of War

Book 9 - Dust and Iron

Book 10 - Clad in Steel

Book 11 - Brave New Worlds (2019)

Book 12 - Warrior's Marque (2020)

The Ragnarok Saga (Military SF)

Accord of Fire - Free prequel short story, available only to email list fans!

Book 1 - Accord of Honor

Book 2 - Accord of Mars

Book 3 - Accord of Valor

Book 4 - Ghost Wing

Book 5 - Ghost Squadron

Book 6 - Ghost Fleet (2019)

Valhalla Online Series (A Ragnarok Saga Story)

Book 1 - Valhalla Online

Book 2 - Raiding Jotunheim

Book 3 - Vengeance Over Vanaheim

Book 4 - Hel Hath No Fury

Blackwell Magic Series (Urban Fantasy)

Book 1 - By Darkness Revealed

Book 2 - Ashes Ascendant

Book 3 - Dead In Winter

Book 4 - Claws That Catch

Book 5 - Darkness Awakes

Book 6 - Spellbinding Entanglements

By A Whisker (short story)

The Raven and the Rose - Free novelette for email list fans!

Dead Brittania Series:

Dead Brittania (short prequel story)

Book 1 - King of the Dead

Book 2 - Queen of Demons

Raven's Heart Series (Urban Fantasy)

Book 1 - Stolen Light

Book 2 - Webs in the Dark

Book 3 - Shades of Moonlight

Other Titles:

Over the Moon (SF romance)

Midnight Visitors (Steampunk Cat short story)

Demon Ex Machina (Steampunk Cat short story)

The Coffee Break Novelist (help for writers!)

You Must Write (Heinlein's rules for writers)

CONNECT WITH THE AUTHORS

Connect with Kevin McLaughlin

Website: http://kevinomclaughlin.com/

Facebook: https://www.facebook.com/kevins.studio

Twitter: https://twitter.com/KOMcLaughlin

Instagram: https://www.instagram.com/kevins.studio/

Connect with Michael Anderle

Website: http://lmbpn.com

Email List: http://lmbpn.com/email/

https://www.facebook.com/LMBPNPublishing

https://twitter.com/MichaelAnderle

https://www.instagram.com/lmbpn_publishing/

https://www.bookbub.com/authors/michael-anderle

www.ingramcontent.com/pod-product-compliance
Lightning Source LLC
Chambersburg PA
CBHW020358110726
47899CB00006B/1767